DOCTOR WHO

GRAVE MATTER
JUSTIN RICHARDS

B B C

Published by BBC Worldwide Ltd,
Woodlands, 80 Wood Lane
London W12 0TT

First published 2000
Copyright © Justin Richards 2000
The moral right of the author has been asserted

Original series broadcast on the BBC
Format copyright © BBC 1963
Doctor Who and TARDIS are trademarks of the BBC

ISBN 0 563 55598 X
Imaging by Black Sheep, copyright © BBC 2000

Printed and bound in Great Britain by Mackays of Chatham
Cover printed by Belmont Press Ltd, Northampton

For Alison, Julian and Christian as ever and for ever.
And for Steve, for asking me to play.

First Generation

Chapter One
Gathering

Even dead men dream. There were curtains at the window, heavy with dust and age, stinking with decay. They were not drawn, and the moonlight spilled on to the moth-eaten carpet and the stained wood of the floor. He could open the window, he had found. He could open the window and reach out into the biting cold of the night beyond, pushing his arms between the bars until his shoulders ached for freedom.

Like pushing his arms into the rubber sleeves. Reaching into the dread-night of the sealed environment. Watching the light flooding into the box as he twisted the latch.

A cloud scudded across the blotchy face of the full moon. There was a taste of mist in the air. The salt-sea smell permeated the room. Out of the corner of his bloodshot eye he caught sudden sight of a tiny dot of light – a star, perhaps. Gleaming alone in the misting sky.

In his bloodshot mind's eye he was imagining the tiny speck of light passing through the stellar clouds, bouncing off the atmosphere of distant planets, grasping at even smaller specks of material, ushering in the mists of space. His hands clenched at the thought, grabbing at handfuls of the gathering mist and feeling them slip through his tortured fingers. He could feel the gaps in his left hand. He could feel the nerves and muscles that were no longer there. He could feel them even now twisting the catch.

It was not an image he welcomed, and he pushed harder against the bars in an effort to break back to reality, to loose the dream and let it slip out on to the moors.

But instead, he saw his gloved hands open the catch, lift the lid, reach in for the contents of three-zero-seven.

'You were right,' he heard himself say, voice filtered by time, by imagination. 'It is genetic.'

And the man in the wheelchair nodded his satisfaction, smiling as if he knew what was to come. What they had unleashed.

He pressed harder still against the bars, so close now he could feel the rough edges of the rusted surfaces through his shirt.

Until he felt the bars give.

'Another drink?'

The woman put her hand over her glass and shook her head. She stifled a yawn.

'You don't mind if I do?' He did not wait for an answer, but refilled his own glass from the decanter. 'Yes,' he said, twisting the glass slowly by its stem, allowing the firelight to flicker on the facets of the bowl as he examined the rich, dark liquid inside. 'Yes, a good day's work.' He turned so his back was to the fire and raised his glass in salute. His thick fingers were a contrast to the delicate stem of the cut glass. 'We're making good progress,' he said.

The woman smiled back. She drained her glass and placed it on a low table beside her chair. 'I'm tired,' she announced. 'It's been a long day.'

The man seemed not to hear. He walked slowly across to the window and tweaked the curtain aside. 'Mist's coming in,' he commented.

'I think I'll say good night.'

He turned from the window, letting the heavy curtain fall back into place. The gaslight on the nearest wall flickered slightly, sending shadows dancing across the man's craggy face, picking out the ridges and pits in his skin. 'We'll need more material,' he said quietly.

The woman stood up. 'So soon?' There was a depth of weariness in her voice.

'Tomorrow.' His face split into a sudden smile. 'Don't worry. I'll organise it.'

Before the woman could reply, there was a knock at the door. Urgent, loud.

'Come,' the man called out. He did not bother to look to see who it was. 'Yes, Rogers, what is it?'

The manservant was flustered. He stood in the doorway as if nervous of entering the room fully. His hands were clasped in front of him, shaking slightly. 'I'm sorry, sir,' he said, his voice tremulous.

The man did turn now, alerted by the tone of Rogers's voice. 'Well?'

'I was taking a drink to –' He broke off, swallowed. 'For the night. And of course to check that –'

'What is it?' The man's face was darkening. His voice betrayed his impatience.

'Well, he's gone, sir.'

'Gone?' the woman asked. She looked from one to the other.

'I'm sorry. The window.' Rogers swallowed again. 'The bars...' He opened his hands, apologetic, almost pathetic. 'Rusted, weak...'

The woman coughed a short, nervous half-laugh. 'But he's ill. We have to find him.'

'I couldn't agree more.' The man pushed his half-empty glass on to the mantel shelf as he spoke. 'We need him.' He kicked a burning log back into place, sending sparks showering across the grate. 'And we need him in one piece.'

He turned and strode purposefully towards the door.

'He could hurt himself.' The woman hurried after him.

'Hurt himself?' There was a note of derision in the man's voice.

'In his present state. He could... anything,' she protested.

Rogers stepped aside to let the man pass. 'The horses, sir?'

The man was already half-way down the panelled hallway towards the front door. 'And the dogs, Rogers,' he called back. He paused in a pool of light cast by a wall lamp. For a moment he was motionless, as if composing himself. Then he turned back, and smiled thinly at the woman. 'Don't worry, my dear. You get some sleep.' His smile hardened, as if setting in position. 'We'll soon run him to earth,' he said, his voice like gravel.

* * *

At least he had all his toes. At the moment.

He had settled into a sort of staggering run, forever falling forwards over the rough rocky ground, but never quite pitching on to his face. There was enough light from the moon seeping through the gathering mist for him to make out the landscape. The landscape which he knew so much better than they did. This was his landscape after all, his home.

He stumbled over an outcrop of rock, lost his balance. This time he did fall. He lay for a moment, staring back up at the grey-blackness. The whole sky seemed to be alive, seemed to be moving as the fog rolled in from the sea. If he listened he could hear the crash of the waves against the base of the cliff. Not far now. Not far at all. And then…?

He pulled himself back to his feet, almost retching for breath. The skeletal outline of a tree was thrusting through the murky air beside him, and he grabbed at the nearest bone-branch for support. His thumb and single surviving finger curled round the damp, brittle wood.

Somewhere at the back of his memory he could hear the crack of pain as they removed his fingers. His brain was a muzzy fog as he watched them, knowing that the pain would follow. Soon. And then, it would happen again. And again.

The sound jerked him back to the present. The howl of a dog somewhere out on the moor behind him. Close to the house, perhaps. The noise was filtered and drawn out by the fog, a mournful baying tinged with a tired sadness that made him yearn to join in. But he knew he must keep silent. They would pick up his scent soon enough. The hounds would be racing over the moors, the horsemen close behind. Soon they would find him, find him and take him… home.

He was stumbling onwards again, hoping it was not far now. Straining to see the edge of the cliff through the night-fog.

He knew it so well, yet he almost missed it. The moorland stopped abruptly, as if cut through by a huge serrated knife. The ground gave way into an abyss of blackness. He teetered on the edge, staring down. The sound of the waves crashed through the night. All he could see was the fog swirling round the base of the abyss, as if stirred up by the wind. As if escaping down a large plug hole. As if drawing him into its very heart.

The hounds were close now. He could hear their voices calling to each other through the night. They had the scent. His scent. His hounds.

It was only now that he knew why he had come here. Now, as he stood staring down at the empty space where the water was. Now, as the hounds were running. There was only one way they would lose his scent, he knew. Only one way out.

He turned to look back. At the same moment, the first of the dogs appeared through the fog. It was in midair, emerging from the gloom as it leaped towards him. He cried out despite himself, raised his arm to ward off the snapping teeth, took a step backwards.

For a brief moment he was poised, half on the edge, half over it. Then the animal connected with his arm, knocking him backwards, falling with him, tumbling head over kicking heels into the abyss.

Before the sound of the sea and the fog swallowed him whole.

Second Generation

Chapter Two
Cortège

The heavy air was split by a sudden scraping, a painful wrenching. The mist seemed to be drawn to the sound, swirling into a sudden gap. It coalesced round a single area, solidifying slowly into shape. A square, box shape. The flash of the lamp on top of the blue box vied with the pale sunlight, struggling to be seen through the thickening air.

Then with a final satisfied thump and a last flash of the light, the TARDIS became real, pushing the mist out of the area it now occupied.

A little later the door creaked open and Peri looked tentatively round the edge, her dark hair framing her face. She sniffed at the misty air, wrinkling her nose up at the scent of the sea. She was about to step back inside when she was suddenly propelled forwards, through the doors, making way for the Doctor to step out on to the moorland.

As Peri stumbled and struggled to regain her balance, the Doctor drew his heavy cloak around him and took several theatrically deep breaths. 'Bracing!' he announced hugely, turning a complete circle as he looked around.

Peri hunched up inside her heavy, dark coat. Beneath it she was wearing a thick velvet dress that reached down almost to her ankles. But she could already feel the cold, damp air working its way through to her bones. 'Not very inspiring, Doctor,' she told him. 'Let's try again.'

'It may not be inspiring to you, young lady.' He was already pulling the TARDIS doors closed and locking them. He turned and set off across the uneven ground without looking for her reaction. 'But to the true genius, inspiration is to be found…' He paused as if trying to recall exactly where it was to be found. 'Everywhere,' he decided expansively. He waved both arms as wide as he could, letting his cloak open to reveal the gaudy coat beneath.

'Huh,' Peri said. She hitched up her dress and ran after him as he set off again.

The Doctor was still speaking, presumably to himself since Peri could not hear what he was saying until she was quite close.

'Oh yes,' he agreed with himself. 'Sermons in stones, books in the babbling brook.' He turned towards Peri as if he believed she had been with him the whole time. 'Inspiration in everything.'

'Huh,' Peri said again.

'Huh,' the Doctor mimicked back. 'Not a very inspired response, if you don't mind me saying.'

Peri seriously considered saying 'huh' again, just to underline the point. But as she hesitated the moment was lost to her.

'Earth,' the Doctor announced. 'Got to be.' He took another deep breath. 'Need to check, of course. When running in a new supply of Zeiton-Seven you have to recalibrate everything. Work out where you are, so you know where you're going. Find out when it is, so you can tell when it will be next. That sort of thing.' He stopped suddenly and drew in a deep breath of mist. 'Mmm,' he decided as Peri caught up with him. 'Taste that sea air. Cornwall, perhaps? Untainted by the excesses of pollution anyway.' He glared at Peri from point-blank range. 'So we're not in your enlightened times.'

'Hey,' Peri snapped back, 'I just live there.'

'Huh,' said the Doctor. Then he suddenly grinned and nudged her with his shoulder as if sharing a deep and meaningful joke. 'Let's get the time and place, and then I can recalibrate the calibrators and we can be on our way.'

'And why do we need to recalibrate the calibrators?'

He stopped dead in his tracks. 'My dear Peri, that is what they are for. You have to calibrate calibrators. Otherwise what earthly use would they be to anyone? It's part of the running in, the resumption of normal service. The calibration,' he finished, a note of desperation creeping into his voice. He shook his head and embarked on a series of profound 'tuts' and whistles.

'Then can we go somewhere warmer once you've sorted out this Zeiton-Seven stuff?' Peri asked. 'Somewhere I can see more than six feet ahead of me?'

'Six feet?' the Doctor asked in puzzlement. 'No, no. Just the two of us.' He held up his hand and raised up his fingers, one by one. 'That makes four feet.'

Peri, however, was staring beyond the Doctor's fingers, out into the mist. 'Six feet,' she said again. 'You need to count him too.'

If Peri had ever taken the time to formulate an opinion of what the Wild Man of the Woods might look like, she would have settled on something pretty close to the figure now emerging from the mist in front of them. He was probably in his mid-thirties, but it was difficult to tell as his face was streaked with mud and dirt. His hair was matted and hung in straggles down his face. Beneath his ragged fringe, his eyes were alert, darting back and forth between the Doctor and Peri. His clothes were as dirty as his face, torn and stained. His feet, Peri could see as he shuffled towards her, were bare and caked with earth and blood.

The Doctor was watching the man, fascinated. He still held his hand out, fingers raised. But he had altered its position just slightly, so that it seemed like a gesture of welcome. In response the man raised his own left hand. Whether this too was a greeting, it was difficult to tell. Perhaps, Peri decided with a gulp, he wanted to show them that he was lacking the two middle fingers. They were gone, missing from the knuckle.

'Hello,' the Doctor said in the same tone as he might use to a five-year-old. Or a puppy. 'Now who might you be?'

Peri half expected him to lean forward and make encouraging clicking noises with his tongue to coax the man forward.

'Live here,' the man said. His voice was weak and barely audible, as if swallowed up by the mist. 'Home.' He waved his good hand, taking in the whole of the visible world.

'Really?' The Doctor looked round. 'Very nice. Do you live here alone?'

'Alone.' The man nodded, his hair flapping heavily round his head.

Then his eyes narrowed. 'They want me back,' he said, his voice a hissing mixture of anxiety and conspiracy. 'First generation,' he added helpfully.

'I see,' the Doctor said, nodding back.

'He's demented,' Peri whispered.

'Oh nonsense,' the Doctor said, shooing her away as he stepped up to the man. The man shrank back in fear. 'Now then, my good man,' the Doctor began.

But the man was already turning and heading back into the mist. He paused just within sight. 'Don't let them get you,' he said. 'Lock you up. Dogs.'

'Thank you,' the Doctor called after him. 'We'll bear that in mind. Won't we, Peri?'

'Yeah,' Peri agreed. 'Right.'

But the man was gone.

The Doctor sighed. 'Charming fellow,' he said. 'Wonder what his name was.'

Peri laughed. 'I doubt if he knew.'

'That's a little uncharitable, you know,' the Doctor admonished as he picked his way onward through the mist. 'I think it's getting thicker, if anything,' he commented.

'He was barking mad,' Peri said as she followed.

'Yes, he did mention dogs, didn't he?'

'Watching too many werewolf movies if you ask me.'

The Doctor was standing still, staring out into the fog. They could barely see a yard ahead now. 'Well,' he said absently, 'even a man who is pure of heart may lose his mind when the wolfbane blooms.'

'What?' Peri stumbled past him, half turning to see what he was on about as she went. She shook her head, deciding she would probably never know. And her foot missed the ground.

Her first thought was that there was a dip in the earth, or a rabbit hole. But her foot kept going and, as her centre of gravity brought her forward, she found she was staring into the space where the ground ought to be.

'Peri!' the Doctor shouted as she continued to fall forwards.

Her arms were flailing now, thrashing in air. She continued to fall forwards until she could hear the raging of the sea far below, could see the broken edge of the cliff.

Then a hand grabbed one of her arms, yanking her backwards with sudden force.

'Thanks,' she gasped, turning towards the Doctor.

Except that it wasn't the Doctor. It was the wild man. He held on to her hand as they stepped back from the edge. His eyes were shining in the watery light, intense as he stared at her, the irises so pale they were almost white. He pulled her even closer.

'Thank you,' Peri repeated, trying to pull gently away from him. But he held on tight to her arm. Over his shoulder, Peri could see the Doctor watching. He nodded, lips pursed in an expression that suggested he thought she was safe.

The man leaned closer still, and Peri could smell his hot rancid breath as he spoke. 'Be careful,' he hissed at her. Then he let go of her arm and stepped away. 'I'm sorry,' he said, his voice suddenly calm, strangely normal. 'Lucidity comes and goes, I'm afraid. A side effect perhaps.' He blinked rapidly several times.

'Side effect?' the Doctor asked.

The man nodded. Then he raised his damaged hand again. 'Or perhaps it's trauma. Because of what they do to me.' They all stared at the hand, at the stumps of his two fingers. Then he clenched his hand into a sudden approximation of a fist, a single good finger pointing through the fog. 'The village is that way.' His body hunched up again, and he staggered away. 'They're good people,' his voice floated back to them. 'They deserve better.'

'What do you make of that?' Peri asked as the mist engulfed the man again.

'Load of rubbish. Absolute nonsense,' the Doctor said huffily.

'What?'

'You can't get better than us, no matter what they deserve.' The Doctor nodded, apparently happy with his reasoning. 'Come along, let's find this village.' He headed off into the mist, Peri stumbling after him, still shaken by her near fall.

'Why can't we go back to the TARDIS?' she asked when she caught him up. There was no reply. 'Doctor?'

'Well,' the Doctor said slowly. 'Unfortunately that nice man was able to direct us towards the village, but didn't tell us which way the TARDIS is.'

Peri considered this. 'You mean we're lost?'

The Doctor frowned. 'Peri,' he said.

The mist thinned as they walked away from the sea. But the air remained damp and cold. After a while they crossed what seemed to be a narrow track, perhaps worn by sheep. It led them winding and meandering across the moorland, and brought them eventually to a rather wider track that ran between two fields. In the distance in one of the fields, Peri could see cows, black and white Friesians, grazing contentedly.

They saw no evidence of farm buildings, though they crossed several other tracks. The land became less rocky, and the track became a cobbled path. The mist began to close in once more, though not to the same extent as earlier on the moor, and Peri guessed they were close to the sea again.

'Watch out for the cliff edge,' she told the Doctor.

'No need,' he answered. 'Look.'

She looked. Through the haze she could see the masts of several small boats, fishing boats perhaps. Peri and the Doctor headed towards them, and found a small harbour built into an inlet. They were all small sailing boats, most of them in a rather dilapidated state. Several torn nets lay across the harbour wall, perhaps in the process of being mended. The wall itself seemed to be built mainly of flint. There was nobody around.

'Small fishing community,' the Doctor said. 'A day off, perhaps. The fish don't usually stop for a bit of sea mist.'

'Perhaps it's Sunday?'

He turned and looked across the landscape. Eventually he pointed along the cobbled road in the direction they had been heading anyway. 'That way, I think.'

'Inspired,' Peri told him. 'The advice of a genius.'

The Doctor glared at her. 'It also happens to be where the church is. And that suggests the village is there too.'

Peri peered into the distance. She could just make out a thin, dark spike sticking up through the mist. As they walked, it resolved itself into the spire of a small church. Sure enough, the road led past the church and its misty graveyard and into the village beyond. They were on a slight rise at the edge of the village, affording them an excellent view down into the community.

Gas lamps stood at irregular intervals along the cobbled street. Although it was daytime, they glowed pallidly in the mist. There seemed to be a single main street through the village. Half-way along was a pub, its sign swinging gently in the breeze. At the far end of the village was another large building. A school, perhaps. There seemed to be a field fenced off beside it.

'Definitely a small fishing community,' the Doctor decided. 'Mid-nineteenth century, would you say?'

'Wouldn't argue,' Peri agreed. 'Gas lamps, cobbled street.'

'Early Victorian school house,' the Doctor added. 'The church is about 1480, give or take half a century, and the pub looks older than most of the other buildings.'

'Great,' Peri said. 'Let's start there then.'

'The church?'

'The pub.'

The Doctor nodded. 'All right. We should be able to get the date and location for the price of a few drinks at any rate.' He jigged his hand in his coat pocket, and the sound of coins chinking together carried discordantly through the heavy air. 'Must have something they'll accept.'

They set off down the street, the Doctor pulling his cloak tight about him once more and looking around with exaggerated interest. Peri followed close behind, head down to keep an eye on the uneven, slippery-damp cobbles. She almost cannoned into him when he stopped abruptly.

'Hello,' the Doctor said quietly.

Peri looked past him. A short way in front of them, a front door to one of the small terraced houses had opened. Standing in the doorway was an old woman. She was small, almost shrivelled, wrapped up well against the cold. Her breath was an uneven, thin trail of steam that mingled with the faint mist, swirling into the air and lost almost at once.

As they watched, another door opened. Then another. And another. All along the street, people were stepping out on to the thresholds of their houses, standing quiet and still as they looked along the street. But they were not looking at the Doctor and Peri: they were facing the other way, looking past the pub towards the distant school.

The Doctor nodded wordlessly to Peri and they stepped to the side of the road. There was a narrow passageway between two of the houses and they stood in the entrance, waiting to see what would happen.

As they waited, Peri looked at the villagers standing silent in their doorways. Like the old woman, they were dressed for the cold; their heavy, dark coats, augmented here and there by mufflers and shawls, swept nearly to the ground. Something struck Peri as odd, and it took her a minute to realise just what it was. Past the old lady she could see a younger couple, in their thirties, perhaps. After that a man of perhaps fifty. A whole group had emerged from the pub and were standing, some with drinks in their hands, watching a house on the opposite side of the road. They seemed a mixed set of people, men and women, young and old. Except...

'Doctor,' Peri said quietly, 'Doctor, there are no children.'

'Perhaps this isn't for a child's eyes,' the Doctor murmured back.

'What is it? What's going on?'

Before the Doctor could answer, another door opened. Peri had to strain to see what was happening. The door was the front door to the house opposite the pub. It was a good way down the street from where the Doctor and Peri were standing, and the remnants of the mist made it more difficult to discern what was happening.

16

As she watched, a group of people came out of the house.

This was not like the group that had come out of the pub. There was an order to this. A formality. A procession.

'I think it's a funeral,' the Doctor whispered in Peri's ear.

And even as he said it, she saw that the distant figures were carrying a large box on their shoulders. Two men either side of it. A coffin. The pallbearers walked slowly to the end of the small front garden of the house, then turned into the narrow street, starting towards the Doctor and Peri.

'Where are they going?' Peri asked. But even as she spoke she knew the answer. They both turned to look at the church behind them.

There was a figure standing at the gate to the churchyard. A priest, his white surplice almost glowing in the misty light, a contrast to the dark and dull clothing of those in the procession and the other villagers. He was in his late middle age, grey and balding. His face was lined but friendly, despite the grim expression. His hands were clasped in front of him, holding a book – a prayer book or Bible. He looked up as Peri turned, and for a moment caught her eye. There was no surprise, no inquiry, no change of expression in his face. Just a faint, slow nod, then he turned his gaze to the approaching mourners.

The funeral procession was moving slowly, the pallbearers taking one step at a time, the coffin rocking gently back and forth as they did so. They were making their way up the street now, followed by a small group of people. Two by two. A woman in full-length black dabbed at her eyes with a handkerchief. An older man put his arm round the woman's shoulder. Behind them were two young men. One stared at the ground, while the other was looking intently, almost fiercely, at the coffin. All were dressed in formal black too. Along the street, heads turned slowly to follow the procession's progress.

Beside her, Peri saw the Doctor suddenly stiffen slightly. He too had been watching the coffin approach. But as he turned his head a little, the Doctor straightened, staring beyond the mourners.

Peri looked to see where the Doctor's attention was fixed. It seemed to be a narrow passageway on the opposite side of the street, further down from the one where they were themselves standing.

At first, she could see nothing. Just the dark opening, the shadows from the houses either side and the faint gleam of a nearby gaslight, diffused through the misty daylight to give an otherworldly glow to the scene. But as she stared, she could see that there was someone standing there, in the shadows. A tall, thin, silhouetted figure. Black against dark grey. It was only when the figure moved slightly, turning as it too watched the procession, that she could see it at all.

As the procession passed between Peri and the figure, she lost sight of it.

The procession was level with the Doctor and Peri. The priest was turning to lead the way along the churchyard path. Peri and the Doctor each took an instinctive, respectful step backwards as the coffin passed by.

Then the second of the two pallbearers on the same side as Peri and the Doctor slipped. Peri saw it happen, as if in slow motion. His shoulder dipped slightly as his shoe slipped on the damp sheen of the rounded cobbles. He adjusted his grip, seemed to regain his balance, stood upright again. But the sudden movement, the change in weight distribution, caused him to slip again, more severely this time.

The man collapsed suddenly, his feet sliding from under him. The coffin tilted alarmingly, falling into the space left by the man's departure. The other pallbearers tried to compensate, tried to strengthen their failing grips on the coffin. The young man with the intent stare ran forwards, seeing what was about to happen.

But he was too late. The coffin continued to tilt, sliding out of the grip of the other men, crashing to the cobbled ground. It bounced on the hard surface of the street. There was a sound of splintering wood as the coffin landed on its edge. Then the lid lifted, jarred open by the impact, and slid sideways.

Peri was right beside it. The gas lamp above cast its pallid light directly into the opening, illuminating the pasty, white face of the corpse. It was a man, not much older than Peri. The stiff white collar of his shirt seemed to merge with the pale skin. The face was contorted, as if in terror, or agony. Or both. The lips rolled back from teeth gritted tight. The forehead was lined, and the eyes – the eyes were bulging forwards as if straining to be free of the dead sockets of the skull. The pupils were wide, dilated, dark against pale irises.

Then abruptly Peri's view was cut off as the lid was pushed back into place. Instead she found herself staring at the young man from the procession. He glared at her, his eyes a fierce contrast to the empty gaze of the corpse, though she seemed to see the dead man's features echoed in his face. He continued to stare at her as the pallbearers lifted the coffin up again, as the Doctor gently put his arm round Peri's shivering shoulder and drew her close to him, as the procession continued on its melancholy way. Only when the last of the mourners was in the churchyard, only when the villagers had withdrawn silent and respectful into their houses and closed their doors behind them, only when the group from the pub had made their solemn way back inside, did the man turn and follow the cortège up the street and into the churchyard.

Chapter Three
Fisherman's Ruin

They continued their walk down the cobbled street in rather lower spirits than they had started.

'I think you could do with a good stiff lemonade,' the Doctor told Peri gently.

'Something a bit stronger than that,' she suggested. 'The pub?'

'The place to meet people.' The Doctor nodded. 'We'll just have a swift drinkie, get the date and the location, and be on our way. A death in a small isolated society like this, especially of a young person, can shake up the community.'

'It shook me up,' Peri agreed. 'Anyway,' she went on, 'they won't have lemonade, will they?'

'Depends what you think of as lemonade.' The Doctor smiled, a thin attempt that was tinged with sadness. 'Let's see, shall we?'

The pub, according to its faded sign, was called the Dorsill Arms. It was perhaps half full of people. They were not exactly in high spirits, but there was an audible buzz of conversation as the Doctor pushed open the door and ushered Peri inside. It was like a switch being thrown. As soon as she crossed the threshold, all talking stopped. Silence.

There were gas lamps round the walls of the room, but they were unlit. The only illumination came from the milky sunlight that struggled through the smeary windows. It made silhouettes of the figures sitting in the bar.

The Doctor stepped past Peri, apparently oblivious to the faces turned towards them as he made his way up to the bar. Somewhere at the back of the room a chair scraped across the stone floor, but otherwise there was utter silence. Peri joined the Doctor, feeling out of place and disconcerted.

Behind the bar stood a large red-faced man with steel grey hair. He was paused in mid-polish, a damp cloth wiping the inside of a pint glass. After a moment, the cloth started working again and the man leaned forward towards the Doctor. It was an intimidating gesture, but the Doctor seemed unmoved.

'Ah,' the Doctor said with a huge smile. 'I see you have a fine selection of local brews.' He ran his finger along the damp top of the bar, tapping it gently as it passed each of the three beer engines. 'Very sophisticated pumping equipment, wouldn't you say?' he murmured as he peered at the handwritten labels on the pump handles. 'What's the Fisherman's Ruin like?'

'Strong,' the barman said. His voice was deep and accented. 'Specially if you ain't used to it.'

The Doctor nodded. 'Excellent. A pint of that then, please.' He smiled across at Peri, who sighed. 'And a glass of water for myself,' the Doctor added. He caught Peri's expression and his smile broadened into a grin. 'All right,' he said, 'you have the water.'

There was still no movement or comment from anyone else in the room. The barman busied himself pulling the pint of beer. 'Liz,' he called out suddenly without looking up from the task.

'Yes, Dad?' The reply came from the room behind the bar area. A moment later a young woman appeared in the doorway. She was about Peri's age, perhaps slightly older, with red hair to her shoulders and a mass of freckles across the bridge of her nose. Her eyes were a startling green, oval and wide. She froze in the doorway as she caught sight of the Doctor and Peri.

'Glass of water for the lady,' her father grunted as he lifted the foaming pint and placed it on the bar in front of the Doctor. The beer was cloudy at the top, the bottom slowly clearing as it settled. A misty froth ran down the outside of the glass and pooled on the wooden surface of the bar.

'Water,' the girl murmured, not moving from the doorway.

'Today, girl,' her father said. It wasn't a harsh rebuke. There was an undercurrent of gentle humour to it.

Her eyes widened still further, and she blinked suddenly. 'Of course. Sorry,' and she disappeared out the door again.

'Sorry,' Peri said. Her voice was a nervous high-pitched sound.

She tried again. 'Sorry if we're intruding,' she said, more controlled now. 'The funeral…'

'Yes,' the Doctor said solemnly. 'My condolences to you all.' He raised his slippery glass carefully and took a mouthful of froth from the top. It left a white moustache traced across his upper lip. 'I'm sorry we did not choose a more propitious time for our visit,' he said, wiping the back of his hand across his lips.

The ruddy-faced barman was watching the Doctor intently. His eyes narrowed. 'We don't have strangers here,' he said levelly.

Peri almost laughed out loud. But somehow the man seemed deadly serious. There was no hint that he was joking or even aware of the cliché.

'Really?' the Doctor asked seriously. 'I am surprised. Such excellent ale as well.' He leaned across the counter, resting his sleeve in the puddle where his glass had stood. 'Why is that, do you suppose?'

The girl was back. She handed a glass of water to Peri. 'Because we're on an island,' she said.

There was the beginning of a hum of voices from the rest of the room now, as people returned to their drinks and conversations.

'You mean,' the Doctor was saying slowly, 'that you don't have strangers here?'

'That's what I said,' the barman said.

'Don't have as in don't tend to get,' the Doctor suggested. 'Rather than actively discourage.'

The barman looked at him sideways. 'Reckon so,' he decided at last. 'We don't tend to get strangers here. Not usually. The rocks and the currents offshore see to that. On days like this you've also got the mist and sea fog.' He leaned across and wiped the area of the bar round where the Doctor was leaning, cleaning away the filmy remains of the froth. 'But you're welcome enough,' he added. 'Just unexpected.'

'Well, that's very kind.' The Doctor smiled. 'Will you have a drink?'

'I might.' The barman smiled back. 'But you've not paid for that one yet.'

'Ah.' The Doctor started to rummage through his pockets. 'An oversight, I do apologise.'

'No problem.' The barman let him struggle with his coat for a few more moments, then added: 'It's on the house anyway.'

'Thank you.' The Doctor seemed genuinely surprised and pleased.

The barman shrugged. 'Reckon you've had the sort of day where you need a drink.'

'It has been a bit traumatic,' Peri agreed.

'Lost in the fog,' the Doctor agreed quickly. 'Our, er, vessel landed on the other side of the island.'

'You're lucky she landed at all,' a voice said from behind them. The Doctor and Peri both turned. The speaker was a tall man with fair hair. He was in his later twenties or early thirties. He was wearing a dark suit and had just walked into the pub. Behind him several other people were coming in, all in dark suits. The mourners from the funeral, Peri realised.

'Dangerous waters round these islands,' the man went on. His voice was clear, without the accent of the barman and his daughter.

The Doctor picked up on this at once. 'Now, you're not local to these islands,' he said, offering his hand.

The man shook it, then nodded politely to Peri. 'Madsen,' he said. 'Dave Madsen. I'm the local doctor, for my sins. And I'm from London,' he added.

The Doctor beamed at him. 'And I'm the universal Doctor,' he said grandly. 'And this is Miss Perpugilliam Brown.'

'But you can call me Peri,' Peri said hastily.

'And you can call me the Doctor,' the Doctor said.

At this point the barman leaned across and tapped the Doctor on the shoulder. 'Robert Trefoil,' he said pleasantly. 'You can call me Bob,' he went on, 'provided you're good enough to move aside and let me and Liz serve these customers.'

Leaving the Doctor to apologise more than profusely for taking up so much space, Peri pushed her way past several tables to find an unoccupied pair of chairs close to a dartboard in the corner of the bar. The table wobbled when she set her water down on it.

The chair wobbled when she sat on it. She was peering at the stone-flagged floor to see how to adjust the table's position when someone sat down next to her.

It was Dave Madsen. He smiled at Peri as she looked up. 'Do you mind?' he asked.

'Oh, er, no.'

'Not at all,' the Doctor agreed as he pulled up another chair. He set his glass down on the table and watched the beer slosh against the sides as the table wobbled.

'Thank you,' Madsen said. 'It's rather a close-knit society, as I imagine you can tell. Islanders, you know. I've been here only a few months, so I'm still an outsider to most of them.'

As he finished speaking, Liz Trefoil set down a pint of ale in front of him. Peri could not help but notice the smile that went with it, nor the way Madsen smiled back. He reached for the glass, his hand brushing against the young woman's as she still held it.

'Most, but not all, I would suspect,' the Doctor said quietly as Liz turned and left.

Madsen half-smiled back, apparently embarrassed. 'As I say, a close-knit group. Almost a family. They all know each other.'

The Doctor nodded, and asked abruptly: 'Talking of families, where are all the children?'

Madsen seemed taken aback for a moment. 'At school, of course,' he said. 'Oh, I see. Well, I imagine they feel that a funeral isn't really children's business.'

'Yes.' The Doctor smiled back. 'They do seem a little, what shall we say, *Victorian* in their outlook, don't they?'

Peri looked to see whether the Doctor's fishing for the date would provoke a reaction. Madsen seemed not to be paying full attention. He was watching Liz pushing past a group close to the bar. On the edge of the group was the young man with the intent gaze, who had put the lid back on the coffin.

'Well, that's hardly surprising, is it?' Madsen said absently.

The Doctor gave Peri a triumphant nod and a grin. 'As you say,' he murmured.

'That's the poor man's brother,' Madsen went on, apparently meaning the young man. 'Mike Neville.'

'The dead man?' Peri prompted cautiously.

Madsen turned back to them. 'William Neville,' he said. 'They were out in that storm the other night. Only William's body has been washed up.' He shook his head and stared at his pint. 'That's why... Three young men.' He shook his head again. 'A terrible blow.'

'Indeed,' the Doctor agreed. 'And so sudden.'

'Yes, that makes it worse,' Madsen agreed. 'Not like the others,' he added quietly.

'Others?' Peri asked. She looked at the Doctor and saw that his eyes had widened slightly.

Madsen looked up, startled, as if unaware that he had spoken out loud. 'I'm sorry,' he said, 'I didn't mean... It's nothing.' He shrugged. 'Just bad luck really. Being the doctor, I guess I'm just closer to it.'

'An occupational hazard,' the Doctor agreed. 'There have been other deaths recently?' he prompted.

'A few. As I say, just coincidence.' Madsen took a swig of his beer. 'The local vet last month. Some sort of allergic reaction. But it's a problem for the farmers like Mrs Painswick. That's all there is here, farming and fishing, so both communities have suffered lately.'

'You said deaths,' Peri said. 'Plural.'

Madsen stood up. 'Lost a couple to a bout of flu last month,' he said. 'Look, I'd better have a word with the families, if you'll excuse me.'

'Of course,' the Doctor told him. But Madsen was already heading back towards the bar.

'What do you think, Doctor?' Peri asked quietly as soon as Madsen was out of earshot. 'Are we in Victorian times?'

'So it would seem,' the Doctor said, staring intently at what was left of his pint of beer. 'The furniture here is all hand-made and reasonably new. The people's clothes and the general architecture, the lack of traffic or pollution, the state of the fishing boats...'

He paused to take another swig of ale. 'All suggests late Victorian,' he said. He sighed. 'But then there's the odd little niggle.'

Peri's hand froze, her water close to her mouth. 'Niggle?' She did not like the way he had said that.

'Mmm. Niggle. Like the way Madsen said "I guess" rather than "I suppose" or "I reckon". Not so very Victorian.'

'Oh.' Peri set her glass down and looked round furtively. Was there some temporal conspiracy here, people travelling back to Victorian times? 'That could just be his manner,' she suggested. 'What else?'

'Nothing much,' the Doctor said. He frowned and pouted as he thought about it. 'The hand pumps for the beer are maybe a bit sophisticated, but not too unusual.'

'So, we take it at face value?'

The Doctor shook his head. 'Where's the fun in that?' he complained. 'No, no, no. We keep our eyes and ears open for the unusual.' He sipped at his beer. 'The anachronistic.' He smacked his lips and held the remains of his pint up to the light from the nearest window. 'The odd.' He nodded to himself, and drained his glass in a single swallow. 'The weird,' he concluded. Then he belched. 'Sorry.'

Peri shook her head and looked at the ceiling. It was grimy and discoloured by smoke and age. 'So we're just going to sit here?' she asked.

'Certainly not.' The Doctor's voice seemed to come from further away than she had expected. She looked across and saw that he had gone. 'I'm going to get another drink,' the Doctor said from just behind her, making Peri flinch with surprise. 'And you,' he whispered close to her ear, 'can just sit here.'

'Thanks.'

'Or,' he suggested as he turned away, 'you could circulate a bit. Converse. Get acquainted. Listen out for...' he shrugged.

'The unusual, the anachronistic, the odd, the weird,' Peri finished for him. 'And the belches. I know.'

The Doctor was half-way to the bar by the time she finished.

She looked at what was left of her glass of water. 'I could do with another drink too,' she thought. 'But something a bit stronger.'

Baddesley had watched the funeral procession from the shadows between two of the houses in the main street. He preferred to keep out of sight of most of the villagers, and he was certain they would rather he was out of sight as well. He watched the accident with the coffin, wondered at the appearance of the two strangers, and waited while the burial took place.

When it was quiet, once the villagers had gone back to their homes and the mourners had adjourned to the pub to drown their memories and regrets, he stepped out on to the cobbled street. He enjoyed walking. It was a liberating exercise. Often he walked just for the exhilaration of it, following the farm tracks or wandering along the stretches of beach and cliff. But today he had a purpose in mind.

Baddesley carried a walking stick. Although he was getting on in years, he did not need it. But the feel of it in his hand, the tap of it on the cobbles, was a pleasant reassurance. He wielded the stick like a sword as he entered the churchyard. He paused at the gate and looked back into the village. Then, satisfied that nobody was watching, he made his way round to where the short service had taken place.

He stood for a few minutes staring down at the newly dug earth. The end of his stick made small circles on the edge of the grave as he considered. Then in a sudden anger of decision he drove the stick deep into the soil. He leaned heavily on the gnarled wood of the handle for a second, then pulled the stick out of the soft earth before turning and striding back towards the main gate.

By the time Peri reached the bar, the Doctor was already in conversation with Robert Trefoil, the landlord.

'Dorsill?' the Doctor was saying. It was evident that the name was new to him.

28

As she approached, Peri saw that the intent young man – Mike Neville – was standing nearby, watching her. He pretended not to, but his glass was angled as he drank so that his piercing blue eyes tracked her progress. She ignored him.

'What's Dorsill?' Peri asked. Behind her she felt rather than saw Mike Neville take a step towards her.

'This is,' the Doctor said. 'Apparently.'

'These islands,' Trefoil said. 'The whole chain is called Dorsill. Too many of them to have names each, not on maps, any road.'

'And this is the largest of the islands?'

'Only two that are any size. This one – what we call Dorsill. And Sheldon's Folly.'

'What an interesting name,' the Doctor said. But his words were lost beneath the loud, slightly nasal voice of Mike Neville.

'What sort of sailor doesn't know the name of the island he's landed on?' he demanded suddenly, shouldering his way past several other people so that he stood at the bar beside the Doctor and Peri. He spoke to the Doctor, but he was staring at Peri.

'Now, now, Mike,' Trefoil said surprisingly gently.

The Doctor smiled amiably. 'Even the most experienced sailor can sometimes make mistakes,' he said reasonably. 'Misjudge the currents, lose the stars on a misty night. Get lost in the fog.'

Mike Neville's eyes widened, the stare seeming to become even deeper. 'What are you saying?' he asked, his voice dangerously low.

The Doctor blinked in surprise. 'Nothing, I don't think. Just that –'

'Are you saying it was my brother's fault they were lost?' Neville demanded. 'Is that it?' He was shouting now. Heads were turning.

Trefoil's face was reddening more than usual. 'Michael,' he warned.

'Not at all,' the Doctor said quietly. 'I didn't know your brother. But I'm sure he was a fisherman of rare ability.'

'Oh are you?' Neville shouted, leaning towards the Doctor. 'Well, he doesn't need your sarcasm. Any more do I.' He put his drink down on the bar and took a step backwards. His fists were clenching at his sides and his intentions obvious. 'You come here with your fancy woman and make out my brother wasn't fit to be out in the boat. Blame him for the accident.' He was raising a fist now.

The Doctor was watching it with surprise rather than anxiety. 'Touched a nerve, have we?' he asked quietly. 'My apologies.'

At that the young man gave a snarl of rage and lunged at the Doctor, his fist starting to crash down. But it stopped before it had got far, held tight in Robert Trefoil's own huge hand. The landlord pulled Neville back and pushed him aside.

For a moment Neville paused, his face crimson with fury. Then Trefoil leaned over the counter and said quietly: 'Now, you don't want me to have to come out from behind here, do you, young Michael?'

Neville blinked. He looked at Trefoil, then at Peri. She tried not to take a step backwards, but she looked away. When she looked back, Neville was pushing his way through the other mourners. They stood aside to let him through. At the door he turned abruptly and looked back. Again, it was Peri he was staring at, she felt his eyes almost burning into her, an almost physical sensation as he looked her up and down. Then he turned and walked out of the pub.

For a moment there was silence. Slowly, the conversation started again, muted and quiet at first but soon building back to the previous level.

'Sorry about that,' Trefoil said. He was still staring after Neville.

'No, no,' the Doctor told him. 'Let me apologise. I obviously upset the poor young man. It wasn't my intention, I assure you.'

'Lost his brother,' Trefoil said, but whether it was meant as an excuse or merely as information, was impossible to tell from his tone. 'Let me get you another drink.'

'You're too kind,' the Doctor said.

'I doubt it,' Trefoil muttered as he started to pull at the pump.

Peri had decided to try the beer. Trefoil gave her a half pint of the brown liquid in a small glass tankard. He was deep in conversation with the Doctor about the chain of islands and their geography. Peri would like to have known about the wildlife and the plants that grew here. But she was still shaken by the incident with Mike Neville, and decided to leave them to it. She made her way back towards the table. A little sit down, to get her breath back, then she would see what she could find out.

She paused before she sat down and took a sip of the beer. She didn't like it. It wasn't thin and fizzy like Budweiser or Coors. It was syrupy thick. It was bitter. While it was not actually warm, it certainly wasn't cold. She stood for a moment, wondering how much of the stuff she had to drink to be polite. And while she stood, a hand tugged at her sleeve.

It was a man at the next table. There were three young men seated round, and a couple of women no older than Peri. They were looking at her, expecting some sort of answer.

'I'm sorry?' Peri stammered.

'I said, you're welcome to join us. Jed here was telling us a story.' The man's voice was accented like Trefoil's, but not as strong or deep.

'Thank you,' Peri said, sitting down on the chair the man indicated, even before she had thought about it. She put her drink on the table and smiled round at the others. 'I'm Peri,' she said. They nodded as if they knew.

They were all smiling, apparently pleased to meet her, Peri saw. All except the one the man had called Jed. He looked anxious, slightly nervous. 'It's not a story,' he hissed across the table. 'It happened, I swear it.'

'What happened?' one of the women asked. 'You've still not told us.'

Jed shuffled his feet under the table. He picked up his pint, looked at it, then set it down again. 'I'm thinking maybe you won't want to hear it,' he said huffily.

'I'd like to hear it,' Peri said. 'Whatever it is.'

The women smiled at her appreciatively.

Jed glared at her. Then his expression softened. 'All right,' he said.

'But I did warn you. It isn't a story.'

'Get on with it, Jed,' the first man said. 'What're you on about?'

''Twas the other morning, at the farm,' Jed began.

'Jed works for Mrs Painswick, up at Heather Hill Farm,' the man said to Peri.

'Do you want to hear or not?' Jed demanded. When there was silence, he went on: 'It was chicken day,' he said.

'Collecting the eggs?' Peri asked.

'Lopping their heads off,' the third of the men said, with obvious glee. He watched Peri closely for a reaction. She tried not to give one.

'Who's telling this story, Ian?' Jed asked.

'You said it wasn't –' the first man began. Then he broke off. 'All right, Jed. Just get on with it.'

'Chance'd be nice,' Jed mumbled. He had a drink, then continued with his tale. 'First chicken it was. Daft bugger. Sat there nice as pie, waiting. Dunno what it thought I was going to do, me with an axe and all.' He had another drink while he looked for the women's reactions. They looked more bored than anything. 'Anyway, I got it on the block, strung out like. It knew then, of course. Struggled and fought, clawed and squealed.'

'And you did it?' Ian asked eagerly. 'You lopped its head off?'

Jed sighed. 'Course I did. Whack.' He mimed the axe slicing down, the edge of his hand hitting the table and making the drinks jump. 'Head on the block. Chicken fell to the floor.'

'So?' the first man asked.

'So, the damned thing got up again. Not the head, but the body. Leaped to its feet and went careering round the yard. Fast as you like.' He stopped for another drink, and Peri could see that there was a sheen of sweat on his forehead now. The memory was upsetting him more than he was wanting to let on.

'So?' the first man asked again. 'That happens with chickens, you know that, Jed. Just trying to scare the ladies, are you?'

'It's a nervous reaction,' Peri said helpfully. 'It's well known.'

'Course it is,' Jed said. His voice was shaking slightly now. So too was his hand as he raised his pint, Peri saw. 'Think I don't know that, Nick? I been killing chickens since I was seven. I know that.'

'So?' the first man – Nick – said again.

'So they usually just run a few yards. Just till their brains realise they're dead, like.'

'And what did this one do?' Peri asked. Despite herself she took a swig of the beer. Her mouth was suddenly dry.

Jed swallowed. He was looking at the table, unwilling, it seemed, to meet anyone's eye. 'It just kept running,' he said. 'Blood stopped almost at once. And it just kept running.' He suddenly reached for his beer and took a long drink. 'Be running still, if I hadn't…' His voice died away and he drank again, draining his glass.

'Hadn't what, Jed?' one of the women asked, her voice was edged with nerves.

Jed's own voice was noticeably shaky now. 'I kept hitting it,' he said. He was staring off into space. 'Again and again. But it just kept on running. Until it was chopped into little pieces, like. And even then…'

'What?' Nick asked him huskily.

'Even then they were… twitching.' He stood up abruptly, his chair scraping noisily across the floor. 'I need another drink,' he said, and stumbled off towards the bar.

There was silence at the table for a few moments. Then Nick said to Peri: 'I'm sorry. Thought he had a joke or something. Break the ice, like. Not some damned fool horror story.'

'That's all right,' Peri said. She realised with surprise that she had almost finished her beer.

'He was making it up, of course,' Ian put in. 'Wasn't he, Nick?' he added nervously. 'Making it up, wasn't he?'

'Yeah,' Nick said, adjusting the position of his glass on the table top. 'Making it up. Course he was.'

The gas lamps were lit now. Their pale light suffused the room with a yellow glow that made everything seem somehow older. Even the people.

The Doctor was half-way through his second pint. He had already decided he had better not have another. It was a strong ale, he could tell. And while his body could metabolise the alcohol so that it had no effect on him (if he wanted), it might provoke unwanted attention if he drank too much of the brew with no apparent effects at all. Also, he was not at all sure he wanted Peri to drink too much. Carrying her across the moorland back to the TARDIS did not altogether appeal, especially as the evening was drawing in.

And he had learned much of what he wanted. He still had not managed to glean the exact date, though, and he was worried by the anachronisms he was spotting. For instance, the silvering on the mirror behind the bar looked just a little too smooth for its own good. But that could be the result of a caring craftsman, a lucky quirk of the manufacturing process, or his own temporal paranoia.

But he knew now where he was. The Dorsill chain of islands was off the south-west coast of Britain. He could find it in the TARDIS data banks, he was sure. All he really needed was the name and approximate location. But in the process of getting that, he was now privy to the islands' climatic conditions (mist, fog, rain), navigation data (don't even try unless you're an expert on local currents and know every rock by name and repute), and population statistics (this small village on the main Dorsill island, and a mansion house on a small island just off the northern edge called Sheldon's Folly). Enough to call it a day, the Doctor decided, as he watched the shadows lengthen and the windows grow dark.

It was just as the Doctor was finally convincing himself that there really was no mystery or excitement to be had here and they should be on their way, that the door opened and a man came in.

He was tall and extremely thin. He walked very upright, which made him seem even taller, especially in the low-ceilinged room. His hair was silvery grey, receding from his forehead. His eyes were pale with age and the skin on his face was like yellowed parchment in the gaslight. It was stretched so tight that his face resembled the skull beneath. He carried a wooden walking stick, holding it in a determined grip in his right hand. As he crossed the room, he held out the stick, pointing it at Dave Madsen, who was standing talking with several people close to the door.

'You, sir!' the man exclaimed. His voice was strong and deep.

Madsen turned, startled.

'Yes, you!' the man said again. 'Why did you let him do it? What on earth were you dreaming of, man?'

Madsen was obviously unsettled by the peremptory address. It was equally obvious that this was an argument he had suffered before. He sighed and tried to draw the man to one side. But the older man refused to budge. 'I don't think this is the time or the place, Sir Edward,' he said. 'I really don't.'

'Oh, don't you?' Sir Edward obviously did.

The Doctor looked quizzically at Trefoil, who leaned forward and whispered: 'Sir Edward Baddesley. Taken Cove Cottage, just outside the village. Nothing but trouble since he came.'

The Doctor raised an eyebrow by way of appreciation and turned his attention back to the argument.

'Of course I let him be buried,' Madsen was saying. 'There was absolutely no need for a postmortem.'

'Huh!' Sir Edward snapped back. 'In your opinion.'

'In my professional, medical opinion.' Madsen was exasperated. 'The poor man drowned. An unfortunate accident. Regrettable.' He glanced at the people he had been talking with when Sir Edward came in. 'Tragic,' he corrected himself. 'But straightforward in medical terms. There's absolutely no mystery, absolutely no doubt. And certainly no need for a postmortem.' He smiled thin apologies to the mourners standing silent witness to all of this.

Sir Edward seemed now to notice the group of mourners for the first time. Suddenly he was quieter. He bowed his head solemnly and mumbled something. Then he turned back to Madsen. 'Be that as it may, I suppose we shall never know now, shall we?'

'Please,' Madsen began.

'Be that as it may,' Sir Edward repeated, over Madsen's attempted reply, 'I hold you responsible. What in God's name were you thinking of, sir? Letting that poor man go to sea with a broken arm. Eh?' he demanded.

It was one of the mourners who replied, pushing his way through the group and standing bristling in front of Sir Edward. He was smaller than the old man, but stared up at him in obvious anger. '"Poor man"?' he repeated. 'You don't even know his name, do you?'

'I –' Sir Edward began.

But it was his turn to be cut off. 'Do you?' the smaller man shouted. Then he turned on his heel and walked across to the bar.

Behind him, Sir Edward Baddesley hefted his stick, held it shaking for a moment. Then he turned and marched out of the pub.

As the Doctor watched him go, he caught sight of Peri standing at the edge of the group by the bar. He guessed she had come over to see what was going on. She caught the Doctor's eye, then looked over at the door. The Doctor considered for a second, then nodded, just enough for Peri to see. He raised his eyebrows slowly in what he hoped would be interpreted as a 'be careful' sort of way. Then he turned towards Dr Dave Madsen. Perhaps there were a few things to clear up before he was on his way.

Outside the pub, the evening was drawing in. It looked darker from inside, but even so, the sky had darkened to gunmetal grey and the streetlights were splodges of light marking the edge of the street.

It took Peri a moment to catch sight of the man. He was walking briskly up the street away from the pub, towards the church. His heavy coat was open and flapped in the breeze as he walked, stick stabbing briskly into the cobbles. He looked, Peri thought, every inch the typical Victorian gentleman.

As Peri watched, the man stopped and turned, looking back. She ducked into the pub doorway, hoping she had been quick enough not to be seen. She gave it a few moments, then peeped cautiously round the wall.

The man was walking on again, and Peri hurried after him, doing her best to keep to the shadows and out of the direct light of the street lamps. He had almost reached the top of the street when he stopped again.

Peri pressed herself back into the gloom, and watched. The man hesitated, still looking round, as if checking there was nobody watching him. Then he slowly pulled something from inside his coat pocket. Peri strained to see, it looked like a small black oblong box. As she watched, he flipped open the lid and pressed his finger to the surface revealed beneath. Peri gasped. He was pressing buttons. A moment later, the man lifted the box to his ear, cradling it almost invisibly in his hand.

She was not close enough to hear what the man was saying, but Peri could see his lips moving. He was speaking into the box – into a sophisticated communications device. Whatever else he might be, Peri now knew, he was not a typical Victorian gentleman.

Chapter Four
Anachronisms

The white face of the clock on the wall had faded to a dull creamy colour behind the stark black of the Roman numerals. The wooden surround was chipped and in need of a good polish. It gave the time as just a shade after quarter past eight, and there was no reason to doubt it was correct.

The Doctor and Peri had returned to 'their' table in the corner of the bar. Nobody bothered them, or seemed particularly interested now. It was as if they had already been absorbed into the small island community, as if they were now part of the social landscape. The Doctor frowned into his beer as Peri quietly described again the device that Sir Edward Baddesley had surreptitiously spoken into beneath the gas lamp.

'I think,' he said as quietly as he ever said anything, 'that it's time we had a bit of a mooch round. See what we can find.'

'You mean here? In the pub?'

The Doctor nodded. 'Check out some of the rooms, see how the people live. Hunt for clues.' His eyes were gleaming with enthusiasm.

'And how do we do that?' Peri asked. 'It's not as if we're inconspicuous.' She stared pointedly at the Doctor's garish multicoloured coat.

'Oh nonsense.' He brushed her comment away with a dismissive wave of the hand that came dangerously close to connecting with his glass. He leaned forward suddenly, and Peri grabbed his glass and moved it away. 'One of us,' the Doctor said, raising an eyebrow in a way that suggested to Peri that he already knew which one, 'needs to excuse herself.'

'Herself,' Peri checked.

'Mmm.'

'Excuse herself.'

The Doctor nodded, and tapped the side of his nose with his index finger. 'You've got it.'

'And then what?'

'Have a look round.' He flung himself back in the chair, evidently pleased with his plan. 'It's perfectly natural. You feel a bit embarrassed having to ask for… you know. So you have an excuse to go snooping about a bit.'

'Ask for the rest room?' Peri said.

The Doctor was leaning forward again immediately, grabbing her hands across the table as he shushed her and looked round. 'I was hoping not to have to say that,' he hissed at her.

'And you think I'm the one to feign embarrassment?' Peri asked.

'Just checking.'

'Try not to attract any attention,' the Doctor advised her. 'Play it cool, as you would say.'

She considered the plan, sniffed, and stood up. 'Just one thing, Doctor.'

'What's that?'

'You've spilt your beer.' She nodded at the table, at the pint glass lying in the middle of it, and the trail of liquid running off the side and into the Doctor's lap.

The Doctor leaped to his feet, pushing his chair noisily aside and exclaiming at the top of his voice in what might have been ancient High Gallifreyan. Or not. Heads turned, people looked. Someone somewhere laughed.

'Try not to attract any attention, Doctor,' Peri told him as she turned and headed towards the bar.

There was a door beside the bar that led out into the rest of the building. Peri tried not to look round as she pushed her way through it. She waited on the other side of the door, expecting someone to call out to her, or to follow and tell her she should not be there. But nothing happened.

On the other side of the door was a hallway. A flight of stairs led upwards, and the hall continued through to the back door of the pub. There were three doors at the foot of the stairs, and they were clearly marked. The ladies' toilet was next to the gents'. Beside them, on the end, the third door was labelled 'Private'. The sign was a hand-painted block of wood fixed to the door at eye level. There was very little chance that someone would miss it.

Peri paused in front of the door, straining to hear if there was anyone on the other side. She glanced back at the door she had come through, the door into the bar. She was half expecting it to open as she stood furtively in front of the door marked 'Private'. After a few moments of nothing happening, she carefully turned the handle of the door and pushed. Maybe it was locked.

It was not locked, though it squeaked alarmingly as she swung it slowly open, prepared to mutter an apology and duck straight out again. In fact, there was nobody inside the room beyond. So Peri crept furtively inside and closed the door behind her.

The Doctor made a big show of brushing himself down. He was, he decided, rather proud of the way he had organised this little diversion, so that Peri could slip away unobserved. Once she was safely through the door by the bar, the Doctor picked up his empty glass and made his own way over to the bar. He handed the glass to Bob Trefoil and accepted a grubby hand towel in exchange.

'For the table,' Trefoil told him as the Doctor dabbed at his trousers.

The Doctor beamed. 'Of course.' He made his way back, mopped up the beer from the table and the floor, then returned to the bar.

'Another one?' Trefoil asked as he took the towel back. His tone suggested that he did not think this would be a good idea. Further along the bar, Dave Madsen cradled the remains of a pint and watched for the Doctor's reaction.

The Doctor took the hint and shook his head. 'I don't think so, thank you. Excellent though it is. Do you brew it yourself?' he hazarded. From the amused expression on Dave Madsen's face as he turned away, the Doctor guessed he had hit the mark.

Trefoil at once launched into a description of yeast and fermentation, and talked about the quality of the island water as the Doctor watched Madsen drain his pint. Trefoil moved on to an explanation of finings, accompanied by encouraging sounds from the Doctor, and Liz Trefoil refilled Madsen's glass. They were both smiling at her father's enthusiasm.

As soon as seemed polite, the Doctor cut Trefoil short. 'Fascinating,' he said. 'I always find the trick is in keeping the temperature right for the secondary fermentation.' He held up his hand before Trefoil could reply. 'We must talk some more,' the Doctor told him. 'Soon.' He smiled widely. 'But if you will excuse me just for a moment, I would like a quick word with the good Dr Madsen before he escapes.'

Trefoil seemed not at all put out by the Doctor's excuse, and Madsen allowed himself to be led away from the bar. They stood a few feet away, Madsen still smiling back at Liz Trefoil as she wiped down the counter.

'I would have rescued you,' Madsen said. 'Eventually.'

'Thank you. Something of a pet subject of his, I assume?'

'Oh, you could tell.'

The Doctor looked at Madsen, then made a point of following his gaze across towards the landlord's daughter. She caught his eye, and looked away embarrassed. 'Sometimes it's very easy to spot where a man's interest lies,' the Doctor said with a smile.

Madsen smiled back. 'Obvious, is it?'

'Well.' The Doctor paused a moment, then went on. 'But I did actually want to ask you something.'

'Please,' Madsen encouraged him.

'The man who was here earlier, Sir Edward Baddesley did I gather his name is?'

Madsen nodded. 'What about him?'

'He was saying that the poor fisherman who died had a broken arm, is that right?'

Madsen blinked, frowned. 'No,' he said, looking down at the floor for a moment. When he looked back, his eyes held the Doctor's. 'No, that's not true. He did sprain his arm quite badly last week, caught it in a net as it was hauled in. I treated him for it, best I could.

42

That sort of muscular problem is best left to mend itself.'

'I see.' The Doctor nodded, stealing a glance at the door by the bar to see if there was any sign of Peri yet. There was none. 'So he was quite fit for a spot of fishing.'

'I can assure you, Doctor,' Madsen said with restrained patience, 'the accident that befell that fishing boat was entirely due to the weather, to the sudden squall. It had nothing whatsoever to do with the poor lad's bruised arm.'

Madsen turned suddenly, and the Doctor realised that Liz Trefoil was standing beside them.

'Hello there,' the Doctor said.

'Doctor,' she replied. 'Father says that you'll be wanting rooms for tonight. Maybe for a few days. Depending on the fog off the mainland.'

'Does he now? That's very kind of him.' The Doctor nodded. 'And it would certainly be useful, I must admit. Our, er, vessel is beached quite a way from here, and I'm not sure we want to go looking for it at this late hour.'

'You'd rather sleep here than on a boat anyway, wouldn't you, Doctor?' Madsen asked.

'More of a ship, actually,' the Doctor said without committing himself. 'Please tell your father he's most generous and we'll happily stay here until we can be on our way.'

'Might be a couple of days,' Liz told him. 'Fog's closing in again, they say.'

'Sometimes it lingers for weeks,' Madsen said. 'We're often cut off, sometimes for as long as a month.'

'Something to look forward to,' the Doctor said with a smile. He watched Liz make her way back towards the bar. 'Do you like it here?' he asked Madsen.

'Yes. Yes, I do.' Madsen was watching her too. 'And not just because...' He paused. 'You know.'

'I do indeed.' They both turned towards each other. 'Tell me about Baddesley,' the Doctor said. 'Why would he assume the fisherman had broken his arm if it was just sprained?'

Madsen shrugged. 'Beats me. Gossip and news travel fast round a community like this. And sometimes it gets embellished on the way. I assume he was misinformed.'

'He didn't seem to think so,' the Doctor said gently. Before Madsen could react, he went on: 'Not a good place to keep secrets then, I suppose.'

Madsen regarded him carefully. 'I suppose not,' he said levelly. 'Baddesley's been here a couple of months,' he went on after a moment. 'Took a cottage on the edge of the village. Cove Cottage, up behind the church. If anyone has secrets to keep, it's him.'

'Oh? Why do you say that?'

'No reason,' Madsen said. 'But why's he here? Hardly a place to retire to.'

'It takes all sorts. Does he say he's retired here?'

Madsen took a long drink of his beer. 'Doesn't give a reason for being here. That's partly why the locals are wary of him. That and the fact he's a government type. They don't hold with any sort of bureaucracy or authority here. There's not even a policeman – we're part of the beat for the mainland.'

'Government type?' the Doctor asked. 'What do you man by that?'

'Oh, he was some sort of civil servant. In London. In the government. So I gather.' Madsen took another drink. 'As I say, they're wary of that sort of thing here. Some of the locals are even saying he's part of the company that put in the bid.'

'The bid?' the Doctor asked. But his question was drowned out by the approaching sound from outside.

The room was almost in darkness. There was an oil lamp casting a hint of light over a low table close to the door, but Peri did not dare to turn it up. If it was dark, she could at least claim she was lost and had not realised this was a private room. It did not look like a living room. There was the table by the door with the lamp on it, and another larger table in the middle of the room. Apart from several upright wooden chairs beside the large table there was practically no other furniture. The small window in the wall opposite the door had no curtains. The floor was bare boards. A stone fireplace stood empty and cold on the wall to the left of the door. On the mantelpiece was a plain cardboard box.

Peri stood just inside the door, letting her eyes adjust to the gloom. After a few moments she went to the fireplace and carefully lifted the lid of the cardboard box. Inside was a flare pistol and several flare cartridges. Peri reached into the box, letting her fingertips stray over the rough metal of the flare gun as she turned to look round the rest of the room.

On the floor beneath the table Peri gradually made out a second box. It was the size of two large shoeboxes standing one on top of the other, and there was something on top of it. She replaced the lid on the cardboard box on the mantelpiece and stooped to look closer at the object on the box under the table. A book.

With a glance back at the door, Peri crawled under the table and lifted the book. She held it up to what pale light there was. It was a paperback, the pages well thumbed and ragged. She looked through it and realised almost at once that it was a set of tide tables. It gave dates, times and water levels for various points along the coast. Presumably it related to the islands, maybe to the mainland coast nearby as well. The dates were month and day. There did not seem to be a year given.

The year had probably been on the cover, but that was torn and frayed. It had once been glossy, an abstract design of blue and black. Did they have glossy paperbacks in Victorian times? Peri wondered. Somehow she felt the book was out of place in this room with its bare boards, creaky door and oil lamp. She tapped the book against her hand as she considered.

Next she examined the box. It was made of metal, she saw as she looked at it. The top inch was hinged and folded back to reveal what was inside. Peri listened intently for a moment, trying to hear if there was any movement from outside the door, but she could hear nothing. Slowly she lifted the lid. Then she sat there, under the table, staring at the inside of the box.

It housed equipment. Communications equipment. There was a

handset, a keypad with numerical buttons. And set into the fascia of the device was a read-out screen. It was blank at the moment, but a tiny red light was glowing at the edge. Peri looked from the bright red of the light to the dull misty glow of the oil lamp by the door. She sat there for a while, looking from one light to the other, frowning, trying to make sense of it all.

Then she heard the noise approaching from outside the window. She snapped the box shut and replaced the ragged book on top of it. She struggled to her feet, almost banging her head on the underside of the table, and left the room at a run.

Outside in the street, the noise had reached an almost deafening roar. Peri caught up with the Doctor as he was standing looking up into the foggy blackness of the sky.

'What is it?' she asked, but he did not answer.

Behind them several of the villagers had emerged from the pub. They were looking bemused and surprised. They too were scanning the sky for any sign of what was making the sound. Madsen and Bob Trefoil joined the Doctor and Peri.

'Can you see anything?' Madsen asked.

'Over to the west,' Trefoil said. 'Towards Sheldon's Folly, by the sound of it.'

They looked where he was pointing. If anything, the sound seemed to be getting louder, cutting through the quietness of the night and chopping through the fog.

'Did you find anything?' the Doctor asked Peri as quietly as he could and still be heard.

She nodded. 'Yes, Doctor. But I didn't like it.'

He looked at her quizzically, and she explained quickly about the communications equipment.

The Doctor nodded grimly. 'Definitely something strange going on here,' he said. Then he took Peri's shoulder and turned her slightly, pointing up into the foggy night. Dimly at first, Peri could make out a faint light. A tiny speck of illumination high in the sky.

'If the weather were clearer,' the Doctor mused, 'I could tell if it was a hawk or a handsaw.'

'It's coming lower,' Madsen observed as the light approached. It was growing larger and brighter as it dropped slowly towards them.

'It's coming down somewhere over there,' the Doctor said. 'I think it's further away than it looks, a trick of the fog and the noise.'

'On Sheldon's Folly,' Trefoil said quietly.

The Doctor watched for a few seconds more, and then turned towards the people standing outside the pub. 'Don't panic,' he shouted loudly, above the sound now receding into the distance. 'I know it's incredible, but what we can see is merely some sort of flying machine.'

The people turned to look at each other, their faces betraying their surprise at his words. Several of them muttered to each other and nodded towards the Doctor and Peri.

'I'm not sure they can cope with the idea, Doctor,' Peri told him quietly.

'Incredible,' Madsen said. 'Absolutely incredible.'

The Doctor nodded. 'Just stay calm, everyone,' he announced. 'There is absolutely nothing to worry about.'

'I'm not so sure,' Trefoil said loudly above the noise. There was the hint of a smile on his face. 'Were you a long time at sea, Doctor?'

The Doctor frowned. 'Why do you ask?'

Trefoil shrugged and grinned suddenly at the Doctor and Peri. 'Oh, nothing,' he said with a glance at Madsen, who was also grinning. 'It's just that anyone would think you'd never seen a helicopter before.'

Peri gaped. 'You just said it was incredible,' she accused Madsen. The sound of the helicopter was dying away now as it disappeared behind the stark silhouette of the church.

'It is,' he agreed. 'Don't you think it's incredible that anyone would take a helicopter up on a foggy night like this?'

Trefoil nodded as he ushered them back inside. 'That Sheldon's an idiot to use the thing at all,' he grumbled. 'Quite against the spirit of Dorsill. But I suppose we have to make allowances.'

Back inside the pub, the Doctor was doing his best to cover his embarrassment, though it seemed only to add to the amusement of Bob Trefoil and the other islanders.

'You know about how we live on Dorsill then?' Trefoil asked at last, giving the Doctor the hint of a way out.

'Oh yes,' the Doctor said loudly and clearly. He coughed. 'Of course. Well,' he admitted, 'the general idea anyway.'

'And the helicopter surprised you,' Madsen said. It was a statement, not a question.

'Of course,' Peri said, wondering what they were getting round to. 'It surprised us.'

'So we thought it best,' the Doctor went on quickly, 'to, well... You know.'

Trefoil and Madsen both nodded at this as if it made perfect sense. 'Just because we don't use the trappings of the modern world,' Trefoil said slowly, 'you needn't assume we don't know about them.' He nodded at Madsen. 'We have contact with outsiders, people who tell us what's going on. Even got a satellite phone in case of emergencies. It's kept in the front room, if you need to tell anyone you've got washed up here,' he offered.

The Doctor and Peri exchanged looks.

'Perhaps,' the Doctor said, his voice at its most reasonable, 'you could tell us everything from your point of view, from your perspective. Just to put us straight.' He smiled winningly.

Trefoil did most of the talking, warming to the topic immediately. Madsen added the occasional comment, giving the perspective of one who had only recently come to the islands. It was, Peri thought as she listened, all quite simple.

In fact, she had heard of a similar situation on a couple of the Channel Islands or among the Amish communities. On Dorsill there was no electricity, no mains gas, no petrol stations. Partly this was because they had never come, partly it was because the cost now of installing these things would be prohibitive, and partly it was because the island community had turned its back on such things. They made a virtue of living off the land, of using horses instead of cars or tractors. They valued their isolation, the cleanliness of the air, the simplicity of their lives.

There were concessions of course. Madsen could, and did, prescribe modern drugs and medication. The street lights were powered by gas cylinders shipped out from the mainland together with the mail and tinned food and fresh fruit, vegetables and meat. There was the satellite phone for emergencies. At this point Madsen grinned.

'I brought a cellphone when I came. Couldn't get a signal. Sir Edward has one too, and he claims it works pretty well. But I never found it did. Wrong network maybe. And anyway, there was no way to recharge it. You soon settle into the ways of the island. It's...' he considered, picking his word with care. 'Refreshing,' he said.

Some of the people made more concessions than others. Travel to the mainland was difficult given the distance and the fog that kept them isolated most of the year. But Trefoil confessed that his daughter ordered clothes from a catalogue and they were shipped out when conditions allowed. She wasn't the only one. A couple of the larger houses had diesel generators and used electricity for lighting and heating. Sir Edward, they were told with more than a hint of discontent, had surreptitiously installed a generator at Cove Cottage.

They talked well into the evening. It was almost midnight by the time the Doctor said: 'So, tell me about Sheldon and his helicopter.'

'Young Mr Christopher it is now,' Trefoil said. The pub was empty save for the four of them and Trefoil's daughter. Liz was wiping down the tables and trying not to make it obvious she was watching Madsen. Peri had seen her trying to catch his eye several times, as if she wanted to speak to him. The rest of them – the Doctor and Peri, Madsen and Trefoil – were seated round one of the tables. Madsen was drinking whisky, turning the glass slowly round and round, so that the chunks of ice floating inside clinked against the side. Trefoil had a glass of water. The Doctor was sitting with an almost untouched pint of Fisherman's Ruin, and Peri had coffee. It was strong and dark with the consistency of syrup.

'Since his father died last year,' Trefoil went on, 'Christopher Sheldon's returned. The prodigal he was. Off to London to study at first. Due back in a few years. Then he stopped coming home for the holidays. Pretty soon he stopped coming home at all. They say he was seduced by the bright lights and the money.' Trefoil grinned. 'Bright lights, maybe. He had money already as we now know.'

'Why's it called Sheldon's Folly?' Peri wanted to know.

'Name of the house,' Trefoil said. 'Big house it is. We call the island Sheldon's Folly now too. Doesn't have any other name, far as I know.'

'And the house?' Madsen asked. Peri had not realised that some of this might be new to him too.

'Sheldon's Folly,' Trefoil said, nodding. 'A sort of joke, it is. Built by Christopher Sheldon's great-great-great-grandfather.' He paused to tap out the 'greats' on his fingers, checking he had it right. 'He never finished it. Spent the family fortune. There are still bits that are just abandoned. Rooms without ceilings or roofs, open to the air.'

'So,' the Doctor said, 'folly as in mistake and folly as in unconventional building.'

'You have it exactly.'

'And folly as in helicopter?' the Doctor suggested.

Trefoil laughed, banging his glass on the table. Water sloshed over the side. 'That too. But we have to allow him his little eccentricities.'

'Oh?'

Trefoil shrugged. 'He still works in London, I understand. Some sort of government scientist. I asked Sir Edward if he knew what

Sheldon does, but he was a bit vague. Don't think they know each other. Anyway, Sheldon needs to travel back and forth and the boats are slow and unreliable.'

'And you let him get away with it?' Peri asked.

'Let him?' Trefoil considered. 'Not sure it's my place to stop him.' He swung round in his chair, waving a hand massively in an arc through the air. 'He owns this pub.'

'Really?' the Doctor said.

'And the village. And the islands.' Trefoil wiped at the damp table with the back of his hand. 'Owns the whole blooming lot.' Then he suddenly downed the drink in one. 'Good thing too,' he said. Then he pushed back his chair and stood up. 'Now if you'll excuse me, I must help Liz lock up. Then I'll show you two to your rooms.' He nodded to Madsen. 'You see yourself out?' he asked.

Madsen finished his whisky while the Doctor toyed with his pint and Peri stared at the remains of her coffee. 'What he didn't say,' Madsen explained as he put his coat on, 'is that Sheldon's only owned the islands for about six months.'

'Oh?' The Doctor was interested. He cocked his head to one side. 'Who owned them before that?'

'The islanders. Some sort of trust as far as I understand it.'

'What happened?' Peri asked.

'Went bust. Legs up. Just ran out of money. The trustees had to sell out.'

'To Sheldon,' the Doctor concluded.

Madsen laughed. 'Oh no, not to Sheldon. Not at first. No, the only buyer they could find was a property developer. They agreed to keep the village more or less intact – most of it is listed, after all. But they wanted to turn the whole of this island into a theme park. Rare animal breeds mixed in with roller coasters and luxury hotels. Couple of golf courses on the other islands. Even a small airport.'

'Hmm. I take it,' the Doctor said slowly, 'that the islanders weren't terribly enthralled by the idea.'

'Too right. They had protest meetings, letters to Parliament, slots

51

on the local news. Not that they saw it, of course. Then Sheldon stepped in. Nobody knew he had any money, they sort of assumed he was broke because of Sheldon's Folly, I think.'

'And he trumped the developers?' the Doctor asked.

Madsen nodded. 'Big time, as I heard it. Bought them off, then bought up the islands lock, stock and barrel. They were a bit apprehensive here at first, but he just told them to get on with it and pretend nothing had ever happened.'

Peri stood up as Madsen made to leave. They all shook hands, and the young doctor turned to go.

'That's a wonderful story,' Peri said to Madsen. 'So nothing's really changed?'

Madsen was facing away from her. He stopped in mid-stride, but did not turn back. 'That's right,' he said, his voice suddenly sounding tired and breaking slightly as he spoke. 'Nothing's changed at all.' He left without looking back.

Chapter Five
Herd Instinct

Liz Trefoil showed the Doctor and Peri to rooms opposite each other at the top of the stairs.

'Not much call for bed and breakfast, I suppose,' the Doctor joked, and she smiled back.

'Breakfast when you want it,' she said. 'Dad'll be up at seven to get things sorted in the cellar. I'm usually not far behind him.'

'Seven?' Peri said. 'I don't think we'll worry you that early.'

'We'll see you in the morning,' the Doctor assured Liz and let himself into his room.

Peri opened the door to her room and went in. There was a single bed made up, and a towel lying across it. She turned to shut the door behind her, but there was someone in the doorway. She gave a stifled shriek, only realising as he stepped into the room that it was the Doctor.

'Don't do that,' she hissed. 'I nearly died.'

'Sorry. You a bit jumpy?'

'I'm a bit tired,' she said. 'What is it?'

'Just saying good night,' the Doctor said. 'What do you think?' he asked her seriously.

'About saying good night?'

'About this place.'

Peri shrugged. 'Seems nice enough. Everyone's very friendly.' As she said it, the light caught the Doctor's eyes and she recalled the young man with his piercing blue eyes who had watched her. The dead fisherman's brother – Mike Neville. 'Almost everyone,' she corrected herself. 'What do *you* think?'

'Oh, I think you're right,' the Doctor said. But he did not sound entirely sure. 'It's just…' he added.

'Just? Just what?'

'I'm not certain. There's something. Madsen's not telling the whole truth for some reason. There must be a reason for that.' He smiled suddenly. 'Probably nothing important. Let's get some sleep, then have a look round in the morning. With luck we can find our way back to the TARDIS in time for lunch and a quick trip round the White Hole of Stelabilis.' He stared off into a corner of the room as he spoke, as if imagining the sights and wonders of the Universe.

'Great,' Peri said. 'But right now I want a quick trip to the land of nod.'

'Mmm?' the Doctor asked, jolted back to the present time and place.

'Good night,' Peri said firmly.

'Mmm,' the Doctor agreed. He closed the door gently behind him.

A shaft of sunlight streaming through the thin curtains woke Peri next morning. She lay still for a while, enjoying the complete lack of traffic sound. The only noise that disturbed her was the discordant crying of the seagulls outside her window. When she eventually twisted her head to see the small alarm clock on the cabinet by the bed, she was amazed to see that it was after eight o'clock.

There was a sink in the corner of the room, and she had been pleased to find the night before that there was plenty of hot water. As she washed, she wondered vaguely if there was anywhere on the island she could get a toothbrush. Perhaps there was a village shop of some sort. A post office? Something to hunt down this morning.

She made her way downstairs, realising as she went that she was already assuming they would be staying for at least another night. Well, she had to admit, she had stayed in worse places. Recently too. The smell of bacon did nothing to dampen her enthusiasm.

The Doctor was in the kitchen. He was wearing a white apron which barely covered his ample form. He was frying bacon over a gas ring.

'Good morning,' he said cheerily. 'Some mod cons at least.'

'That smells terrific,' Peri said, seating herself at the kitchen table. 'Where are our hosts?'

'Trefoil is sorting out his cellar, and Liz went to the farm for milk. I gather there isn't a Mrs Trefoil.' He shuffled the bacon round the pan with a wooden spatula, letting it hiss and spit in the fat. 'The bread's good,' he said without looking up. 'Home made from local flour, of course.'

It was hard to believe that the bright sunny street was the same place as the foggy village of the day before. The Doctor had called down to Trefoil that they were going out for a walk and not to worry about them. 'In case we decide to leave,' he confided to Peri.

'I like it here,' she told him. 'I'm happy to spend a day or two.'

They decided to start with the church. From there they could continue on towards Heather Hill Farm, and then to the TARDIS. Or they could return to the pub for lunch depending on how they felt. The Doctor had hinted that he wanted a quick peep at Cove Cottage where Sir Edward Baddesley was living too, and that was apparently up behind the church somewhere.

They were nearing the top of the street when a door opened. It was like déjà-vu, Peri thought. She was sure it was the same door that had opened as they approached the previous day. And the same shrivelled old lady stepped out.

But this time she was not watching for a funeral procession. She was looking for the Doctor and Peri. She showed no sign of surprise that there were two strangers almost on her doorstep. Peri could believe she had been waiting behind the door, peering out from behind the net curtains in the front window of the small house, timing her exit to coincide with their arrival.

'You're the strangers,' she said. Her voice was high-pitched and cracked with age. She nodded her grey head with something approaching vigour.

'Indeed we are,' the Doctor agreed enthusiastically. 'None stranger,' he added with a smile.

She cackled a dry laugh in return. 'I'm Mrs Tattleshall,' she said. 'Perhaps someone has mentioned…?'

'No,' Peri said, 'I don't think –'

'Of course,' the Doctor interrupted as the old lady frowned with disappointment. 'You remember, Peri. This is Mrs Tattleshall.' He gripped her hand and, to Peri's surprise and Mrs Tattleshall's evident delight, raised the back of it to his lips and brushed a kiss against it. 'Mrs Tattleshall, we have heard so much about you. It is indeed a pleasure to make your acquaintance at long last.'

They stood in silence for a few moments. The Doctor still holding the withered hand and the old lady gazing fondly at him as he smiled.

'I'm Peri,' Peri said. She was tempted to add: 'and I feel sick,' but she was not sure it would be appreciated.

'And I'm the Doctor.' He shook her hand now, and then at last let go of it. 'And we really are very pleased to meet you.'

'Saw you yesterday,' Mrs Tattleshall said. She made it sound something like an accusation. 'At young William Neville's funeral.'

'Alas,' the Doctor said, 'a sad affair.'

'Tragic,' the old lady agreed with something akin to glee in her voice. 'And so soon after breaking his arm.'

The Doctor and Peri exchanged glances. But before either of them could comment on the remark, the old lady was talking again.

'You know,' she said, her voice cracked like an old record, 'I remember when his poor mother first came to the island. Married Big John up at that church. Lovely it was. She wore white.' Her tone suggested that this was not something she had approved of or thought appropriate.

Peri took a deep breath. 'We'd best be getting on, Doctor,' she said, tugging his sleeve. 'Otherwise we'll be late.' She turned so that Mrs Tattleshall could not see her, and then gave the Doctor a huge wink.

'Late?' The Doctor glared at her as if she were mad. Then his face cleared. 'Oh, you mean *late*. Yes, well, I'll tell you what,' he said, 'you go on and I'll catch up with you later.' He winked back. 'I'm sure I can spare Mrs Tattleshall a few moments. If I don't catch you up, I'll see you back at the pub for lunch.'

'Right.' Peri smiled sweetly at the woman. 'It was lovely to meet you,' she said.

'And you, my dear.' But she was still looking at the Doctor.

Peri raised her eyebrows at the Doctor. He smiled back blithely. So she set off towards the church and left him to it. She could already hear Mrs Tattleshall's voice creaking on the breeze behind her, and was pretty certain that the Doctor was there for the rest of the morning.

'He was always headstrong, even as a child,' Mrs Tattleshall confided to the Doctor. 'I remember his poor mother was quite beside herself with his tantrums when he was a toddler. Lie there on the floor, he would, kicking and screaming.' She pulled her ancient coat closely around her and folded her arms. 'You can tell, you know,' she went on. 'Right from the start you can tell how they'll turn out.'

The Doctor nodded sympathetically. 'It seems to run in the family,' he remarked. 'We had rather a run-in with his brother Michael last night in the pub.'

This was obviously not news to the old lady, who nodded in her turn, knowingly. 'Ah, that one – takes after his father, he does, with his nasty temper. Always ready to fly off the handle. He and William used to fight like cat and dog, they did – and now poor William's gone, Michael won't hear a word against him. Gets real touchy. Worked up. If you ask me, he needs watching – it don't take much to turn him ugly.'

Mrs Tattleshall seemed lost for a moment in contemplation of Michael's iniquity. Then she shook herself. 'Where was I? Oh yes, young William – I'm not saying he was like his brother, mind. He wasn't a bad lad, just...'

'... headstrong,' the Doctor put in.

The old lady pursed her lips. 'Oh yes,' she said with feeling.

'If his mother had sorted him out years ago, he wouldn't have been so set on getting his own way all the time. Look what it all came to, him going off in that boat.'

'Oh?'

'And him with a broken arm and all.' Mrs Tattleshall sighed theatrically.

Seeing a way in, the Doctor said quickly, 'I gather from Dr Madsen it wasn't actually broken – just sprained.'

Mrs Tattleshall snorted. A thin reedy sound, which sent a breath of mist streaming out of her nostrils into the cold air. 'Some doctor he is,' she rasped.

'Perhaps you were misinformed,' the Doctor suggested gently. 'These things do get exaggerated.'

The old woman unfolded her arms, then immediately folded them again. 'Maybe,' she said. 'But I know what I saw. Caught it in the net he did. Last week. Tuesday, as I remember.'

The Doctor frowned. 'You were there?'

'Saw the boat come in.' She nodded towards the top of the street, towards where the masts of the fishing boats at the quay were just visible in the distance poking up beside the church. Seagulls were wheeling and crying in the air above them, hopeful of easy pickings. 'I was hoping for some fish for tea. Didn't fancy eating after that.'

'You think the arm was broken?' the Doctor asked.

But she had barely paused for breath. 'Snapped clean through, it was. Blood across the deck. The end of the bone poking out through the poor lad's torn sleeve.' Her wrinkled face screwed up still further as she closed her eyes and shook her head. 'No,' she said quietly, 'didn't fancy any dinner after that.'

The Doctor nodded slowly, looking off towards the distant bobbing tips of the masts. 'No,' he agreed. 'I don't suppose you did.'

Although it was cold, it was pleasant walking in the sunshine. Peri passed the small quay, noticing that several of the boats she had seen the day before were no longer there. Probably out fishing while the weather was fine, she thought. Life had to go on despite the accident.

She kept going, following the track that she and the Doctor had taken into the village the previous day. Peri could now see the fields either side of the path. There was a fence set back from the track on one side and, when she reached a gate, Peri paused. She leaned on the gate looking out into the field. There were sheep, all grouped together in a clump, so that they looked almost like a cloud on the damp grass. They seemed to be moving slowly across the pasture, eating the grass as they went. In unison.

Peri watched for a while. It was relaxing just to stand, leaning on the gate, watching the slow, gentle progress of the animals. She was half expecting the Doctor to arrive, having escaped from Mrs Tattleshall at last. But a part of her was content to stand there alone for a while longer and just do nothing for a time. For a change.

Her reverie was broken by the sound of a dog barking. It was a sudden, sharp sound, from across the field. Peri turned towards the noise and saw a large black dog bounding across the grass towards the sheep. It continued to make a lot of noise as it approached.

She expected the sheep to scatter, to run from the dog. But they did not. Instead they all turned together. Then they seemed to spread out, forming a semicircle with the dog charging into the middle of it. Slowly, the sheep started to move forward.

Peri had never seen anything like it. She did not consider she knew much about sheep, but she did not think this was how they usually behaved. The dog pulled up short as the sheep encircled it. It made a half-hearted attempt to frighten them again by barking and running. Then it seemed to decide that this was going to be more trouble than it was worth, and it backed away. It crouched down on its front legs, snarling as it slowly worked its way back towards the side of the field. The sheep slowly followed, herding it back towards the fence.

At last the dog turned and bounded off. Peri watched as it

leaped over the low fence on the far side of the field and was soon lost to view.

'I must be the only farmer around here whose sheep round up the dogs,' said a voice from behind her.

Peri started with surprise and turned. The woman standing behind her smiled. 'But then I am the only farmer round here,' she added.

The woman was in her late middle age, her hair still clinging to some brown in among the grey. She was wearing a green waxed jacket and jeans. Her face was weather-beaten but kindly, with laughter lines rather than wrinkles. She held out her hand, and Peri shook it nervously. 'Hilda Painswick,' she said.

'Peri. Peri Brown,' Peri replied.

'I'm pleased to meet you. Most people call me Hilly, by the way.'

'Hilly?' Peri smiled, tried not to laugh.

Hilda Painswick saw her amusement. 'Yes, it's a joke really,' she agreed. 'Hilly because of Hilda, and because this is Heather Hill Farm.' She gestured at the fields in front of them. 'But it's stuck, for whatever reason. So now I am Hilly, like it or not.'

'And do you like it?'

The woman raised her eyebrows. 'Between you and me, not much. But it's better than being Madame Pain, which was once mooted as an alternative. So please do call me Hilly.'

From somewhere in the distance came the sound of a dog yelping, a frightened almost pathetic sound, which carried thinly on the breeze.

The Doctor had made good his escape from Mrs Tattleshall. He had checked his watch, tutted, made a point of looking up the street after Peri, and eventually got across the message that really he ought to be going.

He made a point of holding the old lady's arthritic hand for several moments after he shook it goodbye, and of looking into her pale old eyes as he thanked her for the conversation and said how much he had enjoyed it. He knew what it was like to be old and unappreciated.

Once Mrs Tattleshall was safely back inside her house, the Doctor considered. It was a while since Peri had set off. She would be well ahead of him now, and they had agreed to meet back at the pub for lunch if they didn't run into each other before that. Rather than spend the time hunting for Peri and probably failing to find her, the Doctor decided to take a walk down to the other end of the village. He swung round on his heels, drawing in a deep healthy breath of the chilled air.

As he turned, he could hear children's voices, shouting and laughing on the breeze. In the distance, beyond the pub, he could see small figures running, chasing, dashing madly round the school playground. The Doctor smiled. He liked children.

There was an innocent charm about school playtime that somehow attracted him. A microcosm of the Universe in which the evil forces were a nervous bully, the gods were the teachers, and a definition of suffering involved either mild detention or overcooked cabbage. He liked the symmetry of the idea too, he decided, as he set off down the hill. From the old to the young, from the worldly-wise gossip of Mrs Tattleshall to the naive enthusiasm of children. He was looking forward to a friendly chat, he decided.

Peri chatted to 'Hilly' Painswick for several minutes, finding the woman pleasant and friendly company. She glossed over how she and the Doctor had arrived on the island, and tentatively mentioned that she had heard the island's vet had recently died. Peri said she assumed that posed problems.

Hilly looked away at that point. 'Poor George,' she said with a sigh. 'It was so very sudden. Flu apparently.' She blinked, wiped her eye with the back of a gloved hand. 'But we soldier on,' she said. 'Dr Madsen is very helpful.' She took a deep breath and was at once her old self again, the demons of memory banished. 'He helped me inoculate these sheep the other week.'

'Oh?' Peri wasn't sure what to say. Should she change the subject, or just let the woman talk?

'You know, ringworm, that sort of thing. New procedure apparently. George hadn't mentioned it, but Dave Madsen read up on it and called some friends of his at the Ministry of Agriculture. He used to work there, you know.'

'I didn't. No.'

'Some sort of personnel job, I think. Anyway, we'll manage until we can find a proper replacement for George. Dave says he can get whatever we need sent over on the mail boat.' She turned and looked back at the sheep, now clumped together once more as they made their lazy progress across the field. 'One less thing to worry about, and that's always a mercy.'

They talked for a few minutes more before Hilly excused herself. Peri watched the woman striding purposefully across the field, calling affectionately to the sheep as she went. Not that the animals seemed to notice or care.

There was still no sign of the Doctor. Peri wondered whether to head back towards the village. But there were only two possibilities she could think of. Either he was still talking to Mrs Tattleshall, in which case Peri was happy not to be involved, or he had finally managed to escape from her. In that case, if he was following her, she would be able to see him heading towards her, past the distant quay. And since she could not, the only other possibility was that he had wandered off in a completely different direction and had no intention of meeting her again before their rendezvous at the pub.

As she worked through these possibilities, Peri started along the track, heading back towards the open moorland. There was a while yet before she needed to start back towards the pub, and she had half a mind to see if she could find her way back to the TARDIS. It would be good to be able to assure the Doctor it was safe and to be able to lead him straight to it.

Without the fog, the moorland seemed wide, empty and free. The previous afternoon Peri had found it close, oppressive and stifling. What a difference a bit of sunshine made, she thought as she reached the top of a shallow slope and looked down the other side of the gentle hill. She stood for a moment, taking in the view. There was a small wooded area off to one side. In the distance she could see the cliffs and beyond them was the sea. Somewhere in the distance, beyond the coastline, was the smudge of another island – Sheldon's Folly, perhaps.

Peri turned to look back the way she had come. She could not see the village, that was too far away now. But she could see the comparatively ordered layout of the fields of Heather Hill Farm, the track that worked its way between them. And between the fields and herself, a figure was approaching.

Her first assumption was that it was the Doctor. But as it grew closer, Peri could see that although it was a man, he was wearing clothes altogether too ordinary and drab to be the Doctor. There was a fascination in watching the figure slowing growing larger as he strode up the slope towards her. It was only when he was within fifty yards that Peri was able to see who it was.

It was Mike Neville, his piercing blue eyes fixed on her as he approached.

For a moment Peri considered running. But at once she knew that was not an option. Why should she, for one thing? And for another, if he chose to chase her Peri was pretty sure his long legs would soon outrun hers. Better to let him pass by, then return to the village and find the Doctor. Probably the young man was on his way somewhere, probably it was a coincidence that they had met. Probably there was nothing to worry about.

Probably.

She changed her mind when he spoke. 'On your own, are you?' he called from twenty yards away.

'Er, yes,' Peri admitted. But she was sure her nervous voice did not carry to him.

'Without your colourful friend.'

'I'm meeting him soon.' She looked round, hoping he would think she was expecting the Doctor to emerge from the landscape at any moment. There was scrubland, bushes nearby. Maybe she could convince him the Doctor was for some reason hiding there.

Neville was shaking his head. 'Saw him in the village. Heading the other way.' He smiled, all teeth and no effect on the eyes. 'Don't reckon he saw me, though.'

'Oh.' Peri's voice was barely more than a squeak. 'I'd better go and find him then.' She set off down the hill, giving Neville a wide berth.

But he stepped across quickly and caught her by the upper arm. 'There's no hurry,' he said. His breath was hot and smelled of fish. Everything about him smelled of fish.

'Yes there is,' Peri said in a rush. 'I need to get back, let me go, please.'

He didn't. 'But we've got things to talk about, you and me.'

'No we haven't. Let me go.' She pulled her arm free and started to run. But before she had gone two steps, her head was yanked back as he grabbed her hair, pulled her towards him. She screamed in surprise, fright and pain as she fell backwards, collapsed against his body as he pulled her to him.

'Lots of things to talk about,' he hissed. His eyes were wide, the blue of them seeming to deepen as he stared at her. His tongue whipped out and coated his lips with a thin film of saliva that glistened in the cold air. Then suddenly, his eyes widened, and he let go of her.

Peri jumped back at once, staring at him in horror and shock. Neville was shaking his head, his mouth opening and closing. He was looking past Peri, towards the scrubland. Peri turned, to see what he had seen that had stopped his assault.

It was the ragged, scruffy figure they had met the previous day. He was standing on the edge of the scrub, watching them, his head tilted to one side. His face looked even more grimy than it had before, his clothes even more ragged and torn in the better light. He took a step towards them.

Neville backed away. He lowered his head as he went, mumbling. 'I'm sorry, sir,' he muttered. 'I meant no harm, really I didn't. Sorry,' he repeated, 'sorry, sorry.' Then he turned and stumbled quickly away.

Peri watched him go in surprise. Then she turned back towards the grubby figure of the man. The dark stubble of his beard was streaked with mud, and his teeth emerged like tombstones when he grinned at her.

'Are you all right?' he asked, surprisingly kindly. Perhaps he was having one of his lucid moments. 'He didn't hurt you?'

'I'm fine,' Peri stammered. 'Just, you know… upset. He didn't hurt me.' She put her hand to her head as she said it. The roots of her hair hurt like hell. 'I'm sorry,' she went on quickly as the man took another step towards her. 'But I have to go. Really I do.' She turned and ran, wiping the tears from her cheeks as she went, following Neville's stumbling trail back towards the village.

'Goodbye,' the man's voice floated to her as she went. 'Until we meet again.' She did not answer. She did not look back.

There were not many children. Perhaps ten of them, variously aged between five and fifteen. The Doctor stood and watched them over the gate. A woman, perhaps in her forties, prim and proper, schoolmarmish, stood by the main door into the small Victorian school building. She held a mug of tea or coffee. The Doctor could see the heat rising from it as she held it tight in her hands, close under her chin. Occasionally she sneaked furtive sips from the hot liquid.

The children ran past and round her, without comment or worry. It was interesting, the Doctor thought, the patterns they made with their games. There was a symmetry to it. As though each was following the other, taking his or her cue from another child who in turn… and so on. Snakes eating their own tails, he thought ruefully.

The teacher caught his eye and smiled. No problem with strangers, the Doctor decided. She probably already knew exactly who he was – or rather, who he said he was. Probably the rest of the children did too. Not one had glanced across at him, remarked him, noticed his clothing. He was a bit disappointed, actually.

And partly because of this, he pushed the gate open and strode across the playground towards the teacher. The main part of the playground was compacted earth. There was a grassed area off to the side that stretched round behind the school building. It looked like it opened out and became a playing field further round – the Doctor could see goal posts. The children continued their game, running past and round him like shallow water flowing over a stone. He smiled and nodded at them. They grinned and laughed back. And for a few paces life was wonderful.

The teacher released her shivering grip on the mug with one hand for long enough to shake the Doctor's hand. It was coffee, he could smell it now.

'Miss Devlin,' she said. She had a cold. 'You must be the Doctor.'

'Ah, you've heard of me.' The Doctor beamed hugely. 'News travels fast.'

She nodded, her eyes on the racing children as they screamed by. She was quite short, wrapped in a huge coat, mousy-brown hair wisping out from beneath a headscarf. She had a collection of bangles on her left wrist and they jangled as she moved her hand. Or shivered.

'Are you their teacher?' the Doctor asked. 'Their only teacher?'

'With so few of them, it's easy enough despite the age difference. Better a class of eleven happy enthusiastic youngsters than thirty or more little devils all refusing to learn the same thing.'

The Doctor nodded. 'I suppose so. And are they?'

'Little devils?'

'Enthusiastic.'

'Oh yes.' She smiled thinly, to show it had actually been a joke. He smiled back to show that he knew.

'I've been watching them,' the Doctor said. 'So much energy to burn off.'

'You're telling me. They're worse when it's windy. Quieter in the fog.' She shrugged towards her coffee. 'Funny how the weather affects them.'

They watched the children for a while. They were playing a form of tig. For a moment they were all still, frozen in place as the game paused. Then, 'Budge,' shouted one boy. And they were off again.

'I've been watching the patterns they make. When they run.'

She nodded. 'I noticed that too. Just these last few weeks. Perhaps since the weather turned colder.' She sipped at the drink again, barely letting it touch her pale lips as she slurped at it. 'They've been playing better together recently. All ages, all mucking in. The older ones used to stand around, talk.' She made to drink some more, but paused before the mug was even close to her mouth. 'It's time I called them in for lunch, if I can calm them down a bit.'

'Already?'

'It's cold.'

'It is,' the Doctor agreed. 'I like children,' he said wistfully. A sudden thought occurred to him. 'Mind if I show them something? A trick. To calm them down.'

She shrugged again. He took this as a 'yes' and strode out into the middle of the playground. The children seemed to sense that he was here for their benefit and crowded round him. He rummaged in his pockets, wondering now he was committed what he was actually going to do. Yo-yo? Sweets? Ah – cards.

The children watched, respectfully and surprisingly quietly as he pulled the deck of cards from his pocket and shuffled them.

'Show us a trick,' a girl called. She was maybe ten, with large front teeth and a ponytail of dark brown hair.

'Yes, a trick,' others choing.

'All right, I'll show you a trick. Choose a card.'

'Ace of hearts,' a boy shouted immediately from the back.

'I meant from the pack,' the Doctor said. 'But all right.' He cut the cards with one hand and flipped the top half over to reveal the ace of hearts. There was a smattering of applause. He gave it a moment, then shuffled the cards. He made a play of riffling them together, slotting them into place, cutting them. 'Now,' he asked, 'where's the ace of hearts got to?'

'In the middle,' someone called.

'In your pocket,' an older boy said with determination.

The Doctor smiled. He held out the pack, face down. 'What's the top card?' he asked the ponytail girl.

She lifted it carefully. 'It's the ace of hearts.'

More applause.

'Show me how to do it?' the girl asked nervously.

'It's a trick.'

'Oh, please!'

'All right. What's your name?'

'Emma.'

'All right, Emma.' The Doctor looked round seriously at the other ten children. 'Nobody else watch. All turn away now, or it won't be a trick, will it?'

They grumbled and shuffled, and eventually turned away.

He was a good teacher. It did not take long. He showed her silently how to cut the ace to the top. He demonstrated how to riffle the cards and leave it untouched, how to shuffle them without disturbing its position. He let her try it on him once. Then he winked and grinned and clapped his hands loudly together. 'Right, everyone. Emma has a trick. Last one before lunch.'

At the back of the small group Miss Devlin smiled appreciatively.

Then Emma took centre stage. She showed them the ace of hearts, all serious, face a mask of concentration. She put it in the middle of the pack, and shuffled the cards. The tip of her tongue edged out of the side of her mouth as she worked. Then it disappeared as she gritted her teeth and held out the pack to the nearest boy. 'Josh,' she whispered.

He knew what to do. He lifted the top card. And he grinned, one tooth prominently missing as he showed the others. The ace of hearts.

Applause. Then, 'My turn – my turn.'

'I think it's time for lunch,' Miss Devlin said.

'Oh, please.' A cute six-year-old grabbed the cards. 'Let me, let me.'

He showed the ace of hearts. The Doctor and Miss Devlin exchanged amused glances as he slotted it into the pack and shuffled clumsily. He held the pack out to the Doctor who smiled and lifted the top card.

It was the ace of hearts. He felt his own hearts miss a beat.

'That was kind,' the teacher whispered to him as he showed the card.

'Not really,' he muttered back. 'Do that again,' he told the child.

'James,' the boy said.

'Well done, James,' the Doctor said. 'Do it again.'

He did it again.

The Doctor took the cards. He checked them to see that they weren't all the ace of hearts. Well, you never knew. He allowed an older boy to lift the cards from him. And he watched the older boy do the same trick. Perfectly.

'You've done this before,' the Doctor said, realising. He watched as yet another child managed effortlessly to shuffle the ace to the top of the pack.

'No. Never,' they told him. And from their evident delight and glee he could believe it. Though he didn't want to.

Miss Devlin clapped her hands together. 'Lunch,' she announced. 'Now.'

Disappointed, but resigned, the children filed into the school. One of them handed the cards to Miss Devlin at the door. She paused a moment as the children shuffled past, waited for the Doctor.

'How very peculiar,' the Doctor said as the last child went quietly indoors.

'They pick things up very quickly,' she said. 'I was telling Dr Madsen the other week when he gave them their flu jabs. After... you know.'

The Doctor nodded. He was aware of the impact of a death in such a small community, especially from something as apparently minor as influenza.

'They've got even quicker since then, if anything.' She was

shuffling the cards herself now, a nervous gesture. 'The jab worked, though. I always get the flu.' The Doctor wondered where she had put the coffee mug. He would have looked round for it, but his eyes were fixed on her hands as they shuffled the cards. 'But just a slight cold this year. Marvellous what they can achieve these days, isn't it?' She was not aware of what she was doing, wasn't even watching herself as she riffled the cards together again. 'It was kind of you to show them the trick,' she said. 'Thank you.'

'Not at all. I must let you get on.'

She smiled gratefully and handed him the cards. 'They're trick cards, aren't they? That's it, isn't it?'

He smiled, but did not answer. Perhaps it was better she should think that.

'You must come again,' she went on. 'Talk to the children. Sir Edward was kind enough to come and talk to them the other week. They have so little contact with the real world.'

The Doctor smiled back. 'I'd like that,' he said. 'I know the problem.'

He waited until she had gone inside, until the door was closed firmly behind her, against the cold. Then he turned the top card over. And he felt the chill himself.

It was the ace of hearts.

Chapter Six
Digging for Clues

Peri was waiting for the Doctor outside the pub when he got there. He could tell that she was distracted, nervous. He did not ask what was wrong – better to wait until she was ready to talk about it. That would also give him time to decide what he would tell her about his experiences at the school.

He led her into the pub and they each got a glass of water and ordered a ploughman's. 'At least we know the bread will be home-baked,' he told her with a grin.

He waited until they were seated at what was becoming their 'usual table' before asking about her morning. He listened in silence, letting her go at her own pace. She started with an account of her run-in with Mike Neville.

'That's the trouble with strangers,' the Doctor said when she was done. 'They disrupt the normal processes, upset things. Things like procedures, processes. Emotions.'

'Hey, who gets the sympathy here?' Peri wanted to know.

'The man from the woods?' the Doctor suggested. 'I wonder who he is.'

'Just some nutter.' Peri shook her head and attacked a hunk of mature Cheddar cheese. 'He's weird. And talking of weird, you should see the sheep.'

The Doctor paused in the process of pulling apart his bread roll. 'Sheep?' he asked.

'That is strange,' the Doctor agreed when Peri had finished her story. He pushed his plate away, empty. Peri had barely started on hers. She had been doing all the talking. But she seemed calmer now, more herself. Time for the Doctor to do the talking. 'And talking of strange behaviour,' he said, 'I wonder if it's connected to the children.'

'The children?'

'Yes.' The Doctor grinned. 'I've been to school this morning.'

'Learn anything useful?'

'I don't know about useful,' the Doctor confessed. 'But it was instructive certainly.' He gave her a brief summary of his experiences. 'It was as if once one of them could do it, they all could,' he concluded. 'I don't think it was a conscious thing. Not telepathy, even dormant or nascent telepathy. A sort of collective learning.'

'They all go to school together,' Peri said. 'Perhaps they're just used to learning as a group.'

'Hmm,' the Doctor said. He said it in the same tone of voice he would have used for 'No, don't be silly.'

'Is that what happened to the sheep, do you think?' Peri asked. 'Some sort of collective behaviour?'

'Well, it does sound like it,' the Doctor agreed. 'I'm not a great fan of coincidence.'

'Nor am I,' Peri said.

'Hmm. Small world.' He frowned. 'Let's assume that one's genuine, shall we?' He tapped his empty glass on the table as he considered. The noise carried across the near-empty pub and after a few taps he set the glass down again. 'You say that Mrs Painswick –'

'Hilly,' Peri said with a broad smile.

The Doctor continued undeterred and apparently without noticing. 'You say that Mrs Painswick mentioned the sheep had only been behaving like this for a few weeks?'

'I think that's what she implied. I don't remember what she actually said.'

The Doctor let go of the glass and tapped his fingers together. 'And Miss Devlin said that the children had been playing more closely together recently. So what's changed?' He frowned. 'Could it be the weather? She said something about that.'

'But it would be the same every year, wouldn't it?' Peri watched as the Doctor rolled the glass back and forth between the palms of his hands. 'Does it matter?' she asked slowly. 'I mean, is some sort of collective behaviour a problem?'

The glass paused between his palms. 'Not collective behaviour, no,' he conceded. 'Herd instinct, crowd mentality. Not necessarily a problem.' The glass started moving again. 'But what if it goes further than that?' He frowned and set down the glass on the table. 'Collective thinking?' he mused quietly.

'Not caused by a change in the weather,' Peri suggested.

'I agree.' The Doctor sucked in his cheeks. 'For one thing, it wouldn't be limited to the island then.' His eyes widened as he recalled the conversation. 'The teacher, Miss Devlin, said that Sir Edward had spoken to the children a few weeks ago.'

'You said strangers disrupt things,' Peri reminded him.

'I did,' the Doctor agreed. 'I did. How long has he been here?'

'I think last night someone mentioned it was a couple of months.'

The Doctor flung himself back in his chair and folded his hands behind his head. 'You know, I'd like to pay a visit on our friend Sir Edward Baddesley,' he said. 'After all, we haven't introduced ourselves to him yet.'

Liz Trefoil was glad to give the Doctor and Peri directions to get to Cove Cottage. They headed towards the church, almost tiptoeing past Mrs Tattleshall's house with fingers crossed that she would not see them. Once at the top of the street, there was a narrow path past the front of the church and down towards the backs of the houses. Cove Cottage was set back from this. They could hear the sound of the sea as they approached and guessed that there was indeed a cove behind the house.

The garden gate was closed and latched. The Doctor cheerily opened it and marched up to the front door. It was a postcard Elizabethan cottage; half-timbered, with a black thatched roof hanging low over the small upstairs windows. A rose rambled up the side of the door frame and across the lintel.

The Doctor hammered enthusiastically on the door. They waited, but there was no response.

'Nobody home,' the Doctor declared with glee, rubbing his hands together.

'Back to the pub?' Peri asked. She was a little concerned at his attitude.

'Oh, I think we'd better try the back door first,' the Doctor said. 'Then the windows,' he added. He was still rubbing his hands as he led the way round the side of the cottage.

The back door was locked as well. But far from expressing disappointment, the Doctor produced a long thin wire implement, hooked at one end and with a kink in the middle. 'Never fails,' he confided as he slid it into the ancient lock and jiggled it about.

Peri sighed and shuffled her feet as the lock clicked and the door creaked open. 'Is this a good idea?' she asked.

But the Doctor was already inside. 'Come on,' he said, 'don't hang about out there in the cold. There's work to be done, you know.'

They spent about fifteen minutes in the cottage. Peri spent most of that time glancing anxiously out of the window or entreating the Doctor to hurry. By contrast, he spent most of it rummaging through drawers and papers, with no apparent regard for the privacy of the house's occupant or anxiety about being caught.

'What if he comes back?' Peri hissed at him after ten minutes.

'Then he can tell us what he's up to.'

'What *he's* up to? What are *we* up to?' She was practically wringing her hands. 'If Sir Edward –'

The Doctor interrupted her. 'Uh-ha,' he said smugly. He was holding something. A small maroon-coloured booklet. He was tapping it against his palm. 'He's not Sir Edward Baddesley.'

'How do you know?' She was intrigued despite herself.

'Because this is his passport. Look.' He opened the booklet and showed her the photograph. It was a younger version of the man they had seen in the pub, there was no doubt.

'So?' Peri asked.

'So this passport is in the name of someone called Sir Anthony Kelso.'

Peri considered this. 'Why would he lie?'

'Perhaps we should ask him.'

'What, now?' She looked out of the window again. There was no one within sight.

'Now?' he seemed aghast. 'Now! No, of course not now,' the Doctor chided. 'Now we look in the cellar.'

There was a door under the steep, narrow wooden staircase. Peri had dismissed it as a cupboard. But when the Doctor lifted the latch and pulled it open, she saw that it gave on to a flight of stone steps that led downwards. There was noise as well, a faint humming sound and something else – a regular beat.

As they started down the stairs, the noise grew louder. 'It sounds like an engine,' Peri realised.

'It *is* an engine,' the Doctor told her. 'A petrol engine. Or perhaps diesel. A generator – you remember, they told us in the pub that he'd sneaked one in, and they didn't like it.' He reached up and pointed to the bare light bulb that was hanging above their heads from the sloping ceiling. It was so ordinary and expected that Peri had not even noticed it. But it was light down in the cellars. Electrically light.

Sure enough, there was a small generator chugging away in the corner when they reached the bottom of the stairs. The cellar was large – as large, Peri estimated, as the footprint of the house. Like another floor set into the ground. It was open, a single huge room. There were wooden wine racks along one wall, decked with cobwebs. The other walls were whitewashed brickwork. In the middle of the floor was a large trestle table. Beside it was another smaller table with what looked like a metal tool box on it. Along the wall behind were several filing cabinets and cupboards. A few books stood lonely and haphazard on a set of shelves.

'I think we've seen enough,' the Doctor said. 'For the moment, anyway.' He was whispering now, Peri noticed. Perhaps he was getting nervous at last.

'Enough for what?' Peri asked as they made their way carefully back up the steps.

'Enough to know we should keep an eye on our friend Sir Edward,' the Doctor said. 'Or rather Sir Anthony.' He tapped the side of his nose and winked.

'So what's the plan?' Peri asked as the Doctor locked the back door and they made their way back round the cottage.

'Oh, I think you should keep watch on this cottage,' the Doctor said. 'Sit in the churchyard or something and watch out for Sir Edward.' He leaned towards her and added quietly, 'We'll call him Sir Edward for now, anyway, shall we?'

'Then what?'

'Then we'll call him Sir Anthony.'

'No, I mean then what shall I do? Once he returns?'

'Oh, keep an eye on him of course.'

'Great.' Peri paused at the churchyard gate. 'And where will you be?'

'I think I'll go and see the one other prominent member of the community we've not yet had the privilege of meeting,' he told her. 'I'm going over to Sheldon's Folly.'

He turned in time to see the tall, thin man rise up from the scrubland in front of him. He recognised him at once, could even put a name to him – Rogers. As he rose, he lifted a rifle to his shoulder, sighting carefully along it.

For a moment he stood, frozen in position, facing the gun. He knew what it was, why they wanted him back. He knew he could not stand to be caught again. Was Rogers going to kill him? He certainly hoped so. But instinctively he dived away, trying to make the cover of a nearby bush, desperate to make use of what little protection it offered.

He was in midair, almost there, when he felt the sharp pain bite into his shoulder. As he landed, rolled, cried out, he looked down and saw the frayed end of the metal dart sticking out of his grubby shirt. Already the image was blurring, was going muzzy at the edges. He tried to stand, but fell down again at once. He lay there, staring up at the sky, knowing that before long he would see Rogers's face appear above him. When it did, he saw that the man was smiling.

Then the world suddenly pitched round him as he was hauled

up. He stared at Rogers's back, his mind numb, barely realising he was being carried. His arms swung free and limp. His brain swam. Don't open the casket. Don't… But it was too late.

The sound of the sea was a rushing in his ears as the world continued to recede. The staggering, rolling journey down the steep hill was a jolting nightmare of confused images. He landed in the boat with a dull crack that barely registered as a pain in his back. Then the sound of the outboard motor drowned out what was left of his conscious thoughts and he relaxed into oblivion.

When he saw her coming, the Doctor considered his options. He could pretend he had not seen her at all and turn off and head down the street. Or he could brazen it out and try to get away with a friendly 'Good afternoon', though it seemed unlikely that he would succeed. In the end he decided to try to turn the meeting to his advantage.

'Ah, good afternoon, Mrs Tattleshall. The very person,' he said before she could say anything. 'I'm so sorry to trouble you, I know how busy you must be. I'm in rather a rush myself, as it happens,' he confided, glancing round as if to check there was nobody else within earshot. 'I wonder if you could help me with something?'

She seemed surprised at his enthusiastic greeting. 'Of course, Doctor. If I can.'

The Doctor beamed massively, his whole face a picture of glee. 'A boat,' he said.

'A boat?'

'A boat,' he repeated. 'Exactly so. I have an appointment with Mr Sheldon, at Sheldon's Folly.' He opened his hands to show just how much he needed her help. Just how bereft of boat he was. 'Any suggestions?'

Asked a direct question like this, Mrs Tattleshall seemed at a loss for words. 'Well,' she suggested. 'Er. I…'

The Doctor raised his eyebrows expectantly.

'The quay,' she decided at last. 'Old Jim is up at the quay. He can probably lend you a boat.'

'Thank you.' The trick now, the Doctor decided, was to make his escape before she recovered sufficiently to get into her verbal stride.

He was far enough away to be able to pretend he had not heard when she did start. 'They're a rum lot over there at the Folly,' she called after him. 'You mark my words. I wouldn't go over there if they paid me. Specially at night. Noises, lights.' She raised her voice still further in an effort to attract his attention. 'Goings-on,' she pronounced carefully and ominously.

The Doctor half turned and gave her a friendly wave. It did not do to fall out with people. And she had, after all, been helpful.

Old Jim was easy to spot. He was sitting at the edge of the quay biting an unlit pipe and watching the Doctor approach. Old Jim was a name that did not really do the man justice. Ancient Jim, the Doctor decided, might have been more appropriate. His face was deeply lined and stained brown by the elements. His hair was reduced to a flimsy tangle of grey wisps, and his beard was Bernard Shaw white.

The Doctor introduced himself and settled down on the quay next to the old man. 'Mrs Tattleshall says you might be able to lend me a boat,' he hazarded.

The old man nodded. 'A boat, is it?' He chewed his pipe as he considered.

'A boat,' the Doctor agreed. 'Vessel. Embarkation.'

'Mmm. What for?'

'To get to Sheldon's Folly.'

Jim laughed, a cracked and rasping sound. 'That's obvious,' he said. 'Nowhere else really to go.'

'The other islands?' the Doctor suggested.

'Hardly. No, when I say *what for*, I mean what will you give me in return?'

'Ah.' The Doctor understood. 'I'm not sure what I have to offer. A jelly baby maybe? Use of my best yo-yo perhaps? Peace and quiet when I'm gone?'

Jim considered this, his pipe moving slowly from side to side in his mouth. 'Not if that Tattleshall woman comes back,' he said at last.

'Ah, now there I can make no guarantees.'

Old Jim removed his pipe for long enough to say: 'Talked her poor husband to death. She's looking for her next victim now, I reckon.' He clamped the pipe back in. 'You want to watch out,' he said round it.

'I think we both do.'

Jim nodded. 'True enough.'

'She said something about noises,' the Doctor said. 'Goings-on, lights. Said they're a rum lot.'

'At Sheldon's Folly?'

The Doctor nodded.

''Spect they are.'

'She said she wouldn't go over there if you paid her,' the Doctor went on. 'Well, not you personally. Or me for that matter. But you know what I mean.'

'I do, lad.' He removed his pipe and pointed the stem at the Doctor before he had time to remark that he was not used to being addressed as 'lad'. He wiggled the pipe as he spoke. 'They did use to pay her. When the house was empty. Before young Mr Christopher came back. Cleaning and the like.'

'Ah.' This was making some sense. 'And now that Mr Sheldon is back in residence, he has dispensed with her excellent, albeit garrulous, services?'

'That's it. Sour grapes, if you ask me.' He removed the pipe again and pointed at a smudged dark area on the horizon. 'That's Sheldon's Folly. You can take that rowing boat.' He moved the pipe to indicate the small wooden rowing boat he meant. It was tied up to the quayside nearby. A pair of oars was lying down the middle across the low bench seat.

'Thank you,' the Doctor said.

Old Jim nodded. 'It's nice to talk once in a while.'

'Though not to Mrs Tattleshall.'

'That's right. Bring her back safe,' he said. 'The boat, I mean. About an hour if you keep a steady rhythm. Quicker back 'cos of the tide.'

'Thank you,' the Doctor said again, getting to his feet.

'Just one thing.'

'Yes?'

'It's nice to talk once in a while,' he repeated.

The Doctor nodded. 'I've enjoyed it,' he said. 'Let's do it again, shall we? Another day, another time.'

The old man was nodding too. 'Yes,' he said quietly. 'I'd like that.'

The Doctor realised he had learned something else about Old Jim as he arrived at the island. Either the old man was an optimist, or his arms were rather better used to rowing than the Doctor's were. It had taken him an hour and a half, and the autumn sun was low in the sky now. Soon the evening would begin to close in.

The Doctor tied up the rowing boat next to a motor launch at a small wooden jetty which projected from the craggy shore. He spent a few moments staring longingly and jealously at the launch while trying to massage some feeling back into his arms. Then he set off down the jetty and started along the pathway that led from it and wound its way through a thinly wooded area and, he assumed, up to the house.

The house, when he caught sight of it through the trees, was a ramshackle, sprawling affair. It seemed to be a mixture of Gothic and Queen Anne, as if the two styles had been thrown haphazardly together and then finished off years later by a builder who was a devotee of H. P. Lovecraft. The windows were different shapes and at different levels. None of the walls seemed to meet at right angles. The roof rose and dipped as if on a whim. The Doctor stood and stared at the house for a good while, angling and tilting his head as he tried to make aesthetic sense of it all.

When he eventually gave up, he thrust his hands into his pockets and set off towards it. Whistling. As he approached, he could see there were barns and outbuildings, even a coach house, behind and to the side of the main house. They also demonstrated a lack of coherent design or overall style.

The path did not bring the Doctor straight to the front door of the house. It meandered across the front lawn before arriving at the side of the house and then leading past several downstairs windows to arrive at last at the front door. As he passed each window the Doctor made a point of looking inside. The first room seemed to be empty and in darkness. The next window gave into a large drawing room. The Doctor could see a fire burning in the grate, and gas lamps flickering on the walls. He paused, and now he could see there were people in the room.

By instinct more than anything else, the Doctor stepped back into the shadow of the brickwork beside the window. The frame did not fit too well into the mullion, and he could hear voices from inside seeping out through the tiny gaps. He peered carefully round the edge of the window as he listened. He thought he recognised one of the voices.

'Thank goodness you found him when you did,' a man's voice said. 'He could have done himself all kinds of damage.' The Doctor could see the speaker, sitting perched on the edge of a large armchair. He smiled with satisfaction as he recognised Dr Dave Madsen.

'Damage?' Another man's voice. A large, deep voice. Amused.

'I don't mean physical damage,' Madsen responded. There was a trace of annoyance in his voice. 'Anyway, he's in good enough health now. Considering.'

'Excellent.' There was a movement of shadows in the room, and the Doctor could make out a large man walking across to the armchair. He paused in front of it, and handed something to Madsen. A glass, by the look of it. The Doctor peered closer, angling himself so that the sun was not reflected from the part of the window he was trying to see through.

It was a glass. Madsen took it and sipped at the drink. The large man had a drink too. Both the same, by the look of it. Both whisky, from the distant colour.

'I, er, I need more material,' the large man said as Madsen sipped at his drink.

Madsen spluttered in response. 'What, already?'

'As soon as you think it can be done.'

Madsen leaned back in his chair. He was silent for a while. 'I suppose,' he said, and paused. 'I suppose it can't do him any more harm now.'

'I suppose not. The arm, perhaps?'

'The left arm should be all right.' Madsen struggled out of the chair and put his empty glass down on a table. 'I can remove it for you now if you want. While I'm here. Again.'

The Doctor stepped away from the window as the two men left the room. He had not liked the sound of that. He sucked in his cheeks and tapped his fingertips together as he decided what to do. He didn't really know what was going on here. Was the big man Sheldon? And who or what had they been talking about? He turned and walked in the opposite direction from the front door. He needed a few minutes to think, and a look round the buildings would not do any harm.

The double wooden doors to the coach house were open, he saw, as he got close. Inside the dark archway, the Doctor could make out the large spidery form of a helicopter. Its wing tips dipped over the main body. It was painted a glossy black that merged with the shadows and darkness inside the building.

The Doctor continued his tour round the outside of the house, but he saw nothing else of much interest. There was a stable block and he could see horses poking their curious heads over half-doors. He heard dogs barking from another more distant building, though he did not investigate further. His timing was excellent, he reflected, as he approached the front door again. As he watched, it opened and Madsen came out accompanied by a tall thin man dressed in the formal dark suit of a butler.

'House call?' the Doctor asked politely.

Madsen was surprised to see him, and did nothing to disguise the fact. 'After a fashion,' he said. 'What the devil are you doing here?'

'Paying my respects,' the Doctor said. 'To Mr Sheldon.'

'Sheldon?' Madsen frowned. 'I'm not sure...' His voice tailed off.

she got no opportunity to find out, she could simply slip away while Sir Edward was in the cellar. With the body.

The body was slumped in the wheelbarrow still, as if asleep. Peri tried not to look at it. She glanced towards the light from the cellar, wondering if she would see Sir Edward's shadow break the light as he came back up the stairs. She needed somewhere to hide before his return.

She stepped away from the door, feeling the draught created as it slammed shut behind her. But before she could be surprised or worried, a hand closed over her mouth from behind and she felt herself propelled across the room and flung into an armchair. She landed heavily, tried to get up again, but a hand pushed her down. The dark shape of a tall thin man loomed over her, and from a few feet away the twisted corpse echoed her slumped position.

'I think there's some explaining to be done,' Sir Edward said. His voice was solemn, calm. He leaned down towards Peri, his hands on the arms of the chair either side of her, preventing her from getting up. His face was a dark oval, shadowed from the light from the cellar door.

Then the main light in the room came on, and Peri saw him blink in surprise before he straightened up and turned towards the back door.

'Explanations would indeed be very useful,' the Doctor said. He was standing in the open doorway, his hand still on the light switch. 'Hello, Peri,' he added with a smile. 'Sorry I'm late. You been having fun?'

Sir Edward looked from the Doctor back to Peri, confusion evident on his face. 'You, you were at the pub. Last night,' he said.

'And an excellent establishment it is too,' the Doctor told him. He stood beside the wheelbarrow and peered closely at the body. He waved his hand in front of the dead, closed eyes and seemed vaguely disappointed to get no reaction. 'I'm afraid you've missed last orders,' he said quietly.

'You're not from the islands,' Sir Edward said. 'Thank God for that.' He slumped down in a chair close to Peri and wiped his brow with a handkerchief. 'My apologies, I'm a little worn out from the exercise.' His face was flushed red and smeared with grime and sweat.

'Mmm,' the Doctor agreed. 'Digging is exhausting work, isn't it? You want to talk about that? At all?'

Sir Edward looked up. 'You want to talk about it? You catch me red-handed –' He broke off to inspect his hands. 'Black-handed, more like, digging up a dead body, and you want to talk about it?'

'Well, call me old-fashioned,' the Doctor said as he found himself a chair on the other side of the small room and sat down. 'But I like a good story. And I think there must be a good story here.' He stretched out his legs and rested his feet on the side of the wheelbarrow. The corpse within wobbled slightly. 'Don't you?'

'Good grief,' Sir Edward mumbled. 'You're even battier than I am. Thought I'd be clapped in irons, not given centre stage.' He took a deep breath. 'Well,' he said slowly, 'as I was about to explain to the young lady...'

'Peri,' Peri said. 'You were going to explain to me?'

'Er, yes. That's what I was just telling you when your friend here joined us.'

'You can call me the Doctor. And please do go on. You were explaining.'

Sir Edward leaned back in the chair. 'Not sure that I can explain, really,' he confessed. 'It all seems a bit mad now. With the lights on. I mean, in the dark and everything, that's different. But...' He sighed. 'I'm pretty new here, maybe that's why I'm the only one who's worried.'

'Worried?' Peri asked. 'What about?' She was trying to look at Sir Edward as he spoke, trying to ignore the fourth, silent person in the room.

'Well, it sounds silly when you talk about it. Lot of fuss over nothing, probably. But it's got me worried. Anxious. The deaths. Everything.' He leaned forward again, his expression earnest. 'All right, so there was the flu thing. And this fishing accident. Unfortunate. But there are other odd things you notice too.'

'Like the way the sheep behave?' the Doctor prompted quietly.

'Yes,' agreed Sir Edward. Then more quietly, 'Yes, you'd noticed that too?' He shook his head. 'None of them are really that odd in themselves. But taken all together there's a sort of critical mass. Then when Dr Madsen said there was nothing wrong with this fellow's arm, I thought... Well, I'm not sure what I did think actually.'

'You thought,' the Doctor said, 'that here was something concrete you could actually check.'

Sir Edward nodded. 'Yes, I suppose so. That's about it.'

'Did you see his arm broken?' the Doctor asked.

Sir Edward shook his head.

'So Madsen could be right,' Peri told him. 'There could have been nothing wrong with it. Just a sprain.'

Sir Edward shook his head again. 'I don't think so. I've spoken to a few people who saw the boat come in that day. They were all sure that the arm was broken. But they all assume they were wrong or don't want to bother following it up. Just one of those things.'

'And they've none of them spoken to each other about it?' the Doctor asked.

'Don't know. But I assume not.' He smiled suddenly. 'Except Mrs Tattleshall, of course. She's spoken to everyone about it. It was her that put me on to it actually. But somehow her talking about it immediately makes people think it's all an exaggeration or a mistake. Gossip and rumour are her stock in trade, so why should this be any different?'

'Why indeed?' the Doctor wondered quietly. He leaped to his feet and looked closely at the corpse again. The body was dressed in a grubby, mud-smeared suit. The Doctor tugged at a sleeve. 'So what did you intend?' he asked.

'Thought I'd bring the poor chap back here, take a look at him down in the cellar.' He nodded towards the open door. 'The light's better down there. And there's more space. S'pose that's out of the question now, though.'

'I don't see why,' the Doctor said. 'Give me a hand to get him down the stairs, will you?'

Sir Edward stared as the Doctor wrestled the body out of the wheelbarrow and hoisted it over his shoulder.

'Come along,' the Doctor chided. 'There's not that long before it starts to get light. We need him to be done and dusted and back in the ground before the milkman wanders past on the early shift.'

Sir Edward and Peri watched as the Doctor worked. They had lain the body on the large wooden table in the cellar and stripped it to the waist. The skin was pale with a bluish tinge, and there was a sickly sweet smell that Peri tried hard not to think about.

'What now?' Sir Edward asked as they all stood round the table.

'What were you going to do?' the Doctor asked. 'Full post-mortem? Surgical procedures or an external examination?'

Sir Edward shook his head. 'I don't really know,' he confessed. He gave a short, sharp laugh that was strangely devoid of humour. 'I may have run a department at the Ministry of Science, but I don't really have the first clue, I'm afraid.'

'Don't look at me,' Peri said. She shrugged, trying to think of what she could say that might help. 'Shouldn't he have rigor mortis or something?'

Sir Edward nodded as if he had the same thought.

The Doctor had stretched out the left arm of the body and was examining it carefully, pressing the skin and feeling round the elbow joint. 'Not if he's been dead for more than, oh, about forty-eight hours.'

'He has,' Sir Edward admitted, with a trace of disappointment. 'How's his arm?'

'It seems fine,' the Doctor said. He bent it back and forth at the elbow a few times to demonstrate.

'Maybe it was the other one?' Peri suggested.

The Doctor stared at her. Then he frowned and turned his attention to Sir Edward.

Sir Edward shifted uneasily on his feet. 'Not sure,' he mumbled.

'Don't think I asked, actually.'

The Doctor sighed theatrically and started on the other arm. 'No,' he said after a few moments. 'No, this one seems fine as well.' He let the arm flop back down beside the body. 'No sign of a break in either of them. No bruising or contusion either, which is a surprise if it was a bad sprain. I'd expect some sign.'

The Doctor turned his attention to the face of the body. Peri winced as he pushed back an eyelid with his thumb and stared into the exposed eye. After a moment he leaned across the table and repeated the procedure with the other eye. 'Irises are very pale,' he murmured. 'Almost bleached.'

The body's head moved slightly as the Doctor examined the second eye. Peri gasped. 'Look,' she said, her voice husky and strained.

'Hmm?' The Doctor leaned back to see what Peri was looking at.

'His neck.'

The Doctor rolled the head aside to see where Peri was pointing. There were two slightly raised bumps in the neck, adjacent to each other and about an inch apart. In the centre of each was a dark dot.

'Puncture marks?' Sir Edward asked, his voice little more than a whisper.

The Doctor nodded and let the head roll back again. 'Looks like it,' he agreed. 'Looks very much like it indeed.'

'Vampires,' Peri breathed. The word seemed to hang in the air.

Sir Edward gaped.

The Doctor pursed his lips. 'That's ridiculous,' he decided after a moment's hesitation. 'There are dozens of other far more plausible explanations for these marks.'

'Oh?' Peri asked. 'That's good,' she added.

'Dozens,' the Doctor repeated. 'Could be the result of an accident, a fish hook got caught, well, two fish hooks. Something.' He stuffed his hands in his trouser pockets. Then he immediately pulled them out again. 'Or injections of some sort.'

'That's only two explanations,' Peri said. 'Dozens means… dozens.'

The Doctor snorted. 'Well, whatever the explanation is, it's not vampires. Now I think it's time we got this chap dressed again and back to bed.' As he retrieved the dead man's shirt, Peri could see that the Doctor's fingers were crossed.

'I hear you talked to the children up at the school,' the Doctor said. 'Miss Devlin was telling me.'

'What?' Sir Edward said. 'Oh, er, yes. That's right. Couple of weeks ago.'

Peri could understand he had been thrown by the question. They were wheeling a dead body back to its grave at nearly three o'clock in the morning, and the Doctor was chatting about the local school.

'How did you find the children?' the Doctor asked. He was wheeling the barrow, Peri and Sir Edward close behind him. 'Sort of normal, responsive… Individual?'

Sir Edward looked at Peri. She shrugged.

'I'm not sure,' he replied. 'Not really an expert on children myself, so I don't know what normal is.'

The Doctor nodded. They had reached the churchyard gate now and he waited for Peri to come round and open it for him. 'No,' he said quietly. 'Not an area where I have much expertise either.'

Peri was carrying the torch and Sir Edward held the spade. The Doctor set down the wheelbarrow away from the mound of newly dug earth and gestured for Peri to shine the torch into the open grave. At the bottom she could see the coffin, the lid angled across it.

'Could you give me a hand getting him back inside, do you think, Sir Edward?' the Doctor asked as he straightened up again. He paused, then added: 'It is Sir Edward, isn't it?'

'What?' The elderly man turned away, focused his attention on the body in the wheelbarrow. 'Yes,' he said as his face was turned away. 'Sir Edward Baddesley. That's right.'

100

The Doctor and Peri exchanged glances. Peri raised an eyebrow, wondering if the Doctor could see the movement as she held the torch still pointing at the grave. He gave the barest shake of the head, as if to say: 'Leave it for now.' She nodded in return.

'So why did you come here, to Dorsill?' the Doctor asked as the two men hefted the body out of the wheelbarrow and stumbled with it towards the grave. The Doctor set down the feet and jumped into the grave, landing astride of the coffin. He looked up at Sir Edward, who was still holding the body upright under the arms.

'Oh, no reason. Do some walking. Always said I'd find somewhere peaceful when I retired.'

'Just a coincidence then,' the Doctor said lightly as he threw the coffin lid out of the grave. 'Arriving with all this going on.'

'That's right.' Sir Edward shuffled the body forwards, so that the feet dangled over the edge of the grave, and the Doctor guided the body down into the coffin as he lowered it. 'Just a coincidence.'

The Doctor had managed to get the body lying pretty much straight inside the coffin, and folded the hands across the chest. He stood up to admire his work. 'Pass me the lid, will you? I don't think we need to nail it on. The weight of the soil will keep it in place and this poor chap won't complain, I'm sure.' He grinned, his head and shoulders sticking incongruously out of the ground.

Peri shone the torch on the uneven ground where the coffin lid lay, so that Sir Edward could pick his way across and lower it end first into the grave. The Doctor lowered the lid, angling it to fit between his feet and over the top of the coffin beneath.

Peri took a few steps towards Sir Edward, trying to get a better angle for the torch as she shone it down into the grave again. The Doctor seemed to be having trouble getting the lid straight.

'That's funny,' he murmured. 'Seems to be something in the way.' He was bending down now, almost kneeling on the lid as he tried to force it down into place.

Then suddenly he was flung back, losing his balance as the

coffin lid sprang up. Peri's first thought was that he had slipped somehow and see-sawed the lid on the edge of the coffin. But as the torch light spilled over the Doctor struggling to regain his balance, Peri could see the arms reaching up, pushing the lid away. She screamed and dropped the torch.

Sir Edward scooped up the torch in a moment, putting his other hand on Peri's shoulder as he shone the beam into the grave, at the Doctor's feet. The Doctor was kneeling on the lid once more, forcing it down.

'I think maybe we should have brought some nails,' he gasped as he hammered his fists down on the lid. At one edge several pale fingers were working their way out from underneath. The Doctor caught sight of them as he struggled to his feet. He stamped on that edge of the coffin and the fingers withdrew inside. A moment later the wood in the centre of the lid splintered and split apart. A fist emerged from inside, ragged and torn. Dried blood stuck in streaks to the skin, the knuckles were red raw. From directly above the churchyard came a sudden crack of thunder.

Peri screamed again. Sir Edward's grip tightened on her shoulder, and the light from the torch wavered. There was another crack of thunder and the rain started, an immediate torrent pouring down through the damp misty air. The Doctor leaped out of the grave in a single bound, his feet slipping and sliding on the earth at the edge of the hole. Dirt showered down as his feet struggled to gain purchase. It sprinkled over the coffin lid, running off in dark streams as the rain splashed into it.

Finally, the Doctor managed to get a grip on the slippery soil and he shot away from the edge of the grave, tumbling head over heels and landing in a sitting position looking back at the dark hole in the ground. A moment later the coffin lid was hurled after him. It landed on the mound of earth, end first, sticking in upright. Like a tombstone.

One after the other, two pale hands appeared over the edge of the grave. Dead fingers scrabbled at the mud and the matted turf. The Doctor was on his feet again, an arm round each of Sir

Edward and Peri. 'I'm not sure I care for the way this evening is turning out,' he said quietly. He was pulling them gently backwards, none of them able for the moment to turn away from the sight in front of them.

The forearms were visible now, angled to give leverage as Bill Neville hauled himself out of his grave. His head appeared above ground, his dark hair plastered to his scalp by a mixture of mud and rain, and Peri saw with horror that his eyes were open. Wide open. Staring and blank. The irises reflected the wavering torchlight, pale and yellowed. The pupils were non-existent. For a moment the corpse paused in its efforts to pull itself out of the ground.

Then suddenly the body was moving again, and the Doctor was pulling her back, and they were all turning, all running towards the gate out of the churchyard.

It was not until they reached the gate that the Doctor held up his hands for them to stop. He had turned already and they all watched as the dishevelled, muddy corpse staggered slowly and clumsily towards the front gate on the other side of the churchyard. The sound of the creaking hinges carried through the night air as it swung open the gate and set off in a shuffling, stumbling manner away from the village and towards the quay. Its arms were stretched out in front of it, Karloff-like, as it was swallowed up by the swirling mist.

'Oh my God,' Sir Edward breathed. He turned to the Doctor and Peri. 'What do we do?' he demanded, his voice cracked and strained.

'Well,' the Doctor was frowning. 'I think we probably don't want to panic the villagers. Not yet anyway. So I suggest we put the lid back on the coffin and fill in the grave. Then you can have your spade and wheelbarrow back.'

'We can't just pretend this didn't happen,' Sir Edward protested.

'No, but we can leave things tidy.'

'Oh well, that's something,' Peri said, hoping she sounded sarcastic rather than terrified. She sneezed suddenly and loudly.

'Oh great, a cold. That's all I need. Comes from spending most of the night in a cold wet graveyard.'

But the Doctor was not listening. He clapped Sir Edward on the shoulder and led him back across the churchyard towards the open grave. 'Oh come on,' he said encouragingly, 'tonight's been a terrific success after all.'

'It has?' Sir Edward sounded distinctly dubious.

'Oh yes. You came here to confirm your suspicions that there was something odd going on.' He pushed the coffin lid over and it toppled down the mound of earth and slid into the grave. The Doctor started shovelling earth on top of it. 'And I think we've proved there is something distinctly strange happening here,' he said matter-of-factly. 'In spades.'

She was dreaming about the figures. They spun and twisted and danced in her head. Janet Spillsbury had been going over the latest batch of results before she went to bed, and now she was caught in a semi-conscious world where everything that happened did so in the context of a mathematical equation. She was aware that she was thirsty, but could not see the square in the table of numbers that contained a drink. She could hear a banging sound from somewhere, but could not tell what number it was making the noise.

The noise was a monotonous rhythm. Like the way the numbers flowed past her tired eyes as she ran her finger down the page. And suddenly she was awake, and she knew that not everything was related to the numbers, to the results, to the experiment.

The sound was real. It was insistent, regular and constant. It was coming from downstairs. She struggled blearily into her dressing gown, wondering why nobody else had heard it. Where was Rogers, or Packwood? She knew Packwood was a light sleeper.

As she picked her way down the stairs she realised that it was someone knocking at the front door. Rogers slept at the back of the house, so perhaps he could not hear it. But Packwood's room was over the entrance hall. She thought she could hear him stirring above as she reached the front door.

Outside, the first streaks of dawn were cracking across the night sky. It looked like it was going to be a lovely day. It had been cold the night before, she knew. She had heard the rain and the ground was damp. There was a crispness to the morning and it was still very cold. Her breath froze as a mist in the air as Janet exhaled. She stifled a cry and stepped backwards, letting the door swing fully open.

The figure in the doorway lurched forwards. Water was pooling at its feet. The suit it wore was sodden and torn. A strip of seaweed wound round one leg as it took another lurching step. The wide, staring, impossibly pale eyes bored into Janet as she took another step backwards, still unable to shout or scream. The face was a pasty mass of flaccid skin, scratched and weeping seawater. The hair was plastered to the skull.

At last, Janet turned to run. And found that Logan Packwood was standing right behind her. He was fully dressed.

'Oh thank God, Logan,' she managed to say. 'It's –'

'So I see,' he said. His head was tilted slightly to one side as he took in the situation. The walking corpse seemed to have stopped now, as if waiting just inside the doorway.

Packwood sighed. 'I suppose we should have foreseen this,' he said, hooking his thumbs into his waistcoat pockets.

'Foreseen it?' Janet hissed. 'It's…' she struggled to find a word. 'Grotesque.'

'Yes,' he said quietly. 'I suppose it is.' Then bizarrely, incongruously, he smiled. 'But then this whole thing is rather bizarre, don't you think? Thus is real progress made.' He stepped up to the thing on the threshold and examined it with interest, oblivious to Janet's look of disgust.

'I think I'm going to be sick,' she mumbled, hand to mouth as the smell reached her through the cold air.

'Yes,' Packwood said, obviously not listening. 'We need to decide what we should do with this…' He reached out and pinched the limp skin of the cheek, rubbing his finger and thumb over it,

105

pulling it back from the jaw so the blackened teeth emerged in a rictus grin. 'This side effect.'

Janet cupped her hand under her mouth as she ran.

Chapter Eight
Delivery

She pushed her breakfast round the plate, not really hungry. It was difficult to conjure up an appetite after the shock. Coffee, she could manage. Solid food was something else.

'Not eating?' Packwood asked as he devoured his bacon and egg with gusto.

Janet pushed the plate away and shook her head.

'How are you getting on with analysing the results?'

She stared at the plate. 'OK,' she said. 'But I don't suppose it matters.'

'Because of our fisherman friend?' Packwood gave a short howl of laughter. 'I wouldn't let him put you off your breakfast. Teething problems, no more.'

'Teething problems?' Janet stared at him. 'A walking corpse knocks at the door in the small hours and you call it a teething problem?'

Packwood shrugged, dabbing at his full lips with a napkin. 'What would you call it?'

'Sickening,' she murmured, remembering.

Packwood was standing up now, extracting himself from the chair and pushing it back far enough to allow his more than ample bulk to emerge from behind the table. 'I'd like you to finish up this morning if you can. There's something I want you to do at lunchtime.'

'We're going on?' she asked in surprise. 'Despite –'

'Despite nothing,' he snapped. 'Of course we're going on. We can't stop now, Janet. Think what this means. Think what we shall achieve. For everyone.'

'But we can't,' she protested. 'Surely we can't –'

'We *must*,' he hissed at her, leaning forwards, hands resting heavily on the surface of the table. 'For Christopher if for no other reason.' He straightened up. 'You of all people should appreciate that,' he said quietly.

She sat in silence for a moment, her head in her hands, staring at the table mat where her plate had been. Seeing every detail and blemish of the plain burgundy finish, the gold outlines of the edge. 'What do you want me to do?' she asked at last.

'That's better.' There was a hint of relief in his voice. 'We need you, Janet. I need you.' He was behind her, though she had not heard him approach. His huge hand clapped down on her shoulder, squeezing, pulling her back in the chair so she looked up at him towering above her. 'Leave the analysis for now,' he said. 'But I think it would be a good idea if you went over to the main island. Have lunch at the pub. Take a bit of a break. Fresh air.'

'Thank you,' she murmured, wondering what was behind this. She soon knew.

'And while you're there, keep your ears open. I need to know if anyone saw… saw our friend last night.' He let go of her shoulder, his great hand lifting, then coming down heavily as he patted her. 'Let's find out if we're clean on this, or whether there's any damage limitation to be done.'

She nodded slowly as he walked away. 'All right. I'll see what I can do.'

Packwood paused at the door. He tapped a pudgy finger against his chin. 'That strange Doctor who was here yesterday…'

'What about him?'

'A monitor, do you think? Checking? I'd like to know more about him.'

Janet nodded. 'Could be,' she agreed. 'He wanted to see Christopher. Maybe he knows. I mean, maybe he really does know.'

Packwood was stroking his chin now, deep in thought. He shook his head. 'He doesn't know. He might guess. But nobody knows. Only you and I.'

'And Rogers.'

Packwood nodded. 'And Christopher Sheldon.' He closed the

door behind him, so that his last words were almost lost. But she heard: 'Not that he matters now, of course.'

Surgery ran from ten in the morning until noon. Dave Madsen had made it clear that he was always on call, always available. But with no telephones he was also keen to keep anything other than emergencies within certain scheduling limits. So for two hours every morning, except Sunday (when anyone could catch him after church if they needed) he sat in his consulting room and waited to see if anyone knocked at the door. Usually he saw someone, often several people, during the morning. When there was a bug going round then there was often a queue. He had no receptionist, so it was up to the villagers to organise a sensible system.

It was only a quarter to ten when his first caller arrived. Madsen was carrying a steaming cup of coffee carefully to his desk. He had filled it too full, coffee sloshing dangerously close to the lip of the cup. The knock at the door startled him and scalding coffee dripped on to his hand as he set down the cup. 'Damn!' he said as he shook the hot liquid off his hand. 'Just a minute,' he called out.

He was at the sink now, running his scalded fingers under the cold tap. The door opened anyway, he heard it and turned sharply. 'I said –' he started. Then he broke off and smiled. 'Oh, it's you. I'm sorry. I thought it was a punter arrived early with a snotty nose or something.'

Liz Trefoil smiled thinly. 'No,' she said. 'It's me.'

'So I see.' He dried his hand on the towel hooked over the rail by the sink and crossed to her quickly. He hesitated as he reached her. She was not returning his smile. In fact she looked tired and worn. 'You're not ill, are you?' he asked. It sounded odd as soon as he said it.

But it drew a faint smile from her. 'No. I'm not ill.'

'Good,' he said. 'Then I won't catch anything.' He pulled her close, arm round her as he went to kiss her.

'Silly,' she said, pulling back. But she didn't resist for more than a moment. They kissed for several seconds before she again pulled away.

'Are you all right?' Madsen asked, sensing she was nervous, tense.

'I'm fine,' she said. 'I just want to know why you lied.'

'Why I what?'

'I've been thinking about it. All yesterday. I kept hearing your voice, hearing you saying it.'

'Saying what?' Madsen shook his head. 'I'm sorry I didn't see you yesterday. But I was telling the truth. I meant what I said when –'

'Not to me,' she interrupted. 'You lied about Bill Neville.'

He blinked. Felt his stomach lurch and the blood drain from his face. 'Bill Neville.'

'You told Sir Edward that his arm was just sprained.'

'That's right.'

She stared at him, head to one side, hands tight at her sides. 'You know his arm was broken, Dave. It's not like it was a mistake, was it? So why did you lie?'

'Liz.' He shook his head.

'I was here when they brought him in, remember? That afternoon.'

He nodded quickly. 'I remember. Of course I remember, darling.'

'And I saw him.' Her lower lip quivered. 'I saw his arm, bent round. The bone sticking…' She swallowed. 'Sticking…' A sob escaped from her lips and she turned away quickly.

He held her from behind, arms tight round her. 'I know,' he breathed. 'Darling, I know.'

She pulled away and spun round. The tears glistened on her cheeks. 'So why lie about it, Dave? What's going on?' She waited several seconds. 'Tell me!' she demanded.

His own breath was ragged and uneven now as he tried to keep his voice level, reasonable. 'Look, Liz – darling. I would. If I could tell you, I would. Really.'

She just stared at him. Then she looked away. 'Fine,' she said quietly.

'No,' he sighed. 'It's not fine. It's just that… Well, that –'

'That what?' she shouted. 'What, for God's sake? That you love, me but you don't trust me, is that it?' She was shaking her head. Her lip was going again. But before the tears started once more she turned and ran from the room.

He stood absolutely still, his mouth half open. When the outside door slammed shut, he flinched. He walked slowly to his desk and sat down on the chair behind it. He cupped his hands round the mug of coffee, scalded fingers forgotten in the heat of the situation. He stared into the misty brown liquid, surprised more than anything when the first tear splashed into the mug.

He left a sign on the door apologising that surgery would be at three in the afternoon today. Then he walked briskly up to the quay and untied Bob Trefoil's rowing boat. Liz's father wouldn't mind, he was sure. Especially given the circumstances.

By the time he reached the smaller island, Dave Madsen was sweating. He was drained, physically and emotionally. But his muscles did not ache as much as he had expected. Perhaps he was getting used to rowing, although he did very little of it really. Usually Rogers came for him when he had an appointment. But not today. Today was not an appointment. But what he had to say was too important to wait.

The imperturbable Rogers made no comment on Madsen's appearance – either the fact he was there or the state he was in. He showed him into the drawing room and left, saying he would fetch Mr Packwood.

'You should have let me know you were coming,' Packwood said amiably as he appeared a few minutes later. 'Janet's off to the main island in a few minutes. You could have borrowed her boat and taken it back later.'

'Let you know?' Madsen asked. 'What – by carrier pigeon, I suppose? It's about all there is in this godforsaken place.'

'And I thought you were getting on so well with the natives,' Packwood admonished. He paused beside the drinks cabinet and considered. 'Not quite over the yardarm yet, I'm afraid,' he decided. 'I can ring for tea, if you like.'

'I don't want tea,' Madsen snapped.

'Then what do you want?' Packwood's voice was suddenly low and quiet.

Madsen took a deep breath and looked away. 'I want out,' he said.

For a while Packwood did not reply. He crossed to the window and looked out over the grounds of the house. 'You know,' he said at last, 'when Christopher's great-great whatever grandfather built this house, there must have come a time where he knew that the money was gone. He must have realised that he wasn't going to be able to do it, to make his dream a reality. But despite that, he went on.'

'He went bankrupt,' Madsen pointed out.

Packwood whirled round, his eyes blazing. 'He had a vision. A dream. And he was strong enough and brave enough and astute enough to see that although he could not fulfil that dream, it was too late to stop. And whatever happened to him, someone else would realise his vision.' Packwood shook his head. 'He didn't stop, he didn't back out. He had come too far. Just as we have.'

'But it isn't working!' Madsen insisted.

Packwood raised his eyebrows. 'Oh? I thought Janet was analysing the results, not you.'

'I see the results every day,' Madsen told him. 'I live with them, remember. And I tell you it isn't working.'

'And on what exactly do you base this analysis of yours?'

'The deaths for one thing.'

Packwood sat down close to Madsen. 'We've been through this, Dave. Teething problems. There are always teething problems. There have been no more deaths, have there? The fishing accident was just an accident, you know.'

'What? Oh yes, I know. No, no more deaths. Not from…' He rubbed at his forehead with his fingers, trying to massage his thoughts into some sort of coherent order. 'It's just… the ethics of it all.'

'Ah. Ethics.' Packwood rubbed his jaw. 'We've talked about that too, as I recall. The ends justify the means, remember.'

Madsen sighed. 'I'm not sure they do any more,' he confessed.

'But think of the ends, of what we are achieving,' Packwood hissed at him.

'I have,' Madsen told him. He looked up, met Packwood's eyes, held his gaze. 'I have thought about it.'

'Oh?'

'And I've thought about the cost too. The human cost. About what we're doing to these people. I know I agreed to it. But that was before I knew them. Before I was a part of their community.' He reached out suddenly and grabbed Packwood's surprised hand. 'It isn't right, Packwood, what we're doing to them.'

Packwood stared at Madsen's hand as it gripped his own. Then he pulled away and stood up. 'Them?' he demanded angrily. 'Them or *her*?'

'Her? What do you –'

'Liz Trefoil,' Packwood snapped. 'Oh, don't think I don't know about that. News travels faster and further than you'd ever believe in a close-knit community like this.'

'But that's the point,' Madsen was standing too now, almost shouting. 'It *is* a community. It's not a laboratory, these people aren't rats or mice or guinea pigs.' He paused for breath, shaking with emotion.

From out in the hall came the sound of a clock striking noon.

As it struck, Packwood's expression mellowed, his anger seemed to fade. 'Now it really is time for a drink,' he said. 'Will you join me? Brandy?' He waved Madsen back to his seat.

Madsen shook his head. 'No, thank you.'

But Packwood handed him a glass anyway. Then he sat opposite Madsen, swirling his brandy round the large glass as he watched the doctor. 'We've made great progress, you know,' Packwood said. His voice was calm and level again now. He sipped at the brandy and smacked his lips together in appreciation. 'Did I tell you that we've developed a strain that can be administered orally?' he asked.

'No?' He nodded, pleased with himself. 'Makes your job easier,' he said.

'I don't have a job here any more. I'm out of it, I told you.'

Packwood took another sip. 'So you did,' he murmured. 'So you did. Still, it will save you the trouble of all those injections into the carotid artery. No more double doses of the flu vaccine, eh? Just a simple tablet.' He sipped again. 'Or it could be dispersed in liquid, of course.'

Madsen stared at him. Then slowly, carefully he put his brandy down on the table beside his chair.

'Not drinking?' Packwood asked. 'So, we're just awaiting the results of a human test now. We had a successful trial on cattle. Mrs Painswick's cows actually. Seems to work well. No side effects as far as I know. Rogers put it in their troughs the other night. You've not been called out to them in the meantime, I hope?'

Madsen shook his head dumbly.

'Good. Good.' Packwood frowned suddenly at Madsen. 'This brandy is really excellent, you know.'

'I'm not thirsty.'

Packwood nodded slowly. 'I know what you're thinking,' he said, swirling the glass again. 'But I'd hardly tell you this if I was hoping to slip something into that drink, now would I? Nor would I be drinking it myself, of course.' He took another sip by way of demonstration.

'I suppose,' he went on after a short while, 'that we could have used Mrs Painswick herself as a test subject. She will undoubtedly be infected by this strain by now. As no doubt will a few others who work at the farm. But since they may already be infected from other sources like the sheep, it's hardly a control. And Janet says we need a control.'

'And you have a control? A human control?' Madsen asked despite himself.

Packwood was smiling now. It was not a pleasant smile. 'We do,' he said proudly. 'You know, I really don't understand why you won't drink with me. I assure you that brandy is perfectly safe and pure.'

He paused, just for a split second before he added: 'You had a drink last time you were here.'

'Last time?' For a moment Madsen's world tilted sideways. He felt his head swimming.

'Whisky, as I recall. Scotch on the rocks, that's what you asked for.'

'The whisky?' Madsen's throat was dry. 'It was in the whisky?'

Packwood was still smiling.

'No,' Madsen realised. 'No, you drank too. From the same bottle. You're bluffing.' He breathed out in relief. 'You think that if you convince me I'm infected I'll have to go on, to prove it works. Make it work. For my own sake.'

'There is a certain logic to that,' Packwood agreed. 'And you're almost right too. As you realise, there was of course nothing in the whisky. Nothing at all.' His smile seemed to have widened as he drained his glass. Then he leaned forward and picked up Madsen's discarded brandy glass. He stood up, holding the glass carefully by the stem.

Packwood crossed to the drinks cabinet and set down the glasses. He poured himself another brandy. 'I'm so sorry,' he said, 'I forgot.'

'Forgot?' There was something in the tone of Packwood's voice, in his continuing pasted-on smile, that made Madsen feel suddenly sick and dizzy.

'Yes,' Packwood said in the same tone of voice. 'You have ice in your drinks, don't you?' The satisfaction, the pride oozed from his words. 'I never take ice myself. Even if it's made with the purest island spring water.'

Madsen found himself taking back the glass without thinking. His mind was reeling, racing, shying away from the implication.

'The great thing about the orally administered strain of material,' Packwood was saying, his voice seeming to come through layers of water. 'The real advance, is that it's passed on between individuals through bodily fluids. That's why Mrs Painswick will be infected of course. Dairy cows, you see.'

Madsen felt the glass slip from his fingers. He heard the chink of the ice as the drink fell towards the wooden floor, a fraction ahead of the explosion of breaking glass.

'Just think how much further ahead we are now with delivery,' Packwood was saying. 'When it can be passed on to a subject even by a simple kiss.'

Peri sneezed again. She was sitting in the corner of the pub lounge, hands tight round a mug of coffee. So far she was the only person there, apart from Liz, who was tidying up behind the bar.

Peri had been sniffing all morning and had readily agreed to the Doctor's suggestion that she get some rest and then keep an eye on the pub and ask round to find out about any other odd occurrences recently. The Doctor and Sir Edward had agreed to meet again at first light and try to trace the steps of the walking dead man after he left the churchyard, to find out where he had been heading, and perhaps why.

When she had finished her coffee, Peri stared at the empty mug for a while. It was strange how the difficulty of coming to a decision seemed to have no bearing on the magnitude of that decision, she thought. To follow someone wheeling a corpse he's just dug up in the middle of the night was a no-brainer. But whether or not to have another mug of coffee was something that required serious consideration.

She came to a decision and took her mug over to the bar. Liz seemed distracted, distant somehow, this morning. Usually she was smiling and happy, willing to chat. Today she was short-tempered and her face was set in a frown that did not suit it at all.

'Another one?' she asked Peri, taking the mug.

'Please.'

Liz took the mug into the back room without comment. She reappeared a few moments later, the mug filled.

'Thank you.' Peri took the mug and set it down on the counter. 'Liz?'

'Mmm?'

'Are you all right?'

The young woman looked at Peri. There was a sadness in her eyes. Her mouth opened, and she was about to answer when the door to the pub opened and someone came in. She gave a weak, half-hearted smile. 'I'm fine. Really.' Then she turned to serve the woman who had come in.

'Can I have a mineral water? Still, not sparkling.'

Liz retrieved a bottle from under the bar.

'I'll open it, thank you,' the woman said quickly.

Liz shrugged and handed her the bottle. She put a tall glass on the counter. 'Ice?'

'No thank you.' She fished some coins from her purse.

Peri looked at the woman as Liz took the money. She was tall and slim with a neat bob of black hair that reached just to her collar. She was wearing a trouser suit that would normally have been smart but casual. Here in the pub on Dorsill it seemed she was hugely overdressed. She was carrying a large shoulder bag.

'Just visiting us?' Liz asked as she handed over the change.

'Thought I'd take a break. Get some air.'

'Miss Spillsbury works over at Sheldon's Folly,' Liz explained to Peri.

'Really?' Peri introduced herself as Liz retreated to the back room. 'I'm visiting, with a friend,' she explained. 'He went over to Sheldon's Folly yesterday – perhaps you met him? The Doctor.'

The woman regarded Peri for a long moment. 'Yes,' she said at last. 'Yes, I met him.' She smiled suddenly and held out her hand. 'Janet Spillsbury,' she said. 'Shall we find a table?'

'I don't think that will be difficult,' Peri said as she led the way to the table in the corner where she had been sitting. 'You get some sun here, otherwise it's all a bit dark with the small windows.'

'Good thought.'

They settled themselves at the table. Janet set down her bag beside her chair and sipped at her water without enthusiasm.

Peri held her coffee and tried to smell the steam that rose from it, but her nose was blocked and she could barely smell anything.

'So,' Janet said. 'You're visiting.'

'That's right.'

'You have friends here?'

'Not before we came.' Peri smiled. 'We often seem to land up somewhere pretty much at random, you know.'

'Sounds like an interesting life.'

'That's not the half of it,' Peri said.

'So what do you do, exactly? You and the Doctor?' Janet asked.

'I get confused, mostly,' Peri told her. 'And the Doctor, well, he does the confusing.'

'I see.' She obviously didn't.

'What about you? You work for Mr Sheldon?'

'For Christopher?' She was playing with the glass, rolling it between the flats of her palms, looking at the water rather than Peri. 'In a way. We were... colleagues.'

'Oh?'

'We worked on the same research team.'

'But not any more?'

'Mmm?' Janet looked up, for a moment there was a flash of confusion on her face. 'Oh, well, we still have some work to do. You know.'

'You and Sheldon?'

'Ye-es.' She did not sound sure about that. 'But mostly I work with Logan Packwood.'

'So what does Christopher Sheldon do?' Peri asked. 'I mean, it's his house, isn't it? We've heard a lot about him here. From the villagers. They seem to respect him. They owe him a lot.'

Janet nodded and sipped her water. She was staring off into the distance. 'Yes,' she said quietly. 'He was a good man.'

'Was?'

'Sorry?' She blinked.

'You said was. As if –'

'I mean what he did for the islanders was good,' Janet said quickly.

'He is a good man.' She looked away, as if embarrassed. 'One of the best.'

'Sorry,' Peri said gently, wondering what she had said to upset the woman. 'I didn't mean…'

'That's all right. I'm sorry if I…' She shrugged and moved her glass. 'I've known Christopher for years. We've been colleagues for a long time. And friends. Everyone in the department knows him. It's just odd talking to someone who doesn't, I suppose.'

Peri nodded. 'So what are you working on?' she asked brightly.

'We were working on developing a DNA computer,' Janet said. 'If that means anything to you?'

Peri shook her head. 'Nothing at all.'

'Well, we've progressed from that,' she said. 'It's classified, of course.'

'Of course.'

'But we're going to change the world.' There was a wistful note in her voice.

Peri nodded. 'Right.' She laughed. 'I used to want to change the world.'

'But not any more?'

'Oh no,' said Peri. 'No, now we just save it.'

Janet drained her glass and stood up. 'Can I get you another coffee?' she asked.

Peri looked down at her mug. She had barely drunk any. 'I'm fine, thanks.'

'Well, it's been nice to meet you.' She picked up her bag. 'I brought some work to do. I hope you won't think I'm being rude.'

Peri smiled. 'Of course not. I enjoyed the chat.'

Janet smiled back. Then she moved to a nearby table and set her bag down on the seat and her empty glass on the table. There were a few people in the pub now. - the tables were beginning to fill up. Sandwiches and pies were emerging from the back room. Peri watched Janet go to the bar and return to her table with an unopened bottle of water. She caught the woman's eye as she sat down and smiled again.

Janet Spillsbury opened her bag and pulled out a sheaf of papers and a pencil. She did not smile back.

Peri's cold was definitely taking hold, she decided. When she had finished her coffee, she considered lunch. But she had eaten a late breakfast and really wasn't hungry. Probably losing her appetite as well, she thought. Maybe a walk would clear her stuffy head. It looked sunny outside, though she knew it would be cold. But she was sick of sitting in the pub - she needed to get out and do something. Anything.

She made her way to the bar and left her mug on the counter. She caught sight of Mike Neville, sitting drinking alone at a table. He looked up as she passed, and Peri looked quickly away, praying he had not noticed her.

Liz was busy pulling a pint, so Peri just waved and left. She paused outside the pub, debating with herself which way to go. She decided in the end to head out of the village the other way from her previous expedition, past the school rather than by the church and the quay.

But as she turned to go, she saw Dave Madsen approaching from the other direction. He looked dishevelled. His hair was a mess and the cuffs of his trousers were soaking wet as if he had waded ashore from a boat that had not quite beached.

'Hello,' Peri said as he arrived at the pub.

He stared at her with wide eyes. 'Is Liz here?' he demanded. His voice was strained, his forehead lined with concern.

'Behind the bar,' Peri said. 'Is anything –'

But he was gone, pushing his way inside the pub. Peri saw him stumbling towards the bar as the door swung shut behind him.

She shrugged, wondering what the problem was. Lovers' tiff, maybe? Then she buttoned her coat against the cold and set off towards the school.

Liz saw people moving aside suddenly before she saw that Dave was pushing his way towards the bar. She was in the middle of pouring a pint and trying to remember a food order. Behind her she could hear her father in the kitchen getting stroppy with the stove.

'Liz,' Dave was breathless and red-faced. 'I have to talk to you.'

She looked at him, then back at the foaming pint she was topping. Then she looked at the people crowded round the bar waiting to be served.

'I have to talk to you now,' he hissed, leaning across towards her, his sleeve in a puddle of spilled beer.

She reached across and raised his arm, then wiped underneath with a towel before letting him put it back. 'You can see I'm busy here,' she said. 'You'll have to wait a minute.'

'This can't wait.'

She handed the pint across the bar, held up a finger to the next person to tell them to hang on, and went through to the kitchen to give the latest food orders. 'It'll have to,' she told Dave as she went.

He was still there when she got back. As soon as she caught his eye he leaned across the bar again.

'Dave!' she warned him before he could say anything. 'Not now, all right?'

Ned Perkins was laughing as she poured him a pint. She knew why. She had seen him muttering to Harry Strope and both of them looking at Dave. And at her. She frowned at him fiercely as she gave him his drink.

Then she turned to Dave. 'Later,' she said. 'Just come back later when it's quiet. You know how we get at lunchtime, when the boats are in.'

Dave met her angry gaze. He seemed to be about to say something. Then he shook his head. 'It doesn't matter,' he called across the bar. 'There's nothing you can do now. Nothing I can do either.'

'What are you talking about?' She swept several empty glasses off the bar beside him and pushed them roughly into the sink below the bar.

'It's too late. I'm sorry.' He turned away. 'So sorry.' He looked back, just for a moment as he left. Just long enough to mouth 'Goodbye, Liz' to her.

He was obviously in a bad way. Maybe she should not have confronted him about Bill Neville's arm. She smiled back at him half-heartedly. 'Goodbye, Dave,' she called after him. 'See you later.'

The conversations died at the sound of her voice, falling away to a dull background mutter.

'Yeah,' Dave said. 'Yeah, I'm sure you will.' Then he was gone and she was pulling another pint.

There was no chemist on the island, so Madsen did his own dispensing. A locked cabinet in his consulting room contained all the drugs he was likely to need to prescribe. If there was a need for something else, it was shipped out. It came with the mail boat if it wasn't urgent. If it was, then a helicopter would be arranged by the coastguard on the mainland.

He knew exactly what he wanted. He unlocked the cabinet and took out a large glass bottle of tablets.

Madsen's next stop was the kitchen. From one of the cupboards he took a glass tumbler. From another he retrieved a bottle of single malt whisky. It was almost half full. He poured himself a generous measure of the whisky, his hand shaking. Some of it spilled on to the table. He picked up the glass, looked at it, then put it down and sloshed in more whisky. He set the bottle down unstoppered on the table. He had no fridge, and so no ice. Not that he thought he would have wanted it anyway.

He took the drink and the bottle of pills upstairs. His wallet was in his back trouser pocket. He pulled it out, opened it and drew out a photograph. Then he threw the wallet on the cabinet by his bed. He sat down heavily on the bed and took a gulp of the whisky. It burned his throat as it went down. He stared at the black and white photo of Liz for several seconds before he propped it up against his wallet on the bedside cabinet.

They had spent a day on the mainland three weeks ago.

A pleasant happy day. He had insisted on the photo, pushing her laughing into a booth in the back corner of Woolworth's. He put the whisky down beside it and opened the pill bottle. He shook out a pile of pills.

He sat there for half an hour, staring at the picture, crying silently. Every now and then he took a pill and pushed it into his mouth. Then he washed it down with a mouthful of whisky.

When the whisky was gone, he had gone to the kitchen and brought the bottle upstairs. He drank from that. When the pills were gone, he tipped some more out on to the cabinet.

And when his head was so muzzy and tired that he could no longer lift the bottle, could no longer feel the pills as he reached out for them, could no longer see Liz staring back accusingly at him, Dave Madsen leaned back and swung his legs up on to the bed.

He closed his eyes, and slipped away into a sleep from which he knew he would never awaken.

The air was clear and crisp, and Peri could see her breath as she walked. She had no idea where she was going – the village was now long behind her. But she was enjoying the peace and the sunshine. Occasionally she dabbed at her nose with a hanky. Occasionally she stopped to admire the view or to get her breath back. It was a lovely day.

She had circled round a bit after leaving the village, her plan as far as she had one being to see if she could come back round to the church. She reckoned she was heading in roughly the right direction as she was on a track between two fields. If this was Heather Hill Farm, then she knew that on one side its border was close to the quay. In the distance she could see a line of cows marching along another track, an ordered, regimented formation. Single file.

At the back of the line of cows, Peri could see a figure following behind, encouraging them on. Even at this distance she could see that it was Hilly Painswick. Peri waved and was pleased to see the figure wave back.

As the last of the cows entered the field, Mrs Painswick fastened the gate and started across the field towards Peri. She waved again.

'The house is this way,' Hilly said as she climbed over the fence. She pointed up the track. 'Only about a mile. Just the weather for a good brisk walk. And now that the cows are milked I have an hour to myself.' She set off up the track, allowing Peri to catch up with her before she said: 'Come and have some tea. Tell me what you and your colourful friend have been up to.'

'Oh, you know about him,' Peri laughed.

'Everyone knows about him,' Hilly said. 'He's been talking to Mrs Tattleshall, hasn't he?'

The farmhouse was large and square and built of stone. It was surrounded by an assortment of barns and outbuildings, also mainly built of rough, dark stone. The farmyard was awash with mud. Somewhere nearby a horse snorted and was answered by the sudden frantic barking of a dog. Peri sneezed loudly to add to the noise.

The front door was open, and Hilly led Peri inside. The hallway was surfaced with quarry tiles. The kitchen floor was flagged with slabs of pale stone. A large wooden table stood unevenly in the middle of the room. Various cooking utensils and farming implements hung round the walls and from the beams across the ceiling.

'Sorry it's a bit of a mess,' Hilly said. 'But this is a working house.'

'That's fine.' Peri seated herself at the table. 'I hope I'm not taking too much of your time.'

'No, of course not. I love a good natter. And we don't often get the chance to meet new people round here, as you can appreciate. People who have travelled.'

Peri laughed. 'Oh, I've travelled,' she admitted.

'Yes,' the older woman said. 'I know.'

'You do?' Peri's throat was suddenly dry. She could feel herself reddening. She needed to sniff and did not dare.

'Of course.' Hilly Painswick laughed at Peri's consternation.

'Your accent,' she explained. 'We're not completely naive about the outside world here, you know. We may not have televisions, but we do know Americans when we hear them. Rare though that is.'

'Of course.' Peri laughed as her nerves dissipated. 'I'm sorry.'

'Oh, no problem. Now would you like some tea? I don't have any coffee, I'm afraid. Or a cold drink? There are some biscuits somewhere. I was baking just the other day.' She started to look through a cluttered cupboard. 'Or was it last week? Time simply flies by these days, don't you find?' She emerged brandishing a faded tin.

'You know,' Peri said, 'seeing the cows just now… What I'd really like is a glass of cold fresh –'

'Milk?' Hilly smiled as if she had just been paid the greatest compliment imaginable. 'Of course. I'll get some – we keep a churn cool in the pantry. It's difficult in the summer of course, with no real refrigeration.'

She returned a few moments later with a glass filled almost to the brim with creamy milk. 'There you are. You won't get it much fresher than that.'

Peri sipped at the cold liquid. It was surprising how much more flavour the milk had when it was so fresh. 'That's lovely,' she said. 'I can just tell it's doing me good.'

Chapter Nine
Material Evidence

Some time later than Peri was having her milk, the Doctor was drinking tea. He held the cup between thumb and forefinger, his little finger crooked out to the side as he sipped appreciatively.

'Earl Grey,' he said as he set down the cracked cup on a chipped saucer.

'I don't know,' Sir Edward confessed. 'Never could tell the difference.'

The Doctor nodded. They had spent a pleasant few hours walking across the moorland, mainly in silence, enjoying the views and the fresh air. They had skipped lunch by unspoken consent, and the Doctor was slightly upset by what he now had to do. But he did have to do it. 'It's not just tea you have problems identifying properly, is it, Sir Anthony?' he said lightly.

'Isn't it?' The other man sipped his tea without apparent worry. Then he seemed to notice the Doctor's serious expression and he too set down his cup. 'What is it, Doctor? What are you getting at?' he asked, frowning. Then the frown faded and he cleared his throat. 'Oh, I see. Yes, very clever. So you know.'

'You want to tell me about it?' the Doctor asked. 'You're obviously more comfortable as Sir Anthony Kelso than you are as Sir Edward Baddesley.'

'I'm not very good at this cloak and dagger stuff,' Sir Anthony confessed. 'Never have been. Never will be now, I suppose. How did you find out? Recognise me?'

'Only from your passport.' The Doctor nodded towards the desk where he had found the passport.

'You've been through my things?' Sir Anthony was obviously more annoyed at this than he was that his alias had been uncovered. But after a moment he mellowed again. 'I suppose you had a good reason for it, knowing you, Doctor.'

'Evidently,' the Doctor said. 'The tea really is excellent, by the way. And it really is Earl Grey.'

'Thank you.' Sir Anthony sipped at his own tea. Then he set it down again and steepled his fingers as he settled back into the armchair. 'Suppose you deserve an explanation.'

'That depends on the explanation,' the Doctor said. 'If you're fleeing from creditors or persistent lovers then I don't want to know, thank you very much.'

Sir Anthony snorted. 'Wish I'd led that interesting a life,' he said. 'No, the explanation will probably sound as boring and silly as the so-called strange events we were discussing last night. At least, until – you know.'

'We'll see, shall we?' the Doctor said. As he spoke the door behind him swung open slowly. Footsteps crossed the room towards where the Doctor was sitting.

'Ah, there you are,' Sir Anthony said, rising and smiling. 'You're just in time for tea.'

'And for an interesting discussion, I think, Peri,' the Doctor said without turning.

Peri declined the tea, explaining how she had been to Heather Hill Farmhouse for milk and home-made biscuits.

'Good sort, Hilly Painswick,' said Sir Anthony, as the Doctor told Peri they should now address him.

'Hilly?' the Doctor asked in astonishment.

'Don't ask,' Peri told him.

'How are the sniffles, my dear?' Sir Anthony inquired.

'Much better,' Peri said. 'I think the fresh air has helped. I feel fine now.'

'I'm glad to hear that,' the Doctor said. 'And I shall be glad to hear what Sir Anthony has to tell us as well, I'm sure.'

'Ah,' Sir Anthony said. 'Yes. Well. You see.'

The Doctor and Peri both leaned forward encouragingly as he told his story.

'I changed my name in case Christopher Sheldon heard I was here,' he began. 'Probably silly – I mean he'd know me if he saw me.

But I reckoned I could keep my face out of his sight more easily than control who knew I was here at all.'

'You know the elusive Mr Sheldon?' the Doctor asked.

'Oh yes. I was his superior at the Ministry of Science until earlier this year.'

'So he does actually exist then.' The Doctor smiled and sipped his tea. 'I was beginning to wonder.'

'What happened?' Peri asked. 'Did he leave?'

'Oh no. I did. Retired in March. Bit earlier than I anticipated or would have liked, but there you are. But up till then I was responsible for a research department within the ministry.'

'What sort of research?' the Doctor asked.

'DNA computers,' Peri said.

The Doctor spluttered on his tea.

Sir Anthony looked astonished. 'Good Lord,' he said, his voice husky. 'I really am not very good at this secrecy lark, am I? Yes, the DNA computer was a part of my department's research remit. Now how on earth did you know that?'

'From Janet Spillsbury,' Peri said. 'I met her at the pub.'

'Really?' Sir Anthony's expression was grave. 'I didn't know she was here.' He shook his head. 'This could be more serious than I thought. I've never met her, but Janet used to be my department's technical liaison with the European Space Agency.'

'If I may use a jigsaw analogy,' the Doctor said sternly, 'and I think I may, could we perhaps finish doing the edge pieces before we start to fill in the fiddly detail in the middle?'

'What?' Sir Anthony said. 'Oh, I see. Yes. Right.' He settled himself into the chair, tapping the ends of his fingers together.

'Could I ask just one thing?' Peri said. 'What exactly *is* a DNA computer?'

'You want us to explain to you your own single impressive contribution to this conversation?' the Doctor asked sarcastically. He sighed, checked his cup was empty, and then explained. 'A DNA computer works out the solutions to complex equations basically by spinning off strands of DNA for each part of the equation.'

'Oh,' said Peri. 'I see.'

'These strands form chains that represent every possible solution to each part of the equation until the correct formula is found out of the millions of possibilities.'

'Provided there are bounds to the problem,' Sir Anthony put in, 'it's possible to solve the equation even if it takes millions of DNA strands and billions of chains.'

'Useful then,' Peri decided.

The Doctor nodded. 'Potentially. I imagine it's in its early stages of development right now?'

Sir Anthony nodded. 'That was Sheldon's project when I was in charge. Going well, actually. Lots of promise.'

'It's not a good way to solve everything, but it is a way of working out certain otherwise insoluble mathematical problems,' the Doctor conceded. 'Since millions of DNA chains form simultaneously, it is like linking millions of conventional silicon-based processors in parallel, you see. The question is, what has this got to do with what's going on here?'

'Beats me,' Sir Anthony admitted, to the Doctor's vocal disappointment. 'But,' he went on when the noise had died down again, 'I was in charge of all the government's genetic research. And that included Sheldon's DNA computer stuff. I didn't mind that – as I said, it showed promise.'

'But you did mind some of the other research your department was doing?'

Sir Anthony nodded. 'I got in a bit of trouble the other year when I voiced my concerns about genetically modified crops. Remember that fuss? There were a couple of other things I objected to and suggested they shelve. Various people were not very happy about the application of ethics to science.'

'I can imagine,' the Doctor agreed.

'Result, the offer of early retirement. Good package, actually. They didn't want me to refuse.'

'So you took it,' Peri said. 'That's why you left.'

'No, actually. I accepted it, of course. Due to kick in, or rather to kick me out, early next year. But having taken the medicine, as it were, I suppose they decided I wasn't cured.'

'You continued to object?' the Doctor asked.

'When I thought it important, yes. But I don't think that was why they brought the date forward and got rid of me.'

'So why do you think it was?'

'I don't know exactly. That's why I came here. To find out. You see, I got the impression that they were shuffling me off because of one particular project. I don't know what. But there was something coming up that they knew I'd kick up a fuss about. Something sensitive. Something big.'

'But you don't know what?' Peri asked.

'No.'

'So why come here?' the Doctor asked. 'Because of Sheldon?'

Sir Anthony nodded. 'Just so. A couple of days before I left I was handing over some papers to my replacement. Junior yes-man, didn't care for him at all, I might say. Anyway, on his desk was a memo. He covered it up pretty quick when I came in. But not quick enough. I managed to get the gist of it. Basically, it recommending granting Sheldon funding for his project.'

'Was that unusual?' the Doctor wanted to know.

'It was unusual to go to my replacement before I'd even left, given the sums of money it was talking about, yes. But what caught my attention was the breakdown of how the money was to be spent. I didn't see the detail, you understand. Just the main line item. A huge sum of money, as I say.'

Peri and the Doctor were both leaning forwards as they listened. 'To pay for what?' Peri asked.

'This.' He waved his hand in the air.

'This?' The Doctor imitated the gesture. 'What do you mean, *this*!'

'I mean this island. Dorsill. Sheldon was given the money to buy the place out from under the developers and give it back to the islanders.'

'But why on earth would a government department do that?' Peri said.

'Good question,' Sir Anthony agreed. 'So given that I had a rather nice little nest egg and plenty of time on my hands, not to say a welter of curiosity and the hint of a conscience, I thought I'd come down here and find out.'

The Doctor was nodding enthusiastically. 'And have you?' he asked.

'Have I what?'

'Found out?'

'Oh,' Sir Anthony said. 'Well, no actually. No, I haven't.'

'Pity,' said the Doctor. 'More tea, anyone?'

Sir Anthony filled them in on what he had discovered as the Doctor poured more tea.

'I took this cottage,' he explained. 'Lucky to find it. Getting the generator and so on installed was a bit tricky. Had to do it in secret.'

'Everyone knows,' Peri told him. 'They told us down at the pub.'

Sir Anthony looked crestfallen. 'I thought I'd managed that bit quite nicely. Oh well. Do they know about David Madsen as well?'

'Madsen? What about him?' the Doctor asked as he settled back into his seat.

'Not sure really. But his predecessor was an old duffer who suddenly got offered a partnership in Harley Street for no very good reason. Completely unmerited, I'm told. Madsen was the only applicant to take his place. His form arrived the day after the advertisement and he could start at once.'

'Convenient,' Peri commented.

'Indeed. So whatever it is, I reckon he's in on it. Sheldon arrived back here at about the same time, if you want the clincher.'

'Still supposition,' the Doctor said. 'But it does give us something to start with. Perhaps we'll have a quiet word with Dr David Madsen. He was over at Sheldon's Folly yesterday. He could well be involved.'

'I saw him at lunchtime,' Peri offered. 'He seemed a bit distracted. Worried about something.'

'Well, if I was in his shoes,' Sir Anthony said, 'I don't know which

I'd be more worried about – that my patients die, or that they don't seem to stay dead.'

The ceiling was a white void above him. For a while he just lay there, staring up at it, as he did when he woke in the mornings. Nothing odd. Nothing odd at all. Except…

He sat up suddenly, eyes wide. He wasn't dead. He was awake. Awake and alive. Dave Madsen looked at the bedside cabinet, suddenly wondering if the whole thing was a dream. A nightmare. All of it.

Several white tablets were scattered across the top of the cabinet. An empty glass tumbler stood in the middle of them, angled drunkenly because it was on top of one of the tablets. On the floor by the cabinet was an empty whisky bottle, lying on its side.

And he didn't even have a hangover. No ill effects at all. 'Oh no,' he murmured as he rubbed his eyes. 'Oh my God, no.' It was already too late. Too late to resolve anything, too late to help Liz. Too late to die. It wouldn't let him, not like this. Not so easily.

'Logan Packwood.' Sir Anthony nodded. 'Another geneticist, like Sheldon, although he started in computer science of course. Actually,' he went on, 'Janet Spillsbury has some background in genetics, though as I said her main role was with the Space Agency.'

'So what are they all doing here?' Peri asked.

'And how do we find out?' the Doctor added.

'Well,' Sir Anthony offered, 'I was thinking, before you two showed up, that I might call Madge.'

'Madge.' The Doctor nodded. 'Good idea. Who is Madge?'

'My PA at the ministry. She's still there, though I don't think she's quite as important to the new regime as she used to be. But we're friends.' He pulled his mobile phone from his jacket pocket and switched it on. 'The problem is getting a signal. The coverage here isn't really very good. Comes and goes a bit. Sometimes nothing, and sometimes it'll work even in the cellar, clear as a bell.' He looked at the readout on the phone for a while, then smiled. 'Ah,' he said. 'Looks like we could be in luck.' He pressed a speed dial button. 'So long as it doesn't cut out on us.'

'Don't tell her anything you don't have to,' the Doctor warned. 'You never know who might be listening, or who she might talk to.'

Sir Anthony nodded. 'Understood. That's assuming she's there.'

'What do you think, Doctor?' Peri asked quietly as Sir Anthony listened to the phone, waiting for an answer.

'I'm not sure. Not yet. But I don't like it.' Sir Anthony was talking quietly into the phone now. 'I don't like it at all,' the Doctor finished.

'That's right, Madge,' Sir Anthony was saying. 'I'm on Dorsill... Oh, not too bad. Coping. The fresh air does me good I'm sure. Look, I was going to pop over and see young Sheldon while I'm here. Silly not to. Just remind me what he's working on, would you? So I know what planet he's on. You know what he's like.'

He listened for a while. The Doctor and Peri watched expectantly, but there was nothing in Sir Anthony's expression to give them a clue as to what Madge was telling him.

'Really?' he said after a while. 'That secret, eh? Interesting. But you must have some idea...' He listened again for a while, his eyebrows slowly rising.

He used the knife for chopping vegetables and he kept it sharp. Madsen held it up for a moment, letting the afternoon sunlight streaming in through the kitchen window glint on the blade. He had never noticed before how the sharp edge of the blade was scratched and pitted where the sharpener had ground it away. The wooden handle was warm in his sweaty hand. He had already rolled his sleeves up.

A couple of times Madsen had dealt with attempted suicides. One of those was slashed wrists. But like most people the girl had assumed you ran a hot bath and then cut across the wrist. Not the best way, Madsen considered clinically as he stared at his own wrist. He could see the pale blue veins running up to his palm. Cut across and you would hit the bone well before you severed anything major. No, far more effective to slice up the wrist, along the line of the veins and arteries.

He pressed the point of the knife into the pale skin. He could barely feel the prick as it broke through. One advantage at least to all this. Just one. A bead of blood welled up at the point of the knife. He was breathing heavily now as he angled the blade, pushed it in deeper, then sliced it along his wrist.

A thin line of red followed in the wake of the knife. Then it filled out as the blood bubbled up and ran over his wrist. It splashed to the floor. As the blade met the artery, the thick red liquid started to squirt upwards. He knew it was going to happen, but he was still surprised at the force of his heart as it pumped the lifeblood out of his arm.

He smiled, a thin bloodless smile of satisfaction, as he continued to drag the knife through his flesh. Mercifully, there was still no pain. And then, suddenly, the flow of blood slowed. It was already getting sticky, congealing. Madsen pulled out the knife – it made a sucking sound as it came. The line of red was already fading. The blood along his arm was a flaky crust of dark brownish red.

The knife clattered to the floor as he stared in disbelief at his arm. The flow of blood had dried up completely now. He tore at the wound with his fingernails, getting flakes of blood under them. Rubbing the dry blood away like rust.

Beneath it his arm was slowly revealed. There wasn't even a scar. He was holding the wrist, cradling it in his other hand, staring at it transfixed as he slowly crumpled to the floor. The blood was congealing into a sticky mess round his knees as he rocked back and forth. His sobs echoed round the kitchen.

The sun was already low in the sky, though the day was still bright. The Doctor had suggested that Sir Anthony fill them in on what he had learned as they walked. He thought that whatever that might be, a return visit to Sheldon's Folly was called for. Sir Anthony led the way.

'I have a boat pulled up in the next cove,' he said. 'Do a bit of fishing. Rod and line, not nets, you know. It's easier to beach it in the next bay.'

'So, are we any the wiser?'

'A little. Madge doesn't know what Sheldon is working on. It's classified on the computer system. She had a look for me while we were talking, found she didn't have access. That miffed her a bit, I don't mind telling you.'

'So we don't know?' Peri asked.

'Well, she said she did overhear mention of Sheldon's work during some meeting or other the other week. Nothing helpful, though.'

'Anything might help,' the Doctor said. 'However insignificant it may seem.'

Sir Anthony paused to indicate with his walking stick which way they were going. The path was narrow with brambles on one side and the edge of the cliff on the other. 'We go down this fork here. It takes us down the side of the cliff and brings us out in the bay. Not far.' They had to walk in single file. The Doctor led the way, Peri came last. They were all watching their footing carefully as they made their way down the steepening track.

'She said,' Sir Anthony continued as they walked, 'that someone mentioned the "experiment" in relation to Sheldon, though they didn't say anything specific.'

'Pity,' the Doctor said.

'There was some talk about genetic material, whatever that might mean. Oh, and someone was talking about "Gatherer Three", but that may not be related.'

The Doctor stopped so suddenly that Sir Anthony almost collided with him. 'European Space Agency, did you say?' he demanded without looking back.

'What? Oh, yes. Janet Spillsbury, that's right.'

'Then it means that Gatherer Three is certainly related,' the

Doctor told him. He started slowly down the slope again. 'And it also means that things are rather more serious than I had thought.'

'Do I have to ask out loud,' Peri called from the behind them, 'or are you going to tell me?'

'Sorry, my dear.' Sir Anthony picked his way carefully after the Doctor. 'Gatherer Three was a space probe. The Gatherer programme was a joint NASA/ESA project. NASA provided the launch facilities since Ariane wasn't cutting it for this sort of payload. The European Space Agency, in particular Britain and specifically my old department, handled the material.'

'And he means material,' the Doctor called back. 'Don't you, Sir Anthony?'

'Wasn't really involved myself, you understand, though it was under my jurisdiction. But yes. After two prototype trials, the European Space Agency succeeded in launching a deep space probe like no other. Gatherer Three was supposed to travel into the far reaches of our solar system. And then return.'

'As I recall,' the Doctor explained, 'its mission was to skim close to the outer planets and their moons, navigate through the rings of Saturn and the asteroid belt, and then its elliptical orbit would bring it back close enough to Earth for a NASA shuttle to intercept it.' He was almost at the bottom of the cliff now. The beach below was a mass of shingle. 'Isn't that right, Sir Anthony?'

'Well, essentially, yes. Though I'm surprised you know about it. Classified, you know.'

'That wouldn't stop him,' Peri said. 'So when does this space probe go up?'

The Doctor stopped as he reached the bottom of the steep slope. He reached back to help Sir Anthony down the last few feet. 'I think it's already been, Peri,' he said. 'I think that's the point.'

She joined them on the beach, her feet sinking into the shingle. 'You mean, it brought something back.'

'Not that I had heard,' Sir Anthony told them. 'I was still in charge back then. They were examining the samples – each is sealed until it's analysed under controlled conditions.'

'So what did it bring back?'

'Rock, ice, that sort of thing. Boring to you and me, but fascinating to the boffins. Very valuable stuff, I'm told. They examine each sample, then assign it to the expert in that field within the department for further analysis. Then the expert can decide whether to involve others from their field.'

The Doctor was wading across the shingle. In the distance they could see a small rowing boat pulled high up the beach. The sound of the waves on the shingle was a soothing rhythm as they struggled towards it, feet slipping and sliding through the pebbles.

'So what would have to be inside one of the sealed sample containers for Sheldon to be called in as an expert?' the Doctor asked.

'Well, given his pet project and area of expertise was the DNA computer,' Sir Anthony said, 'I suppose some sort of genetic material.' He paused in mid-step. 'Oh, I say,' he murmured.

'Genetic material,' Peri repeated. 'You mean, as in life form?'

Old Jim lived in a small cottage behind the main village street. He could sit on the back step and look out over the moors. He could see the top of the church spire above the other houses, and even the edge of the quay. He loved to just sit and watch the sea, and he loved to wander over the moors with his pipe firmly clenched between his old teeth. His other passions were fishing, though he rarely went out with the youngsters in the boats now, and shooting. But he hardly ever picked up a gun. Everyone knew he had a shotgun – most people knew he kept it locked in a cabinet in his tiny living room.

The only reason for the padlock was that once, in the 1960s, a policeman from the mainland had checked his licence and reminded him that really he should keep the gun under lock and key. The padlock and the clasp it now hung from had arrived on the next mail boat.

Old Jim was out walking the moors when Dave Madsen came for the gun.

Most people in Dorsill never locked their doors. There was no need, and it was inconvenient if others could not just drop by when they wanted or needed. Jim was no exception, and Dave Madsen let himself into the cottage. He called out, but there was no reply. He checked outside the back door to see if Old Jim was sitting watching the world go by. There was no one.

The cabinet was made of old wood. The padlock was strong, but the cabinet itself was not. It did not take Madsen long to wrench the doors from the front of it, leaving splintered wood hanging from the rusted hinges. He pulled out the shotgun, broke it and stuffed in two cartridges. He knew next to nothing about guns. But he did know which way the cartridges went, and which end of the shotgun did what. He hadn't realised there were two triggers, but that made sense. He understood how that worked.

And to be absolutely sure, after he pushed the barrels of the gun into his mouth, he pressed hard on both the triggers.

The sound was deafening in the tiny room. Enough to crack the back window. The fine hairline appeared across the grimy glass a moment before it was splattered red.

The only sound after the echo died away was the body slumping to the ground.

The Doctor had sat down on a bank of shingle and was throwing pebbles as hard as he could out into the sea. Peri was sitting next to him, her knees drawn up under her chin. Sir Anthony preferred, he said, to stand. His stick was pushed into the stony beach and he was leaning on it.

'So how does this explain the walking dead?' Peri wanted to know.

The Doctor threw a stone, watched it arc through the sky. 'If alien genetic material had been introduced into the body...' He paused to watch the pebble splash into the crest of a nascent wave. 'Perhaps that's what the experiment is.'

'How would that work then?' Sir Anthony asked.

'No idea.' The Doctor threw another stone. 'But if we're talking about some sort of – what? Symbiont? Something that lives within the human body, feeds off it.'

'Like a parasite?' Peri asked.

'Yes, but a mutual parasitism. The material gets something from its host. Maybe just a warm place to live.'

'Ugh.' Peri wrinkled her nose is distaste.

'But in return it provides that host with something.'

'Life after death?' Sir Anthony asked with a frown.

'That may be a side effect.' Another pebble splashed down impressively far away. 'Perhaps the genetic material keeps the body healthy, repairs it.'

'Like the fisherman's arm,' Peri realised.

'Exactly. But if the body is too damaged…' The Doctor picked up another pebble and hefted it in his hand, testing the weight. 'Or, no!' He dropped the pebble again and leaped to his feet, stumbling slightly as he caught his balance. 'If the brain dies. Like a drowning, oxygen starvation. Whatever.'

'Then, what?' Peri asked as she pulled herself to her feet beside him.

The Doctor was staring out to sea. Sheldon's Folly was a small dark smudge on the misty horizon. 'If the material doesn't have any effect on the brain,' he said slowly, 'if it has no control, then it might simply just not know that the host is dead. And it keeps repairing the body.'

'But why would it up and walk away?' Sir Anthony wanted to know. 'It was quite active and insistent, as I recall.'

The Doctor waved his arms in annoyance. 'I don't know. I can't answer everything. Look, it's just a guess, that's all. Maybe there is some inherent cerebral influence. Or maybe that comes later.' His voice was rising as he got frustrated and angry with himself at not knowing the answer.

'Most animals have a survival instinct,' Sir Anthony offered. 'Something similar, perhaps?'

'But why do it?' Peri asked as they started towards the boat again.

'What, survive?'

'No, this experiment. Whatever it is?'

Sir Anthony laughed. 'Any idea what the health service costs?' he asked.

'Then there's the licensing,' the Doctor added. 'Imagine the appeal of a material like this. One simple injection perhaps, and then you're cured of everything. For life. Never be ill again. Even recover from the most horrendous and crippling injuries.'

'And the deaths we heard about?' Peri asked.

'Experimental errors,' the Doctor said, 'initial problems. What is it?'

Peri had stopped. Her hand at her mouth. 'I've just thought,' she said. 'The chickens.'

'Chickens?' Sir Anthony asked.

The Doctor walked back to where Peri was still standing. 'Would you care to enlighten us a little further?' he asked with exaggerated calm.

'At the pub, that first evening,' Peri told him. 'One of the men, a farm hand, he was talking about killing a chicken.' She looked straight into the Doctor's eyes as she spoke. 'He said that after he cut the chicken's head off it kept running. Not just a reflex, not just for a few moments. It kept running until he chopped it into tiny pieces.' She looked away, out to sea, towards the black mark in the distance. 'I thought he'd made it up,' she said quietly.

The Doctor and Sir Anthony Kelso looked at each other. Then they both turned as well, so that all three of them were staring out at Sheldon's Folly.

Dave Madsen's body lay on the bare wooden floor of Old Jim's living room. The wood was stained with blood, the walls spattered and discoloured in the dusty light. The back of Madsen's head was a mangled mass of tissue and splintered bone. The front of his skull was almost intact, though the top of his head was a shattered mess. Blood had run down from his staring eyes and out of the remains of his nose and mouth.

Everything was silent. Except for the scratching. One of Madsen's hands was twitching, scraping fingernails across the wooden floor, scrabbling for a purchase. The shattered head turned slowly towards the door. Then slowly, stiffly, the bloodied body of Dave Madsen sat up.

Third Generation

Chapter Ten
Hosts

The school was quiet with so many children off. There seemed to be a bout of something going round. Not enough for anyone to call out the doctor, it seemed. Miss Devlin was not feeling so good herself. Headache. Two aspirins usually did the trick but not today. She had kept her eye on the surgery over the road, Dr Madsen's house. She had seen it was closed in the morning, and had seen him go out in the afternoon. House calls, perhaps?

'I think we'll read quietly this afternoon,' she told the children who were there. The tiny class seemed lost in the Victorian school room. 'Get out your reading books. I want to be able to hear a pin drop.'

There was absolute silence for about five minutes before Timmy Crespin asked impatiently: 'When are you going to drop it, Miss?'

She managed a weak smile. Her headache was not easing.

'I think I'll lie down for a bit, before the evening,' Liz told her father. She was worried about Dave and she was feeling distinctly under the weather.

'Not too swift?' Bob Trefoil asked his daughter. He patted her hand resting on the banister rail as she stood on the third step. 'It does seem a bit close today. I've got a bit of a headache myself.' He went through to the bar. 'I'll give you a shout if I need you,' he called back. But she had already gone to her room. Her head felt as if it was splitting.

Trefoil looked round the bar. Most of the lunch time customers had left. Just a few hangers-on and the woman from Sheldon's Folly still sitting with her mineral water, going through a sheaf of papers.

* * *

Hilly Painswick usually found that five minutes' peace and a glass of fresh milk sorted her out when she was a bit low or run down. God knew it was often enough. Since her husband Geoff had died three years ago she had had hardly a moment to herself. No days off, and the young lads who helped were the ones who weren't up to fishing. Only Benji, her oldest sheepdog, seemed to understand when she was tired and needed a rest. The border collie rested its damp muzzle on her lap. Her eyelids fluttered and Mrs Painswick drifted into an uneasy sleep despite her headache.

'If this genetic material, this life form whatever it is, were in some form of communication with itself, keeping in touch so to speak,' the Doctor was reasoning, 'that might explain the children.'

'The children?' Sir Anthony asked. They were almost at the boat now. Peri was leading the way, slightly ahead of them, straining to hear the conversation.

'Yes, it seems as though you can teach one of them something, something physical, something requiring manual dexterity for example, and then they all have an aptitude for it.'

'Good Lord!' Sir Anthony exclaimed. But it was not clear whether he was commenting on the Doctor's words or what was happening to Peri.

As she reached the boat, several yards ahead of the Doctor and Sir Anthony, Peri could see what looked like a bundle of cloth behind it. Or clothing. Or someone crouching down. Even as she worked out what it was, the bundle unfolded and Mike Neville rose into sight above the boat. Peri froze in surprise and shock. He reached out, grabbing her arm and dragging her to him. Peri gave a shriek and struggled to break free. But he had his arm tight round her neck, was dragging, pulling her round so that he was behind her.

Then she felt the point of the knife at her throat.

'You two!' Mike shouted, his voice hoarse and tense. 'Just back off, all right!'

Sir Anthony took a few steps backwards. The Doctor by contrast made to step forwards, reaching out his hand.

'Back!' Mike screamed, pulling Peri even closer to him.

She could feel his chest against her back and struggled to pull forwards, but without success. 'Let go of me,' she demanded, trying to sound in control. But her throat was being squeezed tight, and the words came out as a strangled squeal of noise.

'No, no,' Mike told her. His breath was oily warm on her ear. 'You're coming with me.' The smell of fish was ripe in her nostrils, and she suddenly wished her cold was still developing. 'You and me, we've got some unfinished business. Things to talk about.'

'Let her go,' the Doctor said gently. He was still reaching out. 'You don't want to do this.'

'Don't you tell me what I want to do, you weirdo!'

'Weirdo?' The Doctor seemed upset at the description. 'Weirdo!? I'll have you know I'm the sanest person I know.' He leaned towards Mike and Peri. 'Which I grant you is not much of a boast in the present company.' His voice hardened. 'Now let her go before we force you to.'

'Force me?' He laughed, a nervous high-pitched sound. 'Think I can't handle a whiney girl and two old men?'

The Doctor straightened up immediately. 'Old men?' he said quietly. Then louder: '*Old men*?' And suddenly he was shouting: 'Old men!'

Mike seemed surprised and worried by the sudden outburst. He pulled the knife from Peri's neck and pointed it at the Doctor. It wavered in his nervous grip.

His hold on Peri also slackened. Slightly. But it was enough. She twisted out from under his arm and started to run.

But her feet were slipping and sinking in among the pebbles. Mike leaped after her, reached out and grabbed her back by her hair. Peri screamed. The Doctor was still shouting. Mike was waving the knife in one hand, still dragging Peri by the hair with the other. Sir Anthony took a step forwards and swung hard with his walking stick, holding it in both hands like a batsman.

It connected with the side of Mike's hand and the knife went spinning away.

Mike cried out and let go of Peri. She staggered back, falling sideways on to the pebbles and rolling desperately away from him as Mike yelled and clutched his hand. She kept rolling, crawling, clawing her way down the beach. Towards the sea.

The Doctor and Sir Anthony were backing away, leaving Mike to rant and shout. Peri managed to pull herself to her feet at last. She kept going, backing away down the slope, watching him as he retrieved the knife with his good hand, and backed away in turn from Sir Anthony who was hefting the stick. He was edging away, slowly, deliberately, he was coming down the beach after Peri. Keeping between her and the Doctor, between her and safety.

She kept going until she felt the wet cold of the wave sloshing round her ankles. Surprised, she turned to find she was at the water's edge. And then she saw the shapes rising up from the waves in front of her. And screamed.

There were two of them, their heads cresting the waves. Peri knew at once that they must be the fishermen, the men who had been out in the boat with Mike Neville's brother. And they were every bit as dead as he was. Their clothes clung to their bodies, moulded on by the sea water. Their hair was lank and matted across their heads. Water was pouring out of the open mouth of one of them as he surfaced, as if his lungs were full of it. It splashed like a stream of bile into the sea.

The skin was pale and puffy, misshapen from the days spent under water. But the eyes were the worst – huge, staring, almost completely white. No hint of a pupil, irises barely discernible. They waded onwards, through the waves, as if drawn to the beach, as if drawn towards Peri as she stood, helpless, rooted, screaming.

Mike was close beside her now, the knife angled towards the hideous forms that were forcing their way through the water, getting ever closer, arms stretched out like sleepwalkers.

The Doctor was shouting at Peri to run. Sir Anthony was

retreating in horror up the beach. Mike was waving the knife, crossing himself with the broken claw of his right hand, his own eyes wide and afraid. The Doctor was running now, stumbling, jumping, down the beach towards her.

Only when the Doctor grabbed Peri's hand and dragged her back, only as the first of the dead men stepped on to the pebbles and she heard the crunch of the stones beneath its feet, did Peri stop screaming. And then she ran. She let the Doctor drag her, hold her upright. She was looking back with morbid, terrified fascination the whole stumbling way.

Behind her Mike was swinging the knife frantically, apparently unwilling or unable to run. As the corpse reached him, he jabbed the knife violently at it, sinking the blade deep into the man's dead chest.

For a moment the fisherman paused, staring down with his bulging eyes at the haft of the knife projecting from his sodden woollen jersey. Then slowly, as if with great care, he reached down and pulled the knife from his dead chest. A stream of discoloured water followed the blade as it emerged.

Mike screamed then, a wailing, terrified screech of sound. Peri finally turned away as the dead man's hands closed round Mike Neville's neck and the screaming stopped.

Janet was not really sure what she was supposed to be doing, other than keeping an ear open for any talk about the resurrected fisherman who had come knocking at Sheldon's Folly. Her own concerns were rather deeper than whether any of the villagers had seen a zombie walking through the midnight mist. Since it was not a subject she thought she could discreetly bring up in conversation, she was not sure how useful she was being.

She had finished going through the latest batch of results, and they gave her further cause for concern. There were anomalies, out of line readings, nothing concrete or substantial. But there was significant deviation from the projections. She would go over them just once more. To be certain.

When she went to the bar to get another bottle of water, she knew there was a problem.

Robert Trefoil was leaning heavily on the bar, his head bowed, rubbing at his temples with his fingertips. Janet could see the top of his head as she approached. She could see the thin streaks of red spreading out through his steel grey hair from the crown. A negative image of how he must have greyed years ago.

And as she stood staring, his left hand clenched into a sudden claw. It was shaking, almost in spasm. He looked up, worried and surprised, did not see Janet as she stood watching. He brought his right hand round and clasped his shaking fist, drawing it into his chest. As he held it tight, tried to stop it shaking, he caught sight of her and attempted a thin smile.

'Can I get you another?' he asked. His voice was shaking too. 'Must have caught a nerve or something,' he added, looking down at his claw-like hand. 'Lost the feeling. Pins and needles.'

Janet put the glass and the empty bottle down on the counter. She tried to keep her own hand from trembling. 'That's all right, I'm finished.'

'Must be a nerve,' Trefoil said. 'It'll stop in a minute.' His shoulder twitched suddenly. He blinked.

'Yes,' Janet said. She was already heading for the door. Trying not to seem in too much of a hurry. 'Yes, I'm sure it will.'

As soon as she was outside she started running towards the quay.

Running across the shingle was like the nightmare where her feet got stuck in glue or treacle. Peri's feet sank into the shifting pebbles as she tried to hurry. The Doctor was dragging her onward, his own feet pushing the pebbles aside, sending them scattering and slipping down the slope under his weight. Sir Anthony was already at the base of the cliff, at the track that wound lazily up and away from the beach.

The two grotesque fishermen were also having difficulty negotiating the beach, but they were still following, making their inexorable way after the Doctor and his friends. Their arms were stretched out in front of them, sea water dripping from their hair and clothes, their eyes staring blankly ahead as they stumbled onwards.

'Come on!' the Doctor shouted. 'Don't dawdle.' He was gesturing for Sir Anthony to start up the path, not to wait for them. In a moment the three of them were staggering back up the steep path. Several times Peri lost her footing and slipped back. Once she managed to get her balance, once the Doctor caught her hand as she flailed and windmilled. Once she fell to her knees with a cry.

At the base of the cliff, the fishermen were starting up the path after them.

'What do they want?' Sir Anthony asked breathlessly.

'You ask them!' Peri suggested.

'I think we should shelve that question until we're in a rather less precarious and perilous situation, if you don't mind,' the Doctor said.

When they reached the top, Peri asked, 'Where now? Back to the cottage?'

The Doctor shook his head. 'I still think our best option is to get to Sheldon's Folly and ask a few pertinent questions of the people there.'

'The quay,' Sir Anthony suggested.

'Good idea,' the Doctor agreed. 'We can borrow Old Jim's boat. I don't think he'll object under the circumstances.'

They had pretty much got their breath back by the time they reached the quay. There was no sign of the dead fishermen following them, but none of them wished to assume that they had given up and gone away.

Most of the boats were gone, out fishing as their owners made the most of the good weather. As they approached the small quay, Peri could make out the shape of a figure sitting hunched on the ground close to the main cluster of small boats. 'Is that Old Jim?' she asked the Doctor.

'Let's see, shall we?'

He was facing away from them, so it was not until they were quite close that the Doctor stopped. 'No,' he said, 'that's not him.' He raised his voice and called. 'Excuse me, could you tell us where Old Jim is? We'd rather like to borrow his boat if it's not too much –' He broke off as the figure slowly turned towards them.

'Trouble,' Peri said.

It was Dave Madsen. What was left of him. He was staring at them now through what was left of his eyes. Slowly, as if afraid more of his body would fall away, he got to his feet. Then he started shuffling slowly towards them.

'You said you thought Madsen was involved,' the Doctor said quietly to Sir Anthony. 'I'd say that was a pretty accurate guess.'

'What do we do now?' Peri asked. Her voice was husky and trembling.

'Run?' the Doctor suggested. He looked expectantly at each of the others. They both nodded. 'Run,' he decided.

She was breathless now, running for all she was worth, desperate to get back to Sheldon's Folly, to tell Packwood what was happening. What had gone wrong.

As she approached the quay, Janet skidded to a halt. She could see people in front of her, at the quay. People running. And they were running from...

She turned to watch the three people running along the quay. One of them was the Doctor, another the girl she had met at the pub. She did not recognise the older man, the one with the stick. And partly because they were heading towards her boat, and partly because she could see what they were running from, Janet ran after them, shouting.

Peri turned at the sound. She heard her name, the Doctor's name being called. She saw Janet Spillsbury running towards them, waving, shouting something about a boat, about having to get to the other island. She saw the bloody mess that had once been

Dave Madsen turn towards her as she ran. Then she saw Janet Spillsbury catch her foot on a cobble and fall heavily to the ground.

She sat there in the road, clutching her ankle. And then Peri saw the silhouetted shapes of the two fishermen from the bay as they rounded the corner behind Janet.

Peri screamed. The Doctor and Sir Anthony both shouted. Janet heard them, turned to see the fishermen close behind her, leaped to her feet and limped frantically towards the quay. Even as she made her way towards the Doctor and Peri, Madsen moved to cut her off.

The Doctor was off and running now, heading straight for Madsen, cannoning into his back, shoulder down like a rugby player. Madsen buckled and went flying. The Doctor grabbed Janet and pulled her up to the quay.

'Boat,' she gasped as she limped along. 'My boat. Over there.'

It was a motor boat. There were two boats tied up close together. One had a grimy outboard motor pitched forwards out of the water. Janet hobbled towards it, gaining speed as she got into the rhythm of moving. Sir Anthony was ahead of her, throwing in his stick and climbing carefully down, trying not to rock the boat too much in the water. He turned to help Peri in after him.

Janet was barely limping at all by the time she and the Doctor caught up with Peri and Sir Anthony. They both jumped down into the boat, so that it shook alarmingly. Sir Anthony was already untying the painter. The Doctor pushed away from the quay with an oar and Janet pulled at the cord on the motor.

Madsen had recovered immediately and was already close to the boat. The two fishermen were not far behind. They clambered down into the next boat as the motor whirred. But did not catch.

Janet tried again. One of the fishermen had the oars now. The Doctor was rowing too, shouting at Janet to get the motor started. But his attempts to row were erratic and ineffective compared with the dead fisherman's steady, strong pull. The rowing boat was gaining on them.

Yet again Janet heaved at the cord of the outboard. This time it coughed into uneasy, smoky life for a few seconds. But then the motor died again, and Janet gave a sob of annoyance and anguish.

'Let me,' Peri offered, trying to move round to grab the cord.

'I can do it,' Janet insisted.

The fishermen and Madsen were almost within reach now. Madsen was standing in the prow of the small boat, reaching out towards them with flailing arms, a few streaks of blond still visible in the matted red tangle of what was left of his hair.

'I just thought –' Peri settled back down.

'I can do it!' Janet screamed at her, and heaved at the cord. The motor spluttered into uncertain life, choking and coughing as it belched out dark smoke.

A dead hand plucked at Janet's hair as she let the cord back in and adjusted the throttle.

Janet dipped the propeller into the water as Madsen grabbed at her. The back of the boat bit low into the sea and the prow rose as it shot forwards. Janet cried out, hand to head as she sank down on the bench in the stern of the boat. Behind them Madsen was left clutching a handful of jet black hair.

'How's your ankle?' the Doctor asked. 'That was a nasty tumble you took back there.' He leaned forward to look as Janet raised her leg and pulled off her shoe.

'It feels fine now,' she said. Her voice was shaking.

'Not even bruised,' the Doctor murmured. 'You're lucky.'

Janet was staring at her foot. Slowly, she slipped her shoe back on. Then she looked round, feeling along the wooden edge of the boat.

'What is it?' Peri asked. 'What do you want?'

'Something sharp,' she replied, her voice quiet but tense. 'Ah.' She had found a screw sticking out of the casing of the outboard motor where it had worked its way loose. The head was standing proud of the metal surround, angled and rough.

Peri watched in astonished disbelief as Janet Spillsbury carefully put the palm of her hand against the screw, then suddenly, violently, dragged her hand downwards. Her face was contorted with pain as she cried out, immediately clutching her hand.

There was a smear of blood down the casing of the motor. The screw was a crimson point in the middle of it. Janet's hand was ripped open, blood welling up and dripping to the floor of the boat.

'I'll get you a tissue. A hanky.' Peri was feeling in her pockets. 'Something to bind it up with.'

Both the Doctor and Sir Anthony were watching Janet's hand bleed. 'No, Peri,' the Doctor said quietly. 'That won't be needed.'

'What?'

'Look.' He nodded at Janet's hand.

She held it up for Peri to see. 'You think I was lucky?' She gave a sad, ironic laugh. 'Quite the opposite.' The blood had congealed already over the hand. It was flaky and dry now. As she spoke, Janet rubbed it away with her other hand, to reveal the unblemished palm beneath. 'I'm infected,' she said, her voice husky and dry. 'Oh God, I'm infected. Like the others.'

The Doctor sat himself next to Janet on the back bench and took hold of the handle for the motor, angling it slightly so that they were headed directly for the dark outline of Sheldon's Folly. 'It will take us a few minutes to get to the island,' he said. 'And I've got nothing much else to do. So why don't you tell us all about it?'

Janet looked up at him. Her eyes were wide and moist with welling tears. 'You wouldn't understand.'

'Oh, I think you'd be surprised.' The Doctor looked into her eyes. 'It came back on the Gatherer space probe, didn't it? Some form of genetic material. Alien genetic material. And you thought you could make use of it.' He shook his head sadly. 'But now you're beginning to realise that it's making use of you.'

'They called Christopher in as soon as they knew it was genetic. That was his thing. The rest of the stuff was ice and dust. Bits of asteroid and the frayed ends of a long-forgotten comet. But sample three-zero-seven, that was the big one. I didn't join until much later of course, so I missed the initial anxiety, the containment problems, the decisions and heart-in-mouth philosophising. Trying to merge what they had with the DNA computer work that was already so far advanced. They were up and running by the time they needed me. Caught up in the excitement and the potential of it all. The implications. When you're that involved, that close, that enthusiastic, it's difficult to realise that things are going wrong.

'Especially when you're changing the world.

'I knew Chris already, of course. I think that was why I had to be on the team, so he could talk to me about it. The ESA liaison stuff was hardly useful by then. He called it Denarian. From DNA, you see. It was pretty clear from the first what the potential was. A universal cure-all was how they explained it to me. I laughed, of course. And then they showed me the test results. The regenerated tissue, the repaired nerve endings, skin grafts. It's funny, it never occurred to me then, only now, now that I see the progression. We never stopped to ask how the stuff knew when to stop.

'I was thinking that in the pub. Just now. This afternoon. As I sat there. You know the old joke about how a thermos flask keeps hot liquid hot, and it keeps cold liquid cold. But how does it *know*? I guess it was like that. We just assumed that was the way it was, the way things happened. Never mind how. Until now. Until I saw what it was doing to Bob Trefoil's grey hair. How it was assuming control, slowly but surely taking over. And then it struck me. The basic instinct of any living thing. And it *is* living, you know. When his hand spasmed, when he lost control. That's how it does it.'

Peri frowned. 'Does it?'

'Survives,' the Doctor said quietly. 'The basic instinct of any living creature is survival.' He let out a long misty breath. 'You know, it's more like the story of the little girl who says she knows how to spell "banana", but she doesn't know when to stop.'

Janet was nodding. 'That's right. Partly it just doesn't know when the human host is dead. And why would it care? It keeps on repairing the tissue, mending the bones. Not the brain of course, we had checked that it doesn't affect the brain. Not in the second generation.'

'The second generation?' Sir Anthony asked.

'But now it's jumped again. Taken another evolutionary step forwards. To a third generation. First it realised that to survive it had to keep the host healthy, look after its own environment. That was what the second generation was about.'

'And now?' the Doctor asked, his face grave.

'Now,' she said, 'it's realised that to survive it needs to take control of the host.' She looked up at him, then at the others. 'Total control.' Then she looked back at the wet boards in the bottom of the boat. 'And I'm in the second generation.'

The island was looming in front of them now, the rocky coastline jutting ragged and forbidding out of a shroud of mist.

'The first generation,' the Doctor said slowly. 'I assume there is one. An incubation period?'

Janet nodded. She was staring straight ahead at the coastline. She did not look at him. 'Yes.' Her voice was a strained whisper. 'Cultivation of the raw genetic material. Within an... incubator. That's right.'

The Doctor angled the boat so that it was heading for the wooden jetty, a boarded pathway into the depths of the mist. 'I don't think it's a conscious thing,' the Doctor said as he brought the boat in. 'I don't think we're up against a planned invasion here. We know from the herding instinct, the way the children assimilate behaviour and abilities, that there's a collective consciousness of some sort. But it certainly isn't conscious in any way that we would understand. It's just a life form trying to survive the only way it knows. Somehow this whole process is its life cycle and you've got plugged in as the necessary symbiotic host.'

'Thanks,' Janet said as she allowed the Doctor to help her out of the boat. Her voice was rich with sarcasm. 'That makes me feel a lot better.'

Sir Anthony stepped on to the jetty and tied up the boat as the Doctor cut the engine.

The Doctor said nothing for a moment. He gave Peri a hand up, then turned back towards Janet. His face was dark with anger. 'It isn't our fault what has happened here,' he said. 'It wasn't us who brought this thing, this scourge to the islands. It wasn't our negligence or lust for scientific advancement that infected you. And it wasn't the islanders either. But they are the ones who are dying because of it. Remember that.'

'I'm sorry.' Her voice was quiet. She looked away, biting her lip.

'You may not like me,' the Doctor went on, his voice also quieter now. 'You may not like what I do, what I shall have to do. But I'm here to help you, and it may be that I'm the only help you have.' He turned away, suddenly bright and cheerful again, marching along the jetty and drawing the others after him in his wake. 'I wonder if Mr Packwood has the kettle on,' he asked the cold surrounding air. 'I think we could all do with a cup of tea to calm our nerves.'

They made the rest of the journey in silence. The strange, misshapen house loomed out of the mist as they approached, seeming to lean down towards them. Peri shuddered at the sight, but the Doctor seemed, if anything, to become even more animated and enthusiastic. As if he were relishing the imminent confrontation.

'Right,' he pronounced, skidding to a halt on the wet grass and turning to face the others. 'A few rules then. You,' he pointed at Sir Anthony, 'are Sir Edward Baddesley, as we all know.'

'If we all know that,' Janet began, but the Doctor raised his finger and his eyebrows to cut her off.

'Nothing is as simple or straightforward as it seems,' he said darkly. 'You,' he dropped the finger so that it pointed at Janet, 'tell me if you begin to feel the slightest suggestion that you are losing control of your body or your mind. Anything at all – dizziness, blurred vision, even a tingling in your feet.' He turned finally to Peri. 'And you...'

'Yes, Doctor?' She stood up straight and thrust her chin out bravely.

'You be very careful, and do as you're told,' he decided. 'Come on.' And with that he turned and headed towards the front door of Sheldon's Folly.

The door swung open even before they reached it. Logan Packwood was standing there, his arms folded, his head tilted slightly to one side as he watched them approach.

'Sir Anthony Kelso,' he said as they arrived. 'How nice to see you again. Come to check up on us, have you?'

'So much for that part of the plan,' the Doctor said with evident disappointment. 'But yes, I think some checking would be in order, don't you? Your precious alien genetic material is out of control. We have to put a stop to this now.'

'Indeed we do,' Packwood agreed. 'Indeed we do.' He stepped aside, as if to let the Doctor into the house.

But before the Doctor could step forward, Rogers was in the doorway. Holding a shotgun. It was levelled at the Doctor's chest.

'The only bit of checking up you'll be doing, Doctor, is in the cellarage.'

Peri watched horrified as Packwood turned to stare at each of them in turn. His eyes lingered on her, his eyes wide and pale with barely a hint of a pupil in the dead iris. She screamed.

Then she turned to run.

And saw the figure behind them, approaching, lurching towards them over the damp grass of the front lawn. It was Bill Neville, his arms out, dead fingers twitching and clenching as he shuffled towards them. Behind her, Peri could hear Packwood's booming laugh as it echoed off the mist and the face of the building.

The only way out was along the front of the house. If she was quick, while the shotgun was pointed at the Doctor, while the Doctor was between her and Packwood. 'Come on!' she shouted to Sir Anthony and Janet.

But even as she made to run, a hand gripped her arm and jerked her back. 'I don't think so, Peri,' a voice said close in her ear.

Janet's eyes were wide and pale. She blinked rapidly several times as she pulled Peri back into the group. 'I really don't think so.'

Chapter Eleven
Sheldon's Folly

It took a while for Peri's eyes to adjust to the near darkness. There was some light, filtering dustily through a grating high in the wall. The Doctor strode across the room, apparently oblivious to the darkness. At once he was swallowed up by the darkness as Peri and Sir Anthony stood nervous and tentative by the door.

'Well, if this is the best cellar you've got, I'm not terribly impressed,' the Doctor proclaimed loudly. The only reply was the sound of the bolt shooting home on the other side of the door, followed by retreating footsteps.

As Peri's eyes gradually managed to cope with the gloom she looked round. The corners and edges of the cellar room were still shadowed and lost, but she could just about make out the stone slabs of the floor and the complete lack of furnishing. Apart from what looked like a low bed against one wall, a slab of dark silhouette against the deeper shadows.

'Is Janet... all right?' Sir Anthony asked quietly.

'Of course not,' the Doctor told him shortly. 'But I don't think she's yet as far under the influence as she would have Packwood and his cronies believe.'

'She'll help us then?' Peri asked.

'I don't think it's up to her,' the Doctor said. He sat down cross-legged on the floor and started to empty the detritus from his pockets. 'It depends how much control what's left of her free will has over her body. And that will be less and less as time goes on.'

'Great,' Peri said. She kicked at the floor. Then she froze as, out of the corner of her eye, she saw the shape that was the low bed begin to stir.

The Doctor was refilling his pockets. 'Nothing much here of use,' he admitted glumly. 'I think we're in for a long stay.'

'Doctor,' Peri whispered. The shape on the bed was rising, staggering to its feet now. 'Doctor!'

'Quiet, Peri, I'm thinking.'

'Doctor, I think you should come over here.' Sir Anthony had seen it too. And now there was the sound of the blankets and sheets tumbling to the floor as whoever or whatever was in the bed emerged and staggered towards them.

The Doctor turned, and visibly jumped with surprise. 'Hello,' he said, no trace of anxiety in his voice. 'Who are you?'

As the figure staggered forwards, Peri could see it more clearly. It was a man, dishevelled and unshaven. He was dressed in tattered and torn clothes, holding his left arm close to his chest, covering it, hugging it with his right arm as he approached. It was the man she and the Doctor had met near the TARDIS, the man who had scared Mike Neville away when he accosted her on the moorland.

'My God,' Sir Anthony breathed, close beside Peri. 'What's happened to you?'

The figure stopped, as if it recognised the voice. Then slowly the man sank to his knees, rocking back and forth, moaning quietly and clutching his arm.

'You know him?' the Doctor asked as he slowly approached the man and knelt down beside him.

'Of course I do,' Sir Anthony said. 'Doctor, this is Christopher Sheldon.'

As the Doctor knelt beside him, leaned forward, Sheldon twisted away so his back was to the Doctor.

'What's… what's happened to him?' Peri asked.

'I have no idea. Seems traumatised.' The Doctor leaned in, speaking quietly, gently. 'I'm not going to hurt you. We're here to help. Are you hurt? Let me see.' The Doctor and Sheldon seemed to merge into a single dark area of shadow as the Doctor leaned closer.

'Maybe it's his fingers,' Peri suggested. 'He was missing some fingers on his hand. An accident perhaps,' she told Sir Anthony.

The Doctor straightened up, separated from Sheldon. 'It's not his fingers,' he said gravely. 'His arm's been severed. Amputated. Gone.'

'Good grief,' Sir Anthony said. 'Doctor, what is going on here?' He glanced at Peri, and the two of them joined the Doctor beside Sheldon's huddled form.

Sheldon looked up at them, his eyes were wide and pale in the dim light. He blinked. 'Know you,' he murmured, pointing at Sir Anthony with a clawed hand. As he moved his arm, Peri could see the remains of his other arm hanging loose from his shirt. The sleeve had been cut away, and a rounded stump of upper arm emerged pale and clean from the ragged material. 'Need a chair,' he gasped out suddenly. 'Wheelchair.'

'No, it's all right,' Sir Anthony said. 'It's your arm, not your leg.'

'Arm?' He looked down at the stump. 'Arm. Needed arm. Took it. Again.'

'Again?' the Doctor asked. 'What do you mean, *again*?'

'Keep taking it. Again and again and again and again and –'

'Yes, yes. All right,' the Doctor interrupted. 'I think I get the idea.'

'Better this arm.' Sheldon nodded. 'This is the arm. The arm that opened the sample casket. Did the gathering.'

'Gathering?' Peri asked. 'Does he mean…?'

The Doctor was nodding. 'Gatherer Three, yes I think so.' He turned back to Sheldon. 'What do you remember? It's very important that you tell us about the casket. That you remember, Mr Sheldon.'

But Sheldon seemed to have collapsed in on himself, huddling closer into the floor, curled up with his remaining arm tight round himself. 'Three-zero-seven,' he muttered. 'Mustn't open three-zero-seven. Mustn't open it. Three-zero-seven.' His voice trailed off into incoherent murmurs and mutterings.

'That was the sample from Gatherer Three,' Sir Anthony said. 'You recall, Janet Spillsbury said –'

'Yes, yes, yes,' the Doctor said, waving him into silence. 'We know that.'

'What did he mean, they took his arm again?' Peri asked slowly.

The Doctor nodded. 'I was wondering that.'

'And?'

'And I don't like what I'm thinking.'

'Care to share it with us anyway?' Sir Anthony asked.

The Doctor stood up and turned towards them. The light catching his eyes and making them gleam as he did so. 'I asked Janet about generation one,' he said.

Peri remembered. 'She said something about an incubator, didn't she?'

'That's right. They would need to cultivate genetic material. Grow it, in effect. In a suitable environment. Somewhere that the Denarian material would thrive.'

'Like an incubator?'

'Ye-es.' The Doctor was pacing slowly backwards and forwards. 'You know how vaccines and viruses are cultivated in eggs, organic material like that. A nice warm, inviting place for them to grow and mature and thrive?'

'Yes,' Peri said. 'But what's that got to do with –' She broke off as she began to see. 'But that's…'

'Horrible,' Sir Anthony finished for her.

'But it's what I think is happening. It explains why this poor fellow is out of his mind. And there's a certain logic to it.'

'Logic be damned!' Sir Anthony said.

'If Sheldon was the first person to become infected, the Denarian would use him as its initial breeding ground. Like a farm for genetic material. And the others, those with a secondary infection, would know to harvest material from him to form the genetic basis of the infection they pass on.'

'He was missing fingers when we saw him before,' Peri said quietly. She hardly dared look at the huddled figure on the floor. She was feeling sick.

'Either they just took fingers before, or the arm had already grown back. The Denarian infection would keep repairing the body as they took the material… A self-sustaining source.'

'But… how could they?' Peri's words sounded lame, pathetic

under the circumstances. But she didn't care.

'Oh, I imagine they started with skin samples. Small pieces of material, like an amount of blood for example. Sheldon would have been a willing contributor in the early stages. It was his project, his dream of a universal cure, remember. But then their needs grew. And the infection within them, within all of them, started to take over. So they started taking more and more. They knew the damage wouldn't be permanent.' The Doctor knelt down beside Sheldon again, patted him gently on the shoulder. 'Except to his mind,' he added.

'And Janet?' Peri asked. 'Did she know?'

'I couldn't say. I doubt she knows it all. Perhaps she thinks Packwood and Madsen are still taking blood samples and skin tissue.'

'Madsen?' Sir Anthony asked.

'He must have been involved,' the Doctor said. 'To perform the operations on Sheldon here. And to pass on the material. Infect the villagers. Run the experiment.'

'And the longer we're stuck in here, the worse it gets,' Sir Anthony said.

'And the less likely that anyone will come to help us,' the Doctor added. 'Frustrating, isn't it?'

It was as if the mist had somehow got inside her head. Her vision was blurry, unreal. Her thoughts were sluggish and forced. Packwood was talking to her through a fog. Telling her his plans, how well it was going. How they were entering the third generation.

'When did you do it?' she asked. Her voice came to her through water.

'Bring you into the fold?' he asked. 'Ensure that you were protected, like me, from the ravages of the flesh?'

She nodded. Her brain felt loose inside her head.

'Weeks ago. When we first came to the island.'

Janet's head was spinning. A succession of images played out:

Dr Madsen telling her she needed a shot of antibiotics as protection. The needle pressing into her arm, puncturing the skin, drawing out a tiny bead of blood. Packwood's reassuring smile – the mirror of his expression now as he stood in front of her.

'You are entering the third generation,' he said. 'I – we – can tell.' He leaned forward, his face distorting in her blurred sight, his grin fish-eye wide. 'Welcome,' he breathed at her. 'Welcome to the fold.'

'You bastard! How dare you? What gives you the right to treat us – to treat me – like this!' she screamed at him. But the words were trapped inside her mind, unable to find escape or expression.

'Thank you,' she heard herself say. And she felt the darkness beginning to push her thoughts aside as it assumed control within her mind.

'Do you think they're just going to leave us here?' Peri asked. It was dark and damp. The light outside had faded and with it what little light spilled into the cellar room had also gone.

'Quite probably,' the Doctor said cheerfully. 'They don't need us, after all.'

Peri did her best to keep her voice level. 'So we're here for… for a while then.'

'Oh, I don't think so.' There was a scuffling noise, which Peri decided must be the Doctor getting to his feet. 'They don't need us, but I think they do still need Mr Sheldon here.'

'Are you sure, Doctor?' Sir Anthony asked out of the darkness.

'Wheelchair,' Sheldon's quiet voice followed Sir Anthony's question.

'And I say potato,' the Doctor added.

But the end of his words was drowned by the metallic scrape of a bolt being drawn on the other side of the door.

'Ah, about time too.' As the light flooded into the room round the edges of the opening door, the Doctor pulled his coat about him, buttoning it up, and stepped towards the light. 'Have you any idea how long we've been waiting down here?' he demanded.

'Have you?'

There was a figure silhouetted in the doorway, frail and slight. Sagging as she dragged the heavy door open.

'Janet!' Peri exclaimed. 'Janet, are you all right?'

'Not really, no.' Her voice was strained and hesitant. 'Not sure how long... how much longer...' She stepped aside to let them out.

The Doctor paused to help Sheldon up the short flight of steps to the door. As he entered the light, Peri could see that his left arm was complete now to the elbow. He looked at Janet as he passed her, a flicker of recognition on his face.

'Oh God, Christopher,' she said quietly, hesitantly. 'What has he done to you?' Her pale body seemed to sag further. 'What have I done?'

'Don't blame yourself,' the Doctor said kindly, his tone a contrast to his shouting on the jetty earlier. 'Now, what's the best way out of here?'

Janet pointed up the corridor and led the way. 'Not easy...' she said. Her voice was strained. 'Words, not easy. Think, say, different.'

Sir Anthony was helping the Doctor to drag Sheldon's weak form after her. Steps led up from the corridor to the ground floor of the house. The corridor itself continued onwards. 'Where does that lead?' the Doctor asked.

'Labs,' Janet gasped. 'Secure. Sealed.'

'I see.'

At the top of the stairs was a heavy metal door. It was standing open. The Doctor ushered everyone out and into the hallway beyond.

'How are you doing?' he asked Janet when they were all in the hallway.

'Can't... can't speak easy,' she stammered. 'Diff- difficult.'

'I imagine the Denarian is taking control of your physical form,' the Doctor said. 'Muscles, nerves, bone, everything. Even your vocal cords. It will get to the mind last of all – for a while you'll be a prisoner inside your own body.'

'And…' the words were a struggle, '…then?'

'And then you won't have to put up with this sort of moral dilemma.' The answer was loud and harsh. It came from in front of them. From Logan Packwood as he stepped out of an alcove and raised a pistol.

'Oh, you can run, Janet,' he said as she stiffened. 'But where would you go? You can't hide from yourself, now can you?' The gun swivelled to cover the Doctor as he too tensed, bracing himself to fly at Packwood. 'No, Doctor, I really wouldn't advise it. I don't need to aim, I can fire indiscriminately until I hit you. Anyone I'm concerned about keeping alive will soon recover from a mere bullet.'

Packwood's smile widened, his pale eyes glistening in the light from a nearby gas lamp. 'Now since you don't seem to care for the accommodation I had prepared, perhaps we should continue our discussions in the drawing room. Mmm?' He motioned for them to continue down the corridor. 'I've asked Rogers to bring in some tea,' he added.

It was grotesque and bizarre. Packwood stood in front of the roaring fire in the drawing room, drinking tea from a cup that seemed miniature in his massive hand. The saucer rested on the mantel shelf behind him.

'I really can't see what you find wrong in all this, Doctor,' Packwood said.

The Doctor and Peri were sitting on a *chaise longue*, the Doctor with his feet stretched out, Peri hunched up on the edge of the seat. Janet was sitting upright and stiff on a chair. Sir Anthony looked at home in an armchair, and Christopher Sheldon was slumped into another armchair beside him, curled up and shivering.

Rogers stood in the doorway, shotgun over his arm, watching the proceedings. And the pale, bloodless corpse of Bill Neville handed them tea.

Peri shrank away as the cadaver offered her a cup. The Doctor leaned across and took it instead, giving a little smile of gratitude. He sipped appreciatively at the tea before setting it down on an occasional table beside the *chaise longue*. There was an oil lamp on the table, giving out a flickering orange light that supplemented the pale glow from the gas lamps round the walls.

'You can't see what's wrong with this?' he asked, nodding towards where Neville was now pouring tea for Sir Anthony.

Packwood watched for a moment, cup raised. Then he took a sip of tea. 'An unfortunate side effect of the process. But where's the harm?' he asked easily. 'The symbiotic partnership is made rather one-sided by the loss of the brain of the human host. But where is the problem? One of the partners in the arrangement survives. Life goes on.'

'A partnership implies choice,' the Doctor said levelly. 'What choice did Neville have? Did you ask him to agree to – this?' He pointed across the room at the walking cadaver.

'Of course not. But what would he have said? Given the choice between a body that can renew and repair itself, or being merely human?' Packwood set down his cup on the saucer on the mantel. 'What would you say, Doctor? Given that choice.'

Peri looked at the Doctor. He seemed frozen in position, his mouth hanging open.

'Well?' Packwood prompted.

'Well, that's not the point,' the Doctor said. But there was a bluster, and uncertainty in his voice now.

'Isn't it?' Packwood demanded. 'Then what is the point, my dear Doctor, if not the assured health and happiness of every human being on this planet? Tell me that.'

The Doctor pointed across the room to where Neville was standing beside the tray of tea things, erect and still and silent. 'That's the point,' he said.

Packwood shrugged. 'But he would have died whatever happened. It wasn't the Denarian that killed him. It was an accident. This way something survives. Oh, there will be social problems to work through, I'm sure. How to cope with the increasing population once death is a rarity. But offset that against the reduced health bills and pensions. Offset that against the suffering that will be banished.'

'But at what cost?' the Doctor shouted at him. 'Think about it, Packwood. How do you know the real, human, internal mental cost?'

Packwood spread his arms. 'I am exactly as I ever was. My mind is my own. You may disagree with my opinions, Doctor, but they are mine. Not some alien material's ideas, my own. The ideals I live and stand for. The ideals that Christopher Sheldon professed and gave so much for.' He gave a short laugh. 'I still fail to see where the problem lies.'

The Doctor took a deep breath. 'You have experimented, without their consent, on a whole population.'

'We needed a controlled and controllable environment with a stable population, Doctor. And it had to be isolated in case there were problems.'

'Problems?'

'But there are no problems. You are being alarmist.'

'But you didn't ask them. People have died.'

'There's no reason to suspect they would not have died anyway. Nothing to link that to the experiment, Doctor. And look at what we have given them in return. Their island is once more their own, not some giant theme park. Surely you can't disagree with that? We are returning to them their freedom and self determination, not taking it away. And we're giving them the first chance to become better, healthier, more robust and fit individuals than ever they were before. As for asking them? Well, I'm sure you know as well as I what Heisenberg would have said about that and its effects on the experiment.' He smiled, the open, generous smile of a man totally at peace with his conscience. 'More tea?' He held his own cup out and allowed the walking corpse of Bill Neville to fill it.

The Doctor rubbed his eyes with the tips of his fingers, then drew his hands down his face. 'You maintain that you still have free will, that your mind is unaffected?'

'I do.'

'How do you know?'

Packwood smiled. 'Ah, that old chestnut. If my mind was not my own, then I would never be permitted to believe that there was any problem, is that your point?'

The Doctor nodded.

'But how can you say the converse, Doctor? How can you suggest that my mind is not my own? On what evidence? In fact, how can you ever be sure about free will under any circumstances given that argument?' He leaned forward slightly. 'Why won't you believe that things are exactly what they seem? That this is as good as it gets? That there is no sinister threat or problem here at all? Have you no trust, man? No sense of proportion?'

'Sense of proportion?' the Doctor fumed. 'Sense of proportion!' He turned suddenly to Peri. 'Tell him,' he snapped. 'You tell him.'

'Tell him what, Doctor?' She was confused, unsure. 'When I was seven,' she said slowly, 'my Auntie Janice died. It was a long illness. I never really understood why it happened. Why it had to happen.' She looked at him, could see the expression of surprise and sudden worry frozen on his face. 'I don't understand now,' she said.

'It should never have happened,' Packwood said quietly. 'And now we can make sure it never happens again. We can never erase your suffering, my dear. But we can save countless thousands, millions even, of others from the same fear and sadness and pain.' He took a step towards the Doctor. 'What right do you have to deny them that, Doctor? Who gives you the right to decide on a whim what is right and what is wrong?'

The Doctor looked round. Janet Spillsbury was still sitting upright and silent, watching. Sheldon was curled up, whimpering quietly. The Doctor did not look at Peri. Instead he spoke to Sir Anthony Kelso. 'You,' he said, his voice husky. 'Surely you understand?'

Sir Anthony cleared his throat. He was looking down at his hands as they lay in his lap. 'I'm not sure that I do, Doctor,' he confessed. 'When I was a lad, at school, I had a friend who had a terrible accident. He fell from a roof, retrieving a rugby ball. Terrible.' He looked up at the Doctor now, met his gaze. 'The poor chap broke both his legs, damaged his spine. They told him that for the whole of the rest of his life he would never walk again.'

He shook his head, his eyes moist at the memory. 'Just seventeen,' he whispered. 'His whole life... gone. What wouldn't we have given for him to regain the use of his legs. We couldn't go back in time and prevent him going after the ball, we knew that. But we all felt the guilt. Every one of us who didn't go up there instead, or with him.' He shook his head. 'I kicked that ball up there, Doctor. Now you tell me that I must live with the consequences. Well, I can do that. I've been doing it all my life. But please, please tell me why.'

There was silence for a while, then Packwood said: 'We have the chance to change the world into a far, far better place, Doctor. Why do you fight against it? Join us, become part of this tremendous effort.'

The Doctor and Packwood stared at each other. Then at last the Doctor turned away. 'No,' he said simply. 'I can't. I won't.'

'And why not?'

'Because it's wrong,' the Doctor said.

At first it had been merely a trickle. A few people slowly, almost painfully, making their way towards the quay. As if drawn. But now it was a steady flow. They marched stiffly out of the pub, out of the houses, out of the misty night. They walked slowly and silently through the thickening darkness and filled the boats.

Liz Trefoil sat beside her father, his hair a mass of red exploding from his head. Old Jim sat stiffly beside them, his pipe clamped in his silent mouth. Across the bay, in a small fishing boat, Mrs Tattleshall clutched her handbag while Hilly Painswick stared out at the blackness of the horizon. Sheep milled round the quay, apparently uncertain what to do or where to go.

One after another the small vessels bobbed out of the harbour, low in the water, making their way ponderously towards Sheldon's Folly. Towards home.

With a sudden burst of energy, the Doctor leaped off the *chaise longue*. 'Mike Neville,' he shouted triumphantly. 'What about Mike Neville?'

Peri's mouth dropped open. Of course, how could she have forgotten? 'They killed him,' she said. 'And then they came after us.'

'Exactly.' The Doctor's eyes were shining. 'If there's nothing wrong in your brave new vision, why was that?'

Packwood's pale eyes blinked. 'I...' he said. He blinked again, the slightest hint of uncertainty in his face. Then it was gone. 'We have to survive,' he said. 'That is paramount.'

'At any cost?' the Doctor suggested.

'At any cost.' Packwood's face seemed to have hardened. Like putty setting. 'But as the Denarian spreads, so the rate of generation increases. It is a short-term problem.'

'Hah!' The Doctor was pacing up and down. 'And you still maintain that your mind isn't affected?' He stopped in front of Packwood. 'Balderdash!' he shouted in the man's face.

The sound of the Doctor's sudden shout seemed to wake Sheldon. He unfolded in the chair and swung his feet to the floor. His eyes were wild, darting to and fro. They fixed eventually on Packwood. 'I remember you,' he hissed. 'The knife. The saw.' His cheeks twitched, his forehead creased. 'The blood,' he coughed out suddenly, a cry of anguish.

'He's delirious, poor chap,' Sir Anthony said.

'I'm not sure.' The Doctor was beside Sheldon immediately.

'The broken glass,' the dishevelled man murmured. 'It saw its chance. Its chance through me. When you dropped the lab beaker. Cut your finger. That was when –' His voice choked off, and he thrust his knuckles against his teeth. 'That was when,' he said indistinctly around them. Then he turned and buried his head in the back of the chair.

173

The Doctor stood up slowly. He patted Sheldon's shoulder gently, then turned to face Packwood. 'Is that how it happened? How the Denarian infected you? A cut finger? You see, even you didn't get a choice.' He took a step towards the *chaise longue*, Packwood watching him all the way.

At the door, Rogers levelled the shotgun, tracking the Doctor's progress, sensing trouble. His eyes were as pale and dead as his master's. Janet turned slowly too. Her own eyes still had a hint of colour in them, Peri could see. Her face was creased up, a mask of concentration, and Peri guessed she was fighting to control her body and her thoughts.

As he walked slowly across the room, the Doctor was speaking quietly but distinctly. 'I think I understand it now,' he said. All eyes were watching him now. Even Neville's head swivelled slowly to follow the Doctor's progress. 'That must have been the crucial moment for the Denarian. The initial first generation host,' he whirled round and pointed to the hunched-up figure in the armchair, 'you, Sheldon. That initial host needed to be preserved intact as an incubator, a *breeder*, for Denarian material. Later generations would have to be cultivated within other hosts. So the Denarian continues to reproduce to saturation point within the original host until genetic, biological contact is made with a secondary host.'

The Doctor stopped in his tracks and pointed at Packwood. 'You,' he accused. 'You are the secondary host, from the blood infection. And I would think that by now you are under complete Denarian control. The third generation.' He continued his slow journey across the room, his eyes locked for a moment with Peri's. 'You probably didn't even realise it was taking you over.' There was something in them. Some message imparted across the space between them as he spoke. 'Even now you might not be able to tell. But when I said it was wrong, I meant it.'

'And what do you intend to do about it, whether you are right or not?' Packwood asked, a trace of amusement in his voice.

'Oh, I intend to stop you,' the Doctor answered seriously.

There was something in the Doctor's voice, an edge to it, that alerted Peri. Packwood had caught it too, she saw that. He looked across at Rogers, and the shotgun froze, pointing at the space where the Doctor had been standing.

But he was no longer there. He was diving headlong to the side of the *chaise longue*, rolling along the floor as the first barrel of the gun discharged and blew a ragged hole in the back of the seat. Peri screamed as wadding and velvet exploded out of the furniture beside her. She leaped to her feet.

As the Doctor rolled away, his hand lashed out at the occasional table, catching the oil lamp a solid blow. Then he was on his feet again, grabbing Peri, shouting to Sir Anthony and Janet, running towards the door where Rogers hesitated with the gun.

The oil lamp hit Neville square in the chest. He dropped the tea pot and it shattered into fragments, bone china spinning across the hardwood floor. A pool of oil spread across the corpse's dry chest, the flames running with it, eating into the fisherman's sweater.

Packwood was shouting. Rogers was swinging back and forth with the gun. Sheldon was screaming something incoherent. Sir Anthony was running after the Doctor and Peri, dragging Janet with him, her eyes wide and empty.

Rogers seemed to recover. The room was filling with oily black smoke, and the second shot did nothing to clear it. The Doctor dived away again, pulling Peri after him. Neville had been thrashing wildly as they passed, the flames now licking along his arms as they flailed in the smoky air. The shot hit him in the side as he turned, propelling him across the room. He crashed against the chair where Janet had been sitting, the fire taking immediate hold on the old upholstery. For a few seconds the chair and the corpse were one, a flaming mass of orange and black. Then the corpse of Bill Neville slipped to the floor, the flames seemingly burrowing into his body as they ate through the remains of his clothes.

The Doctor shouldered Rogers aside. Packwood was shouting through the smoke. Rogers hit the door frame, cannoned off and fell heavily to the floor. Peri was first through the door, emerging through the misty smoke into the hallway, the Doctor close behind. He overtook her on the way to the front door. Behind them Sir Anthony was dragging Janet, and Sheldon was stumbling off in the other direction, deeper into the house.

'Leave him,' the Doctor shouted. 'They won't hurt him. Well, no more than they have already.'

Peri leaned forward, hands on her knees, trying to breathe. Her vision seemed blurred, the world wobbled. The smoke, she told herself. The effects of the smoke. Behind her she was dimly aware of Rogers running after them, shotgun open, jamming in cartridges.

The Doctor was tearing at the bolts, swinging the heavy door open to let in the misty cold night air.

They all froze on the threshold.

In front of them, stumbling, shuffling, lurching out of the mist, were the villagers. Dozens of them, heading straight for the house. The light from the hallway caught their pale faces as they approached. It made their dead, white eyes seem to glow in the night. Ahead of them, two cadavers in fishermen's jerseys and waterproof trousers waded out of the shadows beside the door. And Dave Madsen's corpse, his head a mass of congealed blood and broken bone, reached out for the Doctor's neck.

Chapter Twelve
Sacrifices

The Doctor skidded to a halt on the threshold and pulled back to avoid Madsen's clutching hands.

'Don't move,' Rogers called from down the hall. He snapped the gun shut and ran towards where the Doctor, Peri, Sir Anthony and Janet were standing.

'Ah,' the Doctor said cheerily as Rogers approached. 'Just what we need.' Without further comment, he grabbed the barrel of the shotgun and pulled it. Hard.

Rogers lurched forwards, his brisk pace levered by the Doctor's tug on the gun. He crashed through the group of people in the doorway, and swung round so that he seemed for a moment to be locked in a dance with the Doctor. The Doctor let go of the gun, and Rogers continued, falling back through the doorway, knocking Madsen aside and smacking into the fisherman that stood behind him.

The Doctor immediately leaped forward and shut the door, slamming the bolts home.

'That won't keep them out for long,' Sir Anthony pointed out. 'What about the windows?'

'Toughened,' Janet said, with obvious effort. 'No way in.'

'Sounds good to me,' Sir Anthony conceded.

The Doctor was leading them back down the hall now. 'Except that Packwood can always open the windows and the door,' he said. 'And Janet here is going to succumb to the alien material at any moment. That is, if the house doesn't burn down first, of course.'

'Otherwise OK?' Peri asked.

'Oh yes,' the Doctor admitted. 'Nothing we can't handle. Ah, there you are.' This last was directed at Packwood, who had stepped out of the smoke-filled drawing room as they passed.

177

'Can't catch me!' the Doctor jibed, and neatly side-stepped the large man.

They ran.

'Where are we going?' Peri asked.

'Cellars,' the Doctor called back to her. 'The laboratories that Janet mentioned.'

'Why?' Sir Anthony wanted to know as the Doctor pushed Janet ahead of him to lead the way.

'That's where this started. It's the best place to end it.' He called after Janet and Peri who were racing ahead. 'Not so fast!'

They slowed to let the Doctor and Sir Anthony catch up. Logan Packwood was barrelling after them as they started down the stairs.

Peri made to slam the door shut behind them, but the Doctor stayed her arm. He shook his head. 'We want him down here, with us.'

'Do we?'

'And not letting the others in. One of them is easier to deal with than all of them.'

'So we let him think he's catching us,' Peri said as she chased down the steps after the Doctor.

'Can't keep you fooled for long.'

'And then what?' she asked. They were past the cellar room they had been locked in earlier, heading down the passageway towards the laboratories.

The Doctor paused just long enough to admit: 'I haven't the foggiest. I'm making it up as we go along.' Then he was off again. Until he suddenly stopped sharply outside a door. A heavy door, with a tiny square window set high up in it. 'What about this?' he called after Janet.

She shook her head. 'Not lab,' she managed to call out. 'X-ray room.'

The Doctor beamed. 'Excellent,' he decided and opened the door. 'In we go.'

Packwood was behind them, out of sight beyond a bend in the

corridor, but they could hear his heavy footsteps. He had slowed – he knew there was no way out for them.

'We're lucky he's so arrogant,' the Doctor murmured. 'Otherwise he might just have locked us down here and let his friends in.'

The room was small. There was a hospital bed pushed against the far wall. X-ray equipment stood beside it. On the other side of the room, close to the door, was a heavy lead screen with a small control panel behind it.

'Right, time for a little experiment,' the Doctor decided. 'Behind the screen, everyone.'

The footsteps were approaching now, close outside.

'Maybe he'll go past and we can sneak back out again,' Sir Anthony suggested in a whisper.

'I hope not,' the Doctor replied. 'Right, Peri, I want you to turn this dial here right round.' He caught her hand. 'When I tell you. Then count to three, and turn it back to zero. Got that?'

She nodded. The Doctor motioned for everyone to duck down, so that they could not be seen from the door. Outside, the footsteps paused, then continued down the passage.

The Doctor skipped across to the door and opened it a crack. Then he suddenly, deliberately, sneezed.

A moment later he was across the room, dithering by the bed as if looking for a hiding place. The door swung open and Packwood came in. He paused just inside the door. The Doctor looked shocked, worried.

'Hoping to escape while I pursue your friends, Doctor?' Packwood asked. He took a step towards the Doctor, into the room. 'Not very noble of you, I must say.'

'Well,' the Doctor admitted, 'I think we're running out of options.'

Packwood took another step towards the Doctor. He was level with the screen now. Behind it, Peri's hand was tight on the dial. Janet had her teeth tightly clenched as if afraid she might speak or shout. Or scream. Sir Anthony was crouched down, leaning heavily on his stick.

'Perhaps I shall just lock you in here while I deal with your friends,' Packwood declared.

For a moment the Doctor's eyes widened. Then he smiled back. 'Ah, but in this room the bolts are on the inside of the door,' he pointed out. 'To prevent people wandering in while the equipment is on, I assume.'

Packwood nodded slowly. 'A good point,' he conceded. 'Very well. I'll make it quick for you, Doctor.' He strode across the room, arms outstretched.

'You're too kind,' the Doctor said quietly as the hands reached for him. At the last moment, just before Packwood's huge hands closed on his neck, the Doctor ducked. A moment later he was rolling across the floor, a multi-coloured blur of motion. 'Now, Peri,' he shouted as he went, coat tails whipping round like a Catherine wheel. 'Now!'

Peri twisted the dial.

Just as the Doctor rolled behind the screen. There was nothing to see, just a hum of power from the equipment.

But the effect on Packwood was immediate. He had turned to follow the Doctor. Now he sank to his knees, hands to his head.

Peri twisted the dial back to its original position and slowly, carefully, nervously they all looked round the screen.

Packwood was on his knees, head bowed. As they watched he slumped forward, his hands reaching out at the last moment to prevent him falling to the stone floor. He was breathing heavily.

'What's happened?' Sir Anthony asked in a hushed whisper.

'Well,' the Doctor was already beside Packwood, helping him to the bed. 'From what I know about the Gatherer Three mission, and the area of space it was set to cover, I think it's an area practically devoid of X-ray emissions. Just a hunch, but I did wonder if the Denarian might be a little shocked to come into contact with them.'

Packwood was sitting on the bed, his head in his hands. He looked up slowly, and they could see that his eyes were bloodshot, the irises coloured a pale blue.

'Looks like your hunch was right,' Peri said.

'And we have a weapon now,' Sir Anthony said. 'Something we can use against it.'

'Well, it isn't exactly terribly portable,' the Doctor admitted. 'And unless we get moving, the genetic material will synthesise a cure, a protection as it does with any disease or illness.'

'And another thing, Doctor.' Packwood's voice was husky.

'Yes?' the Doctor asked.

'It doesn't work,' Packwood told him.

The villagers stood silent and still outside the house. Waiting. Miss Devlin was with the schoolchildren in the centre of the group. In front of them, close to the front door to Sheldon's Folly, two dead fishermen stood with Rogers the manservant and the remains of Dave Madsen. Liz Trefoil's expression was a fixed neutral as she stood nearby watching her lover's corpse.

In the midst of the crowd was Mrs Tattleshall, silent in company for the first time in decades, her handbag clasped like a talisman in front of her.

'What?' the Doctor demanded, leaping to his feet. 'But you… that is… What do you mean?'

Packwood sounded tired. But there was a gentleness, a humanity in him that had been lacking. Only now that he showed those qualities did it become obvious what had been missing. He rubbed at his eyes as he spoke. 'I mean, Doctor, that you haven't killed it. I can still feel it within me, regathering its strength. In a few minutes it will be in control again.'

'A longer dose?' Peri suggested. 'Would that do it?'

'Probably,' Packwood conceded. 'It is weak, frightened, hurt. But there's no point really, is there?' He swung his legs up and lay back on the bed, hands resting across his chest.

'Why not?' Sir Anthony asked.

'I imagine an exposure long enough to kill the Denarian would

181

also kill Mr Packwood here,' the Doctor said quietly. 'Kill and cure. Not really an option, I think.'

'So, what do we do?' Janet asked. Her voice was strained, her face betraying the disappointment that there was no easy cure.

'Make the most of me while you can,' Packwood suggested weakly. 'Before it reasserts itself, I will tell you what I know.' He turned slightly on his side. His face was drawn and gaunt. 'You were right, Doctor, for what it's worth. This thing – it saps the will, the power to make decisions. I didn't even realise. I thought… I thought it was me, that what it wanted me to think was what I wanted to think. That its thoughts and decisions were my own.' He slumped back again. 'But really, deep down, somewhere, somehow, I knew.' His body shook suddenly, a sob of anger and misery. 'I can't go through that again.'

The Doctor took his hand. 'Then help us to stop it,' he said. 'There must be a way. Tell us whatever you can.'

'I think you know most of it, Doctor.' His voice was weak, a contrast to the size of his body. 'We started with the chickens. There was no thought at first of a human test, though we brought in Madsen. So even then it knew, was planning, was arranging our thoughts. Otherwise, why would we have brought in Madsen?' He coughed, his body shaking, making the bed vibrate beneath him. 'The island environment was ideal, but for chickens and then sheep. I don't know when it took over, when its thoughts became mine. I see Janet losing her mind, slowly from within. But at least she knows what is happening. That's why it can't let her speak.'

Janet nodded, her brow furrowed with effort and exertion. 'Difficult,' she said indistinctly. 'Want me to say things. Not my words.'

'The process will speed up. Others will succumb quicker as it learns how the human body and mind work,' Packwood said. 'Learns from within. Communicates with itself across the ether. Don't know how. Not thoughts as such, it just… knows.'

'I think,' the Doctor said slowly, 'that there must be a central source.

Someone is host to the main intelligence, a co-ordinating colony of this material that organises the rest of it somehow.'

'Me?' Packwood gasped.

The Doctor raised his eyebrows. 'You do seem the most likely candidate,' he admitted. 'That could be why Janet's infection seems to be marking time, as it were. For the moment.' He cleared his throat. 'So how did you start on the humans?' he asked quietly. 'Tell us what happened.'

'There were problems.' Packwood was struggling now, forcing the words out through clenched teeth. 'Vet died. But that helped as Madsen took over his work. Other adverse – fatal – reactions too as we refined the material. Then the fishermen. One broke his arm, an excuse for Madsen to treat him, and then them all. But their boat was lost in a storm. Bad luck, that.' He coughed again. 'But we still had the children.' He sobbed again, a racking, shaking cry from deep within. 'Oh God, the children.'

'The flu jab?' the Doctor asked.

Packwood nodded, a slight movement hampered by his position on the bed. 'Miss Devlin too. After that, it was one by one.'

'As Madsen treated people, so he infected them? Injections?'

'Yes. In the neck, into the artery. Bloodstream. Usually gave them two, to be certain. Then he tracked how the material coped with whatever illness or complaint they had.' He was forcing the words out now. 'Good... data...'

'So how come they're all infected?' Peri asked. 'It seems like the whole village was out there.'

The Doctor nodded. 'A good question. Madsen can't have treated them all.'

'No,' Packwood agreed. 'Can be passed on by digestion of infected material. Like chicken. Also, developed an oral version. Dispersed it in liquid. Spreads easily. Quickly. Infects everything in the food chain. Not just chickens and sheep.'

'Oh my God,' Sir Anthony breathed. 'We're lucky we escaped it then. I'm glad I haven't eaten chicken recently.'

'Oral version, only recent,' Packwood gasped. 'Cows.'

'Cows?' Peri said. Her head was swimming again, vision blurring.

'Infected their drinking water,' Packwood said. 'Meant the milk was tainted. Then passed on to other animals. Into river water from urine. And on and on.'

Peri swayed, reaching out for the lead screen to steady herself. She was suddenly aware that her cold had not developed, had gone after her visit to Hilly Painswick for tea. 'Milk?' she said weakly. But nobody heard her.

Packwood had levered himself into a sitting position. 'You think I am the source of the problem, Doctor?' He was gripping the Doctor's wrist as he asked.

'Well,' the Doctor said slowly. 'It's only a theory. But it fits the facts so far as we know them. I wasn't meaning to apportion blame.'

'Time to move on,' Packwood said quietly, his voice barely audible. 'Before… before it comes back.' He tapped the side of his head. 'While I am still in control in here.' He managed to stand up, shaky but determined.

'The main laboratory,' the Doctor agreed. 'Let's see what we can sort out. There must be a way. Has to be.' He supported Packwood and together they struggled to the door. The others followed, Peri last, stumbling after them, trying to focus.

Packwood was leaning forwards on the door frame, his head against it, hands either side. The others pushed past into the passageway outside. The Doctor reached out to help Packwood.

Packwood stepped back from the door frame, swaying slightly as the Doctor made to help him. But then he pushed the Doctor suddenly away and stepped back into the X-ray room, slamming the door behind him.

The Doctor was at the door immediately, tugging at the handle. But they had all heard the bolts shoot home and the door refused to move.

Packwood's face appeared at the small window. His voice was cracked and faint through the heavy door. 'Only way, Doctor,' he shouted. 'If it is controlled through me, then there is only one way.'

'No,' the Doctor shouted back. 'No, Packwood, listen to me. We can find a cure. There must be one. Help us!'

Packwood was shaking his head. 'Too late,' his muffled reply came through the door. 'Already losing control again. Now or never. Last chance. Of freedom. For us all.' Then his face was gone.

The Doctor jammed his own face to the thick glass, watching horrified through the window.

Logan Packwood could barely stand. His body fought against the alien material as he staggered across to the control panel behind the lead screen. He could see that the Doctor had set the intensity level to maximum and overridden the timer cut-out. He twisted the dial, listening with satisfaction to the hum of power through the X-ray machine. Then he staggered out from behind the screen, collapsing in the middle of the floor, letting the cleansing invisible rays wash over him, wiping his body and his mind clear.

He was too weak to move now. He could feel his skin beginning to blister. He felt sick. But also, elated. He had done it. If the Doctor was right, the controlling consciousness of the Denarian was dead now. The material within the other infected people would revert to first generation, mindless, healing. It would evolve, slowly, again. But now the Doctor had the time and the knowledge to deal with it.

He tried to crawl back to the screen, to shelter. Maybe this was enough, maybe he could switch off the apparatus and live out what was left of his irradiated life free of the contagion.

He collapsed back to the floor before he even got close.

The Doctor sighed. For a moment he rested his forehead against the cold glass of the window. Then he took a deep breath and turned away.

'How do you feel, Janet?' he asked. 'We should know immediately if the Denarian has lost control.'

'Fine, Doctor,' she said at once. Then her forehead creased, her mouth opened, working silently for a while before she was able to gasp out: 'No, not gone. Still… here… inside.'

Outside the house, the villagers surged forward suddenly, as if on an unspoken order. They started on the door, hammering with their fists at the heavy woodwork. Rogers and what was left of Madsen were at the front. Children pushed through and started on the lower part of the door.

Others moved to the windows of the drawing room, oblivious to the smoke from the dying fire within. Hilly Painswick stood beside Old Jim as they battered their fists against the toughened glass.

The Doctor threw open the door and strode in purposefully. 'I was not wrong,' he exclaimed as he looked round. There was a main table down the middle of the room. There were other work surfaces against the walls. Above one of these was a metal plate set into the wall.

On the far side of the room was a heavy metal door with a keypad next to it. The door had rivets and was braced with more metal.

'Well it hasn't worked,' Peri told him. 'Has it?'

'And now we've lost access to the X-ray machine,' Sir Anthony pointed out.

'There must be another main host. Someone else with the controlling consciousness within them,' the Doctor said. 'Or…'

'Or? Or what?' Peri wanted to know.

'Or I was wrong,' the Doctor admitted sharply and quickly. 'This is not the main lab,' he said thoughtfully as he looked round. 'Or if it is, then I'm more than a little disappointed in the facilities available, though impressed with what's been achieved.'

Behind him, Janet raised her hand. It was a hesitant gesture as if her hand were too heavy for her arm. She pointed a shaking finger at the metal door on the other side of the room.

'Through there?' the Doctor said. 'I see.' He started across the room towards the door, but before he was half way, he suddenly dropped to his knees and looked under the main table. 'Hello there,' he said cheerily.

Christopher Sheldon slowly uncurled, his stained face emerging from the ragged folds of his clothes. 'Oh,' he said. 'It's you again, is it?' Carefully, tentatively, he crawled out from under the table and looked at them all. Then, just as carefully and tentatively, he dropped to his knees and crawled back again. As he went, Peri could see that his arm was completely healed, up to the hand, and she shuddered.

The Doctor walked all round the room. As he got back to the door, he pushed it shut and shot the bolts. 'This is it,' he said grimly. 'This is the end of the road. Here we stand, we can do no other.'

Sir Anthony nodded. 'I agree, Doctor. They'll be through into the house before too long. Maybe they won't find us down here.'

'Oh they'll know we're here,' the Doctor said. 'Won't they, Janet?'

Her eyes were wide, the irises already faded almost to white. 'Everything's fine, Doctor,' she said easily. 'There's no problem. You can open the door.'

'She's gone,' Peri said.

'You don't need to lock me outside, Doctor,' Janet said suddenly. There was an urgency in her voice, an edge.

'I have no intention of locking you –' The Doctor stopped suddenly, and peered closely at her. 'Oh,' he said slowly. 'I see what you mean.'

'What are you talking about, Doctor?' Peri asked.

'I think that's Janet's telling us something, am I right?' the Doctor asked.

'Absolutely not, Doctor,' she replied.

'You see,' he said triumphantly.

'No,' Sir Anthony told him.

With a sigh and exaggerated patience, the Doctor explained. 'The Denarian is controlling Janet's body and her speech centres, much of her brain too I suspect.' He looked to Janet.

She shook her head.

He smiled. 'You see, I'm right. She's communicating with us, despite the Denarian, by saying the opposite of what she means. It will let her say things it wants us to hear, but not what will help. But I think it has no sense of sarcasm or irony.'

'What?' Peri asked.

'Like Americans,' the Doctor said tersely. 'She's lying to us, Peri. And because we know that, she can communicate. Now then,' he went on before Peri could comment, 'tell us, Janet, does that door lead into the main laboratory area? Where we might be able to get at some useful equipment? It's a bit Spartan in here after all.'

Janet shook her head. 'I'm afraid not, Doctor. You won't find anything useful through there at all.'

'Excellent.' The Doctor beamed, rubbing his hands together triumphantly. 'And I would guess that you know the code to open the door, right?'

Janet's expression was frozen on her face. 'Absolutely, Doctor,' she said. 'Of course I do. Logan Packwood would never have been so arrogant as to keep that entirely to himself.'

The door was withstanding the hammering without apparent damage. It was pitted and battered, but showed no signs of giving way.

The main window to the drawing room was another matter, however. Villagers were pulling the bottom of it away from the stone mullion that held it. Another few minutes and it would be out altogether, allowing them into the house. Inside the drawing room the fire was spent, having burned itself out on the armchair and the body of Bill Neville.

As they continued their assault on the window another, smaller, group of villagers emerged from the inky night. They had been round the house, to the barns and outbuildings, to find tools to help with the attack on the house. Robert Trefoil was at the front of the group. He was carrying a sledgehammer, holding it across his chest.

* * *

The sound was muffled but audible down in the cellars. It was a heavy repetitive thump that reverberated through the whole building.

The Doctor was standing by the metal door. He had given up trying to guess the key sequence to unlock it, and had removed the front panel of the keypad. Inside was a mass of coloured wiring that he was staring at without enthusiasm.

'That was upstairs,' Sir Anthony said as the thumping sound continued.

'I'm afraid you're right,' the Doctor agreed. 'They've obviously decided it's time they came to get us. And I don't think it will take long.'

'Can we get out?' Peri asked.

'Not upstairs we can't.' The Doctor returned his attention to the wiring, picking out strand after strand and examining the connections. 'Best to keep the door shut and try to barricade it.'

Sir Anthony examined the table. 'No good,' he decided. 'It's fixed to the floor.'

'So we're trapped in here, with no way to keep them out for long,' Peri pointed out. Her voice was strained. 'And we can't even get into the lab where we might find something to help.'

The Doctor turned slowly to answer. 'Peri,' he said, 'would you please try not to state the obvious with such assertion? We're all well aware of how much trouble we're in, thank you very much.'

'There's no other way out of here,' Janet said.

'You see,' the Doctor said indistinctly. 'Even Janet there agrees.' His voice was indistinct as he had the ends of several wires between his teeth now. He added yet another, and then gave a sudden high-pitched yelp. The wires fell from between his teeth. 'That one was live,' he said in a peeved voice. Then he started scrabbling through the loose ends. 'Which one was it?' He tentatively tapped the bare end of a wire against his hesitant tongue. 'Not that one.'

'It was the red one,' Peri told him.

'Thank you.' The Doctor turned back to the keypad, pulling out a length of red wire. He paused, then he dropped the wires again. He turned to Janet. 'You said there was no other way out of here, didn't you?' His voice was low and thoughtful. 'So, where is it?'

'I told you,' Janet replied evenly 'there's absolutely no other way out of here.' She pointed up at the square of metal set into the wall above a workbench. 'That is not, I repeat not, a coal chute behind there, and there is no way you can get outside through it.'

They all stared at Janet. Then they stared at the metal plate. The Doctor leaped on to the workbench and reached up. He could just get his fingers behind the bottom of the plate and worked at it frantically. After a few moments the plate lifted away, and fell with a clang to the work surface below. It bounced to the edge, then fell to the floor with another, louder clang as it hit the stone.

Behind the plate was revealed a square hole. It was just possible to make out a steep chute running at an angle upwards. The hole was about two feet wide and eighteen inches high. The Doctor stood on tiptoes atop the work bench to peer into it. 'I'm not sure that it really is a coal chute,' he announced loudly into the opening. His voice echoed round inside the empty space.

A moment later a cloud of black dust fell out and splattered across the Doctor's face. He coughed, wiping at his eyes. 'Definitely a coal chute,' he decided.

'So what do we do now?' Sir Anthony asked. 'I don't know about anyone else, but I'm hardly up to climbing out of here through that thing.' He nodded at Sheldon, still huddled under the table, rocking back and forth and singing to himself. 'I don't think Christopher here is up to it either. Janet?'

'I think it would be very easy to climb out,' she said.

The Doctor finished dusting himself down and jumped from the workbench to land squarely on the floor beside Peri. 'One of us needs to get out,' he said calmly, 'and send for help.'

'How?' Peri asked.

'Well, climb.'

'No, I mean how do we send for help?'

The Doctor looked to Sir Anthony. 'Do you have your mobile

phone about your person?' he asked. 'We should have thought of that earlier. It may not work down here of course, but once out, Peri can call up help from your friends at the ministry.'

Sir Anthony's face fell. 'It's back at the cottage,' he confessed. 'I don't tend to carry it round. There's rarely a chance of a signal, so I just got out of the habit, I suppose.'

'Wait a minute.' Peri was frowning. 'What do you mean "Peri can call up help"?'

The Doctor looked round, wide-eyed with surprise. 'Well, I don't know who else you think could do it,' he told her. 'Sir Anthony and Sheldon are obviously out of it. Janet would only be able to tell them that everything here is hunky-dory, thank you very much, and I...' He set his right hand on his left breast and struck a theatrical pose. 'As you are so fond of pointing out, Peri, I have a statuesque and well-toned physique which is sadly just a little too ample to fit through that hole up there.' He smiled. 'Which leaves...?'

'OK, Porky,' she said. 'Point taken. You just want me to crawl up that chute, get out at the top, avoid the roaming zombies, get a boat back to the other island, find Sir Anthony's phone and hope that I can get a signal. Then I call some people who have no idea who I am and hope they'll agree to send some sort of help. But we don't know what. Is that it?'

The Doctor sucked in his cheeks and nodded. 'You seem to have the general idea,' he agreed.

As he spoke, there was the sound of running feet from outside the door. A moment later, the first blows hammered against the door. It shook under the impact, the sound echoing round the room.

'Except,' the Doctor added, 'that you missed the bit about haste, urgency and speed.'

Peri looked at the Doctor. Then she looked at the door. 'Right,' she said, 'give me a bunk up, then.'

'The phone,' Sir Anthony told her as the Doctor hoisted Peri on to the workbench then jumped up after her, 'is in the top left drawer of my desk at the cottage. The ministry is speed dial three. I assume you know how to work a mobile phone?'

The Doctor was just lifting Peri into the chute. She had her arms stretched out above her head, reaching into the narrow shaft. 'No,' she said. 'Not a clue.'

The Doctor gently set her down on the work surface again.

They found a scrap of paper, and Sir Anthony scribbled down hasty instructions.

'You'd better give her the home number of your friend, what's her name?' the Doctor said.

'Madge. Good thought.' Sir Anthony added a phone number to the bottom of the paper, then handed it to Peri. She stuffed it into her pocket.

'Right,' the Doctor said. 'Here we go again.' Behind him the door frame was splintering under the relentless onslaught. He lifted Peri into the chute. 'Try to brace yourself against the sides and wriggle upwards,' he suggested.

'Thanks, Doctor,' she told him. 'What a good thought.'

But the Doctor had disappeared from the bottom of the chute. He was already working at the wires behind the keypad that controlled the lock of the metal door to the main lab. The last thing that Peri heard from below as she eased herself up the shaft was the sound of splintering wood, and the terrific crash as the door was knocked out of its frame.

Chapter Thirteen
Close Calls

There was no time to waste and little to be gained by wondering what was happening in the room below. Peri had managed to worm her way up the chute. It seemed to go on for ever, and there was no sign of a light at the top. It was night, Peri reminded herself, she would see nothing until she arrived, probably. However, a little moonlight or the sight of a star would have been encouraging.

She continued to wriggle upwards, bracing herself against the steep sides and pushing up with her toes, then pulling with her hands. Fortunately the chute was made of brick or stone, she could not see which, so there were handholds and niches the whole way. The disadvantage was that it was rough and grazed against her legs and her arms, dug into her sides, rubbed painfully on her cheeks and nose if she rested her head.

The sound and light from below had receded into nothingness. That was her only indication that she was making any progress. Even so, Peri was worried that she was slipping back as far as she pushed upwards each time, without realising. As her journey continued, still with no end in sight, her worry turned to anxiety, and her anxiety to fear. By the time she reached the top, she had no idea how much later, tears of frustration and terror were streaming down her dusty cheeks.

She heaved herself forwards again, reaching out, and her hands hit the metal plate that covered the top of the chute. For several seconds she was unable to work out what was wrong, what she had hit up against. Then slowly, it dawned on her, and she lowered her head and sobbed. Her hands battered on the metal plate, making a hollow clanging sound. But it refused to budge.

She was feeling sick again. Though whether this was because of the situation or the Denarian gradually taking hold within her,

Peri neither knew nor cared. She continued to batter at the metal plate, her only options to break through it or to slide back down to the room below and whatever was waiting for her there.

The first indication that her thumping at the plate was doing any good was a breath of fresh air against Peri's cheek. At first she was merely glad of the cool, clean air inside the stuffy chute. But then she realised that it must mean there was a gap somewhere to allow the breeze through. A gap that had not previously been there. She renewed her attack on the plate, pushing herself further up the chute to try to bring more force to bear on it.

When the plate gave way, it did so suddenly. With a metallic wrenching, the whole dented rectangular sheet of metal ripped away from the opening, and Peri found herself looking out into the night mist.

With a sense of relief greater than she could recall ever feeling before, Peri hauled herself out of the chute. It emerged about two feet above the ground at the back of the house, and she climbed out on to the gravelled driveway that circled the house. Her feet crunched noisily on the small stones as she stumbled. She froze, scared that someone might have heard. Her feet had pins and needles, and it took her a moment to regain her sense of balance after the disorientation of the climb.

After a few moments there was still no sign of anyone about, and Peri decided they must all now be inside the house. Nevertheless it was with exaggerated care and caution that she made her way round to the front of the house. She needed to get down to the jetty and find a boat. With luck she could row it across to the main island before anyone even knew she was here.

She had been assuming that the villagers were the only threat. But it became apparent, as she reached the front of the house and set off across the lawn, that this was not the case.

At first she thought they were bats, black shapes swooping through the misty night sky, screeching at the pale shape of the moon. But as one dipped low over her, Peri saw that it was an owl. The creature's sharp clawed feet were extended downwards as it flew, ripping at the air. Instinctively, Peri ducked. And a claw ripped through the top strands of her hair. She screamed in fright, surprise and pain.

She assumed it was an accident, that the owl had simply not seen her. But then it came round for another try. And others joined it. She ran on, desperately waving her arms above her head, thrashing at the owls. They screeched and howled as she hurled herself along the narrow path through the trees. Claws tore at her hair, whipped at her cheeks. Then suddenly, they were gone. The night air was empty again.

Peri did not stop to wonder where they had gone – she simply gave silent thanks that they were no longer after her. Perhaps she had blundered through some territorial area, or disturbed them while feeding. Her mind struggled to rationalise the attack as she neared the jetty. Then she saw the fox.

It was crouched down at the near end of the jetty, as if guarding it. As Peri approached, the fox's head snapped upwards and it stared directly at her. Saliva dripped from the side of its jaws as it opened its mouth slightly at the sight of the girl. Its pallid eyes gleamed through the mist. And at that moment, Peri realised what she faced.

They had talked about the infection spreading into the food chain. The fox, the owls too, were infected. They probably did not know why they were doing it, but they were out to stop Peri reaching the main island of Dorsill. She ducked back into the shadows of the trees.

As Peri considered what to do, the fox leaned forward, its snout close to the ground as if smelling her out. Slowly, it started forwards, keeping low, its body moving fluidly over the path as it crept towards Peri. Behind it she could see the jetty, could see several small boats tied up along its length. From somewhere came the screech of an owl, answered immediately by another.

'Peri?' The voice was from the woods behind her. 'Is that you, Peri?' A woman's voice.

It took her a few seconds to identify the direction. She peered into the darkness, barely able to discern a dark figure on the path. 'Who is it?' she called out, her voice trembling.

'It's me, Liz.' The figure took a step forwards, illuminated now by a shaft of moonlight that sent the mist scurrying away into the trees. 'Come back, Peri. Everything's all right, you know. There's no need for this.'

She was right, of course. Peri knew that. Somewhere inside her mind she knew that all she needed to do was wait and everything would be fine. For everyone. Especially for herself.

Liz Trefoil leaned her head to one side as she waited, silhouetted hair falling sideways. 'What do you say, Peri?'

Peri opened her mouth, about to answer, about to say that yes she knew everything would be fine. But then she saw the other figure, the dark shape behind Liz in the shadows.

It was Madsen, the silhouette of his head jagged and broken.

And suddenly Peri's mind was clear again. She turned back towards the jetty. The fox's mouth opened in a wide hiss of anger and anticipation. Peri ran towards its jaws.

She almost left it too late. The fox snapped at her heels as Peri leaped over it. Almost. Then she landed on the edge of the jetty, already running, sprinting for the nearest boat.

No, not the nearest. The next one. The one with a motor, she could now see even as the moon receded behind the mist again. Peri slipped the rope from round the stumpy pole of the jetty and jumped down into the boat, feeling it lurch beneath her as she landed, as she rocked with it and almost fell.

The fox was racing towards her. Liz Trefoil was running too, Dave Madsen stumbling after her. Peri grabbed the motor's starter cord and pulled. She pulled so hard she almost lost her balance. The fox jumped, was in the air as the motor caught.

The blades of the propeller were in the water already, and they bit immediately into the water. The boat lurched, tipping backwards as the prow lifted and the whole boat shot forwards. The fox's front paws scrabbled on the stern of the boat, scuffling, desperate to gain purchase. It managed to pull itself up on to the edge of the boat, eyes glinting, cruel and pale with anticipation. Its jaws opened wide.

Just as Peri slammed the blade of an oar into it, sending the fox howling into the water.

She sat down, angling the motor and setting the boat towards where she hoped the main island was.

Behind her, above the sound of the motor, she fancied she could hear the steady dip and pull of the oars as another boat set off after her. But, she told herself, it must be her imagination.

There was a strange air of similarity between the journey on the boat and Peri's climb up the coal chute. Again she was heading into the darkness with little or no way of judging how far she had come or exactly where or when she would eventually arrive. She just prayed that her memory of the position of the island was not flawed, and that by keeping the motor in the same position she was not going in circles. She tried not to consider what the effects of tide and current might be on her trajectory.

She also hoped that she was going at a speed sufficient to keep the owls from attacking her again. But in the event it was not owls she needed to worry about.

Peri's first intimation of trouble was when the boat was thumped in the side with a jarring thud. She was almost knocked from the wooden seat by the outboard, the impact was so sudden, so unexpected and so violent. Then came another. And another.

There was precious little moonlight, and what there was served mainly to illuminate the swirls of mist that clung to the surface of the water. But beneath the smoky texture of the night, Peri could make out a dark shape circling in the water. Barely more than a long shadow, it undulated through the sea, coming round in a wide arc before hurtling towards the boat. A long, thin tail became visible thrashing it through the water as the creature attacked again.

Then a triangular fin sliced through the mist, and Peri realised it was a shark.

There was water in the bottom of the boat now, sloshing over the side as the whole thing shook and trembled beneath the onslaught. One of the planks that made up the floor of the boat was loose, shaken out of place and more water was pushing up through the gap, washing round Peri's feet.

The shock of the sudden cold water over the tops of her shoes caused Peri to cry out in surprise and alarm. She pulled her feet up on to the seat, sitting angled sideways, clinging to the spluttering motor. The boat rocked again, and she was pitched off the seat and on to the floor, landing with a splash.

The boat was low in the water and getting lower. The motor had been skewed sideways and was driving the boat in a circle, churning it through the same water again and again. In the middle of the white water, the shark's fin moved with deceptive laziness through the mist.

As the boat came round for the third time, getting lower with each lap, Peri fancied she could make out a dark shape in the distance. An island. What she did not know was whether it was the main island she had been aiming for, or one of the other smaller islands. Perhaps it was Sheldon's Folly again. But she hardly cared. It was land.

She watched for the shark to be at the furthest point away, then jumped. Peri hoped – prayed – that the motor would distract the shark from any noise that Peri made in the water. She broke the ice-cold surface, spitting and coughing water, checked her bearings and struck out towards the dark mass in the distance.

Behind her the boat chugged to an uneven halt, shipping water, sinking.

The engine cut out.

She was lucky in two ways, Peri decided as she waded ashore. Three if she counted the fact that she was actually on the right island and not far from Cove Cottage – she could see the church spire standing proud against the night sky.

The first piece of luck was that the shark seemed to have lost her, or given up, or been distracted by the death of her boat. The second was that she had discovered that swimming no longer tired her anything like as much as it used to. The Denarian had not yet taken control of her mind, but it was sorting out her body. She put her hand to her face, feeling for the cuts and scratches where the owls had attacked her. Sure enough, there was just the hint of a ridge of healing skin.

So it was in a mood of something close to elation that Peri made her way through the deserted village, past the church, towards Cove Cottage. She was shivering from the cold, upset almost that she still felt it. The back door of the cottage was unlocked, and Peri fully expected her luck to hold. From now on it had to be easy. Get the phone from the desk, call for help, sit back and wait. The Doctor would have found a way to escape the villagers, she was sure of that. Everything suddenly was going to be fine.

Except...

Except that the phone was not in the top left drawer of the desk.

It wasn't in the top right drawer either. Or any of the others. By the time Peri had emptied the entire contents of the desk on to the floor and sifted through them twice, she was frustrated to the point of tears. She spent half an hour going through the kitchen and bedrooms, even the cellar. She checked the living room again, turning out every drawer and cupboard. Nothing.

In a final desperate rush of inspiration she went through the pockets of Sir Anthony's coats, hanging on pegs by the back door.

Still nothing. The phone was nowhere in the house, she was sure.

And with that knowledge, Peri sat down in the middle of the mess that had once been inside the desk, and cried.

To the Doctor's well-hidden amazement, the door had sprung open as he touched two wires together more or less at random and in barely disguised panic.

He had bundled Sir Anthony into the room, grabbed Sheldon by what was left of his collar and hurled him after Sir Anthony. For a moment he had wondered whether it might not be best to leave

Janet outside. The villagers would not harm her after all. But no, he decided, he needed her help and she was not yet quite fully under the alien influence. He pushed her after Sheldon. Then he pulled the wires apart and ripped one of them right out of the wall to prevent anyone else hitting on the same lucky combination.

He hesitated just long enough to see the door to the room begin to topple forwards, to make out the shapes of the villagers behind, to see Trefoil wielding the sledgehammer, before he followed. The Doctor slammed the door shut, relieved to hear the lock click into place as it closed. He leaned back against it for a few moments, eyes closed, hoping that Peri was all right.

Then he pushed himself away from the door and looked round to see just how much trouble they were in.

Actually, he decided as he surveyed the equipment in the lab, they were surprisingly well off. A well-equipped workbench in the middle of the room with high stools round it. Plenty of glassware – always impressive, that, he mused. There was even a huge plastic tank full of, he guessed, pure water in the corner of the room.

And since the Doctor had both Sheldon and Janet with him, there seemed to be no shortage of alien material, whatever specimens might be stored in the large fridge in the corner. There was another upright cabinet next to it. Time to explore that later. The only important question now was whether he could come up with a suitable solution and produce it. In quantity. In time. Effectively.

'Right,' the Doctor said with a bravado and confidence he did not, in all honesty, quite feel. 'Let's get started, shall we?'

As she sat sobbing in the mass of papers and letters from the desk, it came to her. Peri's mind was going back over events, wondering how things could have worked out differently, how they could have come to a different conclusion. How she could have escaped sitting on the floor, crying, out of touch with the rest of the world while alien material that infected her began to take hold. She found herself playing through the different moments when she and the Doctor could have just left. Could have decided that there was nothing of interest happening here after all and simply returned to the TARDIS.

One of these moments was when it became apparent to them that they were in the twentieth century not the nineteenth or earlier. And as she considered this, as she remembered how she and the Doctor had thought they had spotted anachronisms in the environment and the attitude of the people, Peri recalled stumbling across the tide tables and the satellite phone in the pub.

She sat for a minute more, her mind numb from the shock of realisation. Then she hauled herself to her feet and ran from the cottage.

The mist parted for her as she raced down the main street of the village towards the pub. Her feet clattered on the cobbles and several times she slipped but managed to catch her balance. It was a good five-minute run to the pub, but she was barely out of breath when she arrived. The door was standing open, and she stepped inside.

It was dark. One gas lamp was burning above the bar. Otherwise the main lounge was unlit. The entrance to the hall was a dark outline, the door standing open. Peri made her way carefully towards the dark area, arms stretched out in front of her. She hit a table a glancing blow and caught her foot on a chair leg, making the chair scrape noisily on the stone floor. Her steps became more hesitant. It seemed to take an age to reach the doorway.

Then suddenly, it seemed, she was there. She stepped out into the hall. A light was burning somewhere upstairs, so there was a pale glow of illumination in the hall. Enough to make out the door to the room where the phone was.

Enough to make out the shape of the figure coming down the stairs. Enough to see it was Liz Trefoil, her hair glowing like fire in the dim light.

Enough light too that when Peri turned she could see that Dave Madsen's bloodied head was all but healed, the bone at the back of his skull knitted together in a jagged binding of white that zigzagged through his matted hair. He stepped towards her.

Peri did not stop to think. She slammed the door to the bar shut, felt it connect with Madsen on the other side, heard him stumble backwards and fall against a table or chairs.

Liz was coming down the stairs fast, racing Peri for the door to the private room. She got there first, turning in triumph, smiling. Her teeth caught the light, almost glowing, as Peri put her head down and barged into her. Peri's shoulder hit Liz in the stomach. The wind went out of her in an explosion of breath and Liz sagged.

Peri pulled her away from the door, scrabbling for the handle as Liz slumped to the floor. Peri opened the door.

But Liz had a hand on her ankle, squeezing, pulling, dragging Peri down as Liz struggled to get up. Her smile was fixed on her face. Her eyes were wide ovals of white staring blankly up at Peri.

Peri slipped, her leg pulled from under her. She was face down, head and shoulders through the doorway, struggling to crawl forwards, towards the phone, she could see the phone. Her hands scrabbled on the stone flags, her nails clattered on the floor. Liz was crawling over her, dragging herself up Peri's leg, nails biting into the flesh through her clothing.

With an effort, Peri managed to roll herself on to her back. She could see the woman clawing her way up towards her face. She shook her leg, trying to break free, but without success. And behind Liz she could see the door to the bar opening again as Madsen came to help the young woman.

Desperate, frightened, and with a renewed sense of urgency, Peri pulled back her free leg. Then she kicked violently, viciously, at Liz's face.

The smile broke, blackened holes appearing in it as Peri kicked again. And again. The grip on her leg loosened and Peri rolled clear, her leg bloodied from the nails, and from the cuts and gashes in Liz's freckled face.

As she pulled herself inside the room, Peri kicked the door shut. She leaped to her feet, feeling the pain in her left leg as she put weight on it. There was a bolt at the top of the door, and Peri slammed it home. She dragged the table in front of the door. The single oil lamp gave enough light for her to see the box that contained the phone, and Peri slumped down beside it as the hammering on the door started.

She lifted the handset. The readout on the box that housed the phone lit up to read: 'Dial'. Peri stared at it for a moment. She considered dialling 999. Or would it be 911? And what would she say and who would believe her? No, better to stick to the plan and call Sir Anthony's former PA. She would at least know who to contact.

The paper on which Sir Anthony had written Madge's number was in Peri's pocket. She scrabbled for it, aware that the hammering on the door now sounded more hollow, sounded as if the wood was beginning to splinter. She looked round as she fumbled for the paper, wondering how she could get away once she had made the call. The window was an obvious route. It looked like it opened. Diamonds of glass held together by strips of lead. She dragged the phone over so that she was sitting under the window as she finally found the piece of paper and pulled it out of her pocket.

She had folded it in half, she remembered. Now she stared at the paper is horror and disbelief. It was rough to the touch, a single thick sheet sealed by the water when she swam ashore. The number was somewhere inside the mass of pulp.

Peri hardly noticed that the hammering at the door had stopped. She desperately, delicately tried to prise the layers of paper apart with her broken nails. Or could she recall the number? No way – she had barely glanced at it.

The pain in her leg had subsided, the bleeding stopped. She could feel the muscles knitting back together, and shuddered as she thought about how Madsen's skull had also knitted back together. But with no brain inside, just a cavity. A hole. But she could not wait for her nails to grow back, she thought as she tore at the paper.

Finally she managed to lift a layer away, to reveal the scrawl of instructions and numbers below. The ink was faded and had run, but if she angled the paper she could just about make out Madge's number.

'Dial' the phone still demanded.

Was that an eight or a nine?

She dialled. Must be an eight.

'Connecting' the display on the phone read and Peri sighed. There was a series of rapid clicks from the handset's earpiece. Then, suddenly and mercifully, a ringing tone. Come on, come on.

When the phone was answered, after about a dozen rings, Peri realised she had no idea what to say.

'Hello?' said a sleepy voice in her ear. A female voice, at least. Had to be the right number.

'Hello?' Peri stammered back. 'Is that – is that Madge?'

A pause. Was it Madge?

'Yes. Yes it is. Who's calling, please?'

'You don't know me,' Peri said. She stopped. Why had the hammering at the door stopped? Had they given up? Never mind. Concentrate… 'My name's Peri.' Not important, get on with it. 'I'm sorry about getting you up, I'm a friend of Sir Anthony Kelso.'

'Oh?'

'Yes. I'm here on Dorsill with him. He asked me to call you.' At last, getting somewhere. Her brain was working again.

'Is he all right?' the woman – Madge – asked. There was concern more than tiredness in her voice now. 'Nothing's happened to him, has it?'

'No, no. That is –' Peri sighed, tried to gather her thoughts. 'No, he's fine. Really. Don't worry.'

A sigh of relief from the other end of the phone. 'Thank God. I've been so worried. How is he getting about?'

Peri's brain froze at the question. Tried to decipher it. 'Getting about?' she asked, even as part of her brain was telling her to ignore the small talk and get on with it.

'Well, on the island. There can't be many roads or paths.'

Peri's mind was a fog now. She tried to concentrate on what the woman was saying, tried to focus. 'No, not many.'

'So how is he managing? You know – in the wheelchair?'

Peri's hand tightened round the phone. The fog had lifted from her brain now, and her mind was racing through the implications. Leave it, she decided, leave it and get help. Worry about it later.

But even as she came to this decision, even as the woman's voice was calling again in her ear: 'Hello? Hello, are you still there?' the window above and behind Peri exploded.

Diamonds of glass scythed through the air in a tortured wrenching of leading. Several of the tiny panes exploded as they hit the floor. Peri screamed. The woman was shouting down the phone, asking what was going on, the hands were reaching in, down, for the phone.

The handset was ripped from Peri's hand as she tried to shout back. The curled wire connecting it to the box that housed the main body of the phone ripped free, dangling by Peri's face as the hands reached in at her. Madsen's face loomed close to hers, upside-down, lopsided as he leaned down through the shattered remains of the window.

Chapter Fourteen
Under the Influence

The appearance of Madsen's face, upside-down, flecked with dried blood clinging like rust to his forehead and cheeks, galvanised Peri into action. As his clammy hands grabbed for her through the shattered window, Peri sprang away, half rolling and half crawling across the room. She kept going, a bundle of frantic movement, until she collided with one of the uprights of the fireplace.

She sat with her back to the fireplace, watching in shock and horror as Madsen levered himself through the remains of the window. Slowly, she pushed herself upright, her back pressed against the fireplace. Madsen's head and shoulders were inside the room now as he fed himself through, negotiating the mass of tangled leading that clung like a fisherman's net to the window.

As she stood upright, Peri's shoulder connected with the mantel shelf. She gave a small cry of surprise and slight pain. Something fell to the floor, landing at her feet with a thud. At the same moment, Madsen finally flopped forwards into the room. He made no effort to break his fall, mirroring the cardboard box as it fell. The lid sprang off on impact.

Madsen was getting up now. Was starting towards Peri.

The box at her feet.

The lid off.

The flare pistol inside, dull metal lit by the flicker of the distant oil lamp.

Peri grabbed the pistol as she ran for the door and dragged the table away. She had no idea if it was loaded. She had no idea how it worked. She had no idea if she could – or would – use it.

Behind her, Madsen's footsteps were heavy on the bare boards of the floor. As she dragged the table clear, Peri turned.

And found Madsen close behind her, reaching out, leaning

towards her. The lamplight washed round his image so that he shimmered, almost unreal.

When she brought the flare pistol up, that was unreal too. As unreal as the pressure of her finger on the trigger, as the click of the hammer, as the whoosh as the gun fired, as the thudding jolt of the recoil.

The flare hit Madsen full in the chest from just feet away, knocking him backwards, hurling him across the room in a staggering, stumbling backward run. He collapsed in a heap, hands battering at his chest as the orange-yellow tail of the flare bored into his clothing. Then abruptly his whole torso erupted into a red fireball that burned into Peri's retina. She closed her eyes tight as she turned away. But she could see the imprint of the last image, could still see Madsen's flailing body engulfed by the waves of fire that rippled and ran across and around his body.

The astonishment and horror were also burned into Liz Trefoil's eyes. She was waiting behind the door as Peri pulled the bolt and swung it open. The girl was paused, arms outstretched, fingers grasping at air as she stared past Peri at the burning figure now slumped on its knees as the flames pooled round it. The red of the flare made Liz's hair glow like fire as Peri reached out, grabbed it, and dragged the young woman into the room. She kept dragging, then pushing, hurling Liz across the floor towards the pool of fire.

Peri did not stop to see how far Liz travelled before regaining her balance. She was out of the door in an instant.

The door into the bar was locked, or bolted. Peri guessed that the back door of the pub would be barred too. They had been taking no chances on her escaping. That left only one route. Up the stairs. She raced back, just as Liz emerged from the smoke. Liz grabbed at Peri as she ran past, caught at her, almost managed to take hold. But Peri pulled free and started up the stairs, two at a time. Behind her, Liz Trefoil began to follow with slow deliberate steps.

Madge Simpson sat in her kitchen, snuggled inside a towelling dressing gown. The kettle was on. A mug stood ready beside it with a tea bag stuffed inside. She tried to make sense of the girl's phone call. She had seemed confused, distressed. And then there was the screaming, the shouting before she was cut off.

Never one to panic, Madge considered her options carefully. She could call the police, but she wasn't really sure what she could usefully tell them. She could ignore it and go back to bed, but her conscience was unlikely to allow her to sleep much afterwards. She could wait for the girl to call again, assume that there was nothing more wrong than a broken connection. Or she could call the ministry and see if anyone there knew what was happening. But she was loath to do that – she knew that Sir Anthony had not wanted anyone but herself to know where he was. There would be a reason for that. With Sir Anthony there was a reason for everything.

The kettle started to boil, and she came to a decision. She would make the tea, give the girl another few minutes to call back. And if there was still nothing, Madge would call the one number she did have. Perhaps, just perhaps, she would be able to get through. If not... Well, she would worry about that when she needed to.

Janet Spillsbury was sitting on a laboratory stool, her fingers knitted together in her lap, twisting all the time. She stared straight ahead, her pupils tiny dots in her wide, pale eyes. The Doctor spared her the occasional glance as he worked. He did not want her to succumb completely to the alien influence without his realising, though he had no idea what to do if and when she did.

Sheldon was sitting cross-legged on the floor, rocking back and forth and humming. The sound was just loud enough to be annoying. The Doctor tried to tune it out, almost succeeding. Sheldon was nursing his healing hand, clutching it close to his body. Stubby fingers had sprouted from the stump of his new palm. It was somehow fascinating to watch the genetic healing process, and at the same time grotesque.

The Doctor tried to concentrate on the view through the microscope. It was a sample of blood he had taken from Sheldon's new arm. That had seemed like the best place to start hunting for the alien material. Sir Anthony was standing nearby, his old, grey eyes watching the Doctor intently, as if assessing his progress, his proximity to success.

Eventually the Doctor looked up. 'I think I've managed to isolate the Denarian material,' he said, with a certain amount of pride. He gestured for Sir Anthony to take a look. He did.

'Means nothing to me,' the elderly man confessed as he stepped away from the bench. 'What's the next step?'

'Well, I've doctored this sample, if you'll forgive the expression.' The Doctor grinned. 'Now I can synthesise a solution of the pure alien material.'

'Thought that would be the last thing we need,' Sir Anthony grumbled.

'Yes,' the Doctor said with exaggerated patience. 'But once we have that, we know what we're fighting and I can develop an antidote, something that will neutralise it genetically.'

'Simple as that?'

The Doctor raised an eyebrow. 'I very much doubt it,' he confessed. 'Now, could I have just a little bit of peace and quiet, do you think?'

As he worked, the Doctor tried to ignore the sound of Sheldon's humming, the intense stare of Sir Anthony, the nervous movement of Janet's fingers. He slotted two test tubes of material into a centrifuge and turned it on. And frowned.

It was making the most peculiar noise. A high-pitched buzzing. Almost like...

And it did not seem to be coming from the centrifuge at all, now he came to listen properly, the Doctor decided. Insistent, regular. Almost like...

Almost like a mobile phone ringing.

Out of the corner of his eye, the Doctor saw Sir Anthony reach into his jacket pocket. He fumbled for a moment, then the sound stopped.

He had his phone.

Hidden in his pocket.

And the Doctor had sent Peri back to the main island to get it.

Suddenly a lot of things were clear to the Doctor. Not least that he needed help. 'So,' he said without looking up from the centrifuge, 'you do have your phone with you. And it can get a signal even down here.'

Sir Anthony was standing absolutely still. Sheldon had stopped humming. Janet's fingers were still. The centrifuge spun to a halt.

'That's why you really came here, to Dorsill, isn't it?' the Doctor went on, still not looking up. He removed the test tubes from the centrifuge and placed them carefully in a wooden rack beside it on the workbench. 'Not that I think you knew, not really. Any more than you really, consciously knew you had the phone with you when you sent Peri off to find it. You've been consciously struggling to ascribe motives to your subconscious actions all along, haven't you?'

He did look up now, fixing Sir Anthony with a steely stare. He had assumed the man's eyes were pale with age. Now he could see how wrong he had been. 'I guess you must have been infected even before Packwood.' The Doctor took a step towards Sir Anthony. 'That's why it's you that is the host for the controlling, sentient part of the Denarian. Isn't it?' He reached out his hand suddenly. 'The phone please.'

Just for a second, the Doctor thought Sir Anthony was going to give him the phone. He reached into his pocket. But when his hand emerged, it was holding a small, flat pistol.

The Doctor hesitated. He was just too far away to grab Sir Anthony's hand. Too close to risk trying to dive away. So he stood still and slowly raised his hands, fingers splayed out. 'So why did you let me get this far?' the Doctor asked quietly.

'Partly because you're right, Doctor,' Sir Anthony told him. 'I really didn't know what I was doing. But I see it all now. I see the great vision that Packwood held. I see how it ends.'

The Doctor nodded as if he understood. 'Partly?' he prompted.

'And partly, Doctor, because I am an old man.'

'I wouldn't say that,' the Doctor murmured.

'I may have the advantages of the Denarian enhancement within me, but I fear that my frame is still brittle and frail. I can heal, I grow stronger, but for the moment I am still an old man who feels the cold.'

'Ah, of course.' The Doctor turned slightly to see Janet Spillsbury push herself off the stool and approach them. 'So you were waiting for Janet.'

'Or Peri,' Janet said quietly, behind him. 'But I was further advanced.'

'Peri?' The Doctor's eyes widened. 'You don't mean Peri is infected too?'

'Of course,' Janet said. 'Couldn't you tell?'

'Oh, Peri,' the Doctor breathed.

'Everyone is infected,' Sir Anthony said. 'Or will be. Soon.' He turned slightly to address Janet. 'Would you do the honours, please?' As she moved to take the test tubes the Doctor had placed in the rack, Sir Anthony went on: 'I really must thank you, Doctor, for synthesising a pure Denarian solution. Most useful.'

The Doctor turned enough to see Janet push the needle of a syringe into one of the test tubes. She drew out a portion of the clear liquid into the syringe.

'I think it's only fair to point out,' the Doctor said, 'that I'm a little further on than I led you to believe.'

'Oh?'

Janet paused, holding the syringe upright, the needle glinting in the harsh lighting of the laboratory, a bead of liquid escaping from its tip and running down the side of the needle.

'Yes.' The Doctor smiled winningly. 'You see, that's actually the antidote, not the Denarian.'

Sir Anthony nodded. 'I see,' he said. 'You guessed that I was infected, so you synthesised the cure without letting on. Is that it?'

'In a nutshell.'

'Rubbish,' Sir Anthony barked at him. 'Not a very good bluff, Doctor. I expected better.' He nodded to Janet, and she approached the Doctor, syringe levelled. 'If that were true, Doctor,' Sir Anthony was saying, 'you would hardly tell me. Would you?'

'Double bluff?' the Doctor suggested. It sounded lame even to him. The syringe was close to his arm. 'Would you like me to take my coat off?'

Janet hesitated. And as she hesitated, Sheldon suddenly launched himself across the room at her. None of them had seen him rise slowly from the floor, none of them expected this. Janet fell heavily. The syringe skidded from her grasp and scuttered across the floor. The Doctor was sent sprawling, one arm half out of the coat he had been intending to throw at Janet.

Sir Anthony took a step backwards, turning to aim the gun. The Doctor managed to disentangle his arm from the sleeve and flailed at the gun with the coat. A bullet rocketed into the ceiling of the lab with a dull echoing explosion of sound.

Janet was scrabbling for the syringe. Sheldon was standing up. Sir Anthony was trying to get his gun out of the lining of the Doctor's coat, dragging the still-entangled Doctor back and forth as he did so.

Then Sheldon was on Sir Anthony, punching him with his good hand, ignoring coat, gun, Doctor. 'I'll put you back in that wheelchair,' he screamed, his face contorted with fury and pain.

Abruptly, Sheldon went rigid, his head snapped back and his back arched as Janet Spillsbury plunged the syringe into his upper arm. He gave a short, high-pitched wail, and sagged, flopping to the floor. As he fell he dragged the Doctor's coat with him. It fell over him as if covering a corpse.

The Doctor stood in his waistcoat as Sir Anthony, again, turned the gun towards him. Janet was already refilling the syringe from the second test tube.

Between them the coat moved. Sheldon emerged slowly, painfully from beneath. He sat staring into space, the coat wrapped round him as he huddled inside. His voice was slow, deliberate, calm. 'I thought it was such a triumph,' he said with complete lucidity. He turned to look at the Doctor, his eyes clear and bright.

'That was before… it was when a small blood sample was enough. Or so it seemed. A miracle cure. Sir Anthony, crippled since his teens, walks again.' He gave a short laugh, shook his head. 'A drop of blood, the odd nail clipping.' He lifted his hand and stared at the stubby blunt fingers that were reforming. 'A small price for the use of a man's legs.' He drew a deep breath. 'But what a terrible cost it turned out to be.'

The Doctor said nothing. He stared down in sympathy at the pathetic figure sitting on the multicoloured island of his coat. He barely noticed the triumphant expression on Sir Anthony's face, hardly saw Janet approaching with the syringe, scarcely felt the sharp impact of the needle as she drove it through his shirt and into the fleshy part of his upper arm.

The image of Sheldon swam before his eyes as he swayed on his feet, reaching out desperately for support that wasn't there.

The only real plan Peri had was to escape. She had no idea how that plan could be put into action. At the top of the stairs there was a landing with doors off it. Peri had run past her own room and the Doctor's, fearing that Liz Trefoil was close behind her. She had no idea which of the rooms ahead of her could be locked, or which had windows that would open sufficiently for her to get out, or how to get down to the ground from them. Apart from falling.

As she dithered, as she heard the steady tread on the bare boards behind her, Peri saw the hatch in the ceiling. There was a handle attached to it and, almost by instinct, she took a running leap, reaching up as high as she could, and grabbing the handle, dragging the hatch down.

A steel ladder swung down as the hatch opened, clattering as it extended to the floor. In a moment, Peri was climbing, two steps at a time, not daring to look back, hearing a cry of anger from Liz Trefoil.

As soon as she was at the top, Peri pulled the ladder back up, telescoping it back into the attic area. She dragged the hatch shut, and looked round for something to jam it.

It was light. Not very light, but a dusty, grimy moonlight filtered into the attic from somewhere. It was enough for Peri to make out the broken handle of a broom nearby and ram it through the ladder and hatch mechanism in the hope it would prevent Liz from opening the hatch from outside.

It was also light enough for Peri to make out the outlines of boxes and crates stacked and strewn haphazardly across the rafters. There were clusters of shadows and dark recesses to the attic area. And, at the far end, allowing the hint of moonlight to creep inside, was a window.

Feeling with her feet for the rafters, Peri made her way slowly towards it. There was a creaking and straining from the hatch behind her as the broom handle struggled to hold its own against Liz's efforts to open it. Peri could imagine the girl standing on a chair from one of the bedrooms, pulling at the hatch handle. She hoped the makeshift wooden bar would hold.

As she approached the window, her eyes grew more accustomed to the pale light and she could make out shapes within the shadows. And as she worked out what they were she could also hear them, crying softly and shuffling. There must be a hole in the roof somewhere. Not big enough to be of any use to her, but of a sufficient size to admit the seagulls that had made their homes here inside.

Or was it their home? Wouldn't people downstairs in the building have heard them? And would so many live so close together? As she stepped cautiously across the boards, Peri fancied she could see tens – hundreds even – of the birds perched on the roof supports and beams. And as their eyes blinked and stared in the grimy vestiges of light, she saw that they were watching her. Every one of them.

A rustle of wing feathers in the gloom. Then a sudden rush. Peri was running now, trying to measure her frantic steps to hit the wooden struts and not plunge through the ceiling of the floor below. The sharp feathers were at her face, flapping in her hair. A blur of motion, loss of clear vision, the world moving, shaking in a whirlwind of confusion.

Then the claws and beaks. A rip at her cheek, tearing at her hair, screeches of anger cutting through her screams as she ran, pushing her way desperately through the tangle of birds. She could feel her clothes being shredded from her, her foot crunched on something that let out an almighty scream of high-pitched pain, and she dared not look down as she slipped on its remains.

An eye close to hers, pale yellow, unblinking, moving suddenly aside to be replaced by a sharp beak that rushed towards her. Peri batted it aside, feeling her finger tear on the sharp point, knowing it had connected sideways with her cheek, seeing the blood drops as red splodges in her field of vision. A spray of red mist.

She threw her hands in front of her face again, gave up worrying about what her feet were doing, staggered, stumbled, slipped, fell forwards heavily, connected with feather, claw, beak, warmth. Then an all-embracing shattering of glass as she plunged head first through the window. A shower of glass, feathers and squawks accompanied her as she plummeted downwards, the lights of the pub a blurry haze above and behind her. The ground a huge dark mass in the night as it hurtled upwards, blotting out everything. A sickening, bone-shaking crunch as she connected with the ground.

Then nothing. At all. In the night.

The villagers crowded into the room outside the laboratory seemed to know what was happening. There were only a few of them waiting in the room. Bob Trefoil stood at the front, still holding the sledgehammer across his chest. Beside him stood Rogers. Most of the others now waited silently throughout the house and the grounds, as if protecting it from the night outside.

The villagers who remained in the cellar room waited patiently, silently, as the door swung ponderously open. Janet was covering the Doctor with the gun while Sir Anthony opened the door. Sheldon was sitting on the floor again, looking glum but with his eyes now close to normal. Gone was the intense, manic stare. His face seemed more relaxed somehow, less anxious.

The Doctor stood by the workbench, leaning against it for support. Slowly, he straightened up.

'Doctor,' Sheldon said quietly as he too stood up. 'Doctor, I'm sorry. For all this.' He gestured round the lab. 'My fault.'

'You seem suddenly very lucid, Mr Sheldon,' the Doctor said. It sounded as if it were an effort for him to speak.

'Yes,' Sheldon admitted. 'But not for long, I don't think. I can feel the new material taking hold already. Much quicker this time.'

'Of course.' It was Sir Anthony who answered as he gestured for them to leave the room. 'The strength of the Denarian grows as it spreads, as it extends its influence. And this time there was no casual, slight infection. You've been injected with pure material. Already it is coursing through your veins. Already it's working its way into the synapses and the cerebellum, neutralising, controlling, superseding. It won't be long now.' He was grinning, his face a parody of how Packwood's had been. 'You are indeed fortunate,' he said.

'Doctor,' Sheldon hissed as the two of them walked slowly towards the door, Sir Anthony ahead of them, Janet behind – with the gun. 'Doctor, we don't have long, either of us, before it takes complete control. Third generation control. Whatever we do, we have to do it now.'

The Doctor turned towards him, as if to reply. His face was fixed in a huge grin, all teeth and drawn-back lips. 'It is done,' he replied, his voice at its normal volume, echoing round the room for all to hear. 'Finished.' A huge, grandiose intake of breath. 'I welcome the new reality,' he said grandly, arms outstretched.

Janet smiled back at him as she passed them, following Sir Anthony out of the room, to join the small group of villagers. They were all smiling in greeting – rictus and terrifying.

Sheldon stumbled, almost fell. The Doctor caught him. 'You need never stumble or fall again,' he said. 'Not now. Not now that we are Denarian, now that we are enhanced, better, superior.'

In the doorway Sir Anthony and Janet waited, welcoming, expectant, and the Doctor strode towards them, Sheldon shuffling desolate and afraid behind. As he reached the door, the Doctor threw his arms out again, turning a full circle as he declaimed: 'We are become life!' Then he threw back his head and laughed.

Chapter Fifteen
Overdosage

As he turned, laughing, the Doctor's outstretched arm knocked Sheldon back into the room. As Sheldon staggered back, the Doctor continued to turn, his arm coming right round, catching the edge of the heavy metal door and swinging it shut.

Sir Anthony cried out in sudden disbelief and alarm. Janet started forwards. But she was just too late. The door clicked massively shut and the Doctor lowered his arms. He stopped laughing and his face was grave as he helped Sheldon to a stool.

'You're absolutely right,' the Doctor said. 'We don't have much time at all, I'm afraid. How long do you think you can hold out against it?'

Sheldon was shaking, whether from fear or the alien influence he wasn't sure. 'I don't know,' he admitted. 'I can feel it within me. Stronger, more obvious this time.' He looked closely at the Doctor. 'But what about you?' he asked. 'How long...?'

'Can I hold out?' the Doctor asked. He smiled, a genuine open smile rather than the manic possessed grin of the Denarian. 'My metabolism isn't bothered by that sort of genetic nonsense. There's more than enough going on inside here already.' He patted his chest. 'That sort of alien material would be neutralised and rejected immediately.'

'You're immune?'

'Evidently.' The Doctor sat himself down on the stool next to Sheldon. 'But that doesn't surprise me. In fact, I was rather counting on it. Unfortunately I don't think my immune system is straightforward enough to duplicate and transplant into the entire population of these benighted isles. Even if I thought that was a good thing to do, we'd only be swapping one alien metabolism for another.'

Sheldon just stared at him.

The Doctor waved a hand dismissively in the air. 'Doesn't matter.' He hunched forwards, hands clasped together on the workbench. 'What I'm interested in is why you are suddenly so much better. Since you received a second dose, you seem rather more coherent, if you don't mind me saying. Rather more what I imagine to be yourself.' He raised a quizzical eyebrow. 'Now that may be something we can duplicate. Do you think?'

'Twenty-seven oh six.'

'Are you sure?' Janet asked.

Sir Anthony Kelso nodded. 'His late wife's birthday. Packwood used it as his code for everything. Even as the password for his secure systems. Had to speak to him about it, actually.'

Janet nodded. She returned her attention to the mass of wires sticking through the hole where the keypad had been, on the wall by the door. Most of them were still connected. It was just a case of replacing the few wires the Doctor had ripped out or moved to other connections. She did not think she could duplicate his sabotage. But she could repair the system, she was sure.

'Anything else? Anything at all?' the Doctor asked.

Sheldon shrugged. 'My fingers stopped growing,' he said. 'Started again now.' He held up his hand to show. His fingers ended in gnarled nascent knuckles.

'When you got the injection? From Janet?'

He nodded. 'That's when my head cleared.'

'Good. Excellent.' The Doctor jumped down from his perch on the stool and started pacing up and down. 'Check my logic as I go, would you?' he asked. 'What's that?'

'Sorry?'

The Doctor had stopped in front of the tall metal cabinet by the fridge. He pulled the handle and the whole frame of the cabinet rattled in response. 'Hmm,' he muttered. 'Important enough to be kept locked. Where's the sign about the leopard?' he wondered.

'You mentioned logic,' Sheldon reminded him.

'Oh, yes. That.' The Doctor gave a huge pull at the cabinet's handle and the door screeched open. Inside, mounted on a rack, were four rifles. 'Interesting,' the Doctor decided as he took one out.

'Guns?'

'Dart guns,' the Doctor told him. He pulled a clear plastic container from a shelf in the cupboard and angled it so that Sheldon could see the tufted end of the darts.

'Oh yes,' Sheldon said. 'I remember those. Anaesthetic darts.'

'You can load them with any fluid,' the Doctor said. 'Less risky than creeping about with a syringe, wouldn't you say?'

'What did you have in mind?'

The Doctor replaced the gun and the darts and turned to face Sheldon. 'First dosage,' he said. 'It gave you the initial infection. Though you didn't know it. Insidious, slow, creeping progress. Right so far?'

Sheldon agreed.

'Let's not worry how rapidly it actually assumed control or went through the generations,' the Doctor said. 'What strikes me as important is that a second, concentrated dose had such an interesting effect on you. It seemed to counter the initial infection.'

'But retained its own healing qualities,' Sheldon pointed out.

'You mean it pulled your mind together?' The Doctor nodded. 'True. Very true. Yet the physical healing that was already in progress was halted.' He tapped his lips with a finger. 'Packwood said that the initial generation of Denarian had no effect on the brain. That comes with the later evolution of the material.'

'So?'

'So...' The Doctor continued to consider. He was pacing again, finger still on his lips. He stopped in mid-step and whirled. 'A battlefield,' he said. 'Don't you see?'

'No, actually, I don't think I –' Sheldon broke off. 'Or maybe I do,' he admitted. 'Are you saying that the two batches of material battled it out inside my body?'

'Exactly. That's why your fingers stopped healing. Until the battle was over.'

'But which material won?'

'Oh, the new batch,' the Doctor told him. 'It healed your mind. Did it straight away.'

'No battle to be fought there,' Sheldon said slowly. 'Because the initial material I was infected with didn't get to my brain.'

'Exactly.' The Doctor sat himself down on the stool again. 'But suppose, just suppose for a moment, that the second, more advanced batch of Denarian saw the initial infection as just that – as an infection.'

'Something to be fought.'

The Doctor nodded. 'It purifies the body, makes it as healthy as it can. It saw the alien material as an infection rather than as its daddy. Provoked a sort of allergic reaction to it. Like scorpions stinging each other to death. Don't realise they're relatives.'

'That's possible,' Sheldon agreed. 'There's no sentient or intelligent control of the process. It affects the brain later, we know. But within the host systems, the body, it just sort of gets on with it.'

'What we need,' the Doctor said slowly, thoughtfully, 'is a batch of first generation material that will defeat the Denarian within the infected people's bodies. It doesn't affect the brain, so the side effects would be confined to the healing process, to what you originally intended.'

But Sheldon was shaking his head. 'No, you're forgetting, Doctor, the original material won't go near the brain, so it won't destroy the Denarian there. It won't have any effect, won't matter which batch wins out inside the body. The brain isn't a battlefield, remember?'

'So we need a hybrid, perhaps.'

'What we need,' Sheldon said, 'is a form of Denarian that will defeat the existing infection and cure the host, and then do nothing more.'

'Maybe if it's exhausted and dies in the battle, just as it wins,' the Doctor said. 'Or just peters out somehow. A limited life span, perhaps.'

'Fight fire with fire that then burns itself out,' Sheldon said quietly. 'Can it be done?'

The Doctor was on his feet, rubbing his hands together briskly and surveying the equipment on the workbench in front of him. 'I have absolutely no idea,' he confessed. 'But it should be fun finding out.' He turned to face Sheldon. 'Could you give me a hand?' he asked. 'Er, not literally of course. Though a small blood sample might come in... helpful.'

The fog had lifted and the stars were clear points of light sparkling like ice in the cold night air. Peri lay staring up at them for a while before she realised that she could not move. On the branches of a nearby tree she could see a line of seagulls watching her, and her blood ran cold. But they made no move to attack. Didn't even seem curious.

For a while she thought she might be dead, staring up through lifeless eyes at the eternity of the firmament. Then she decided she had broken her neck and was paralysed. But she could feel. She could feel the ground cold underneath her, the rough gravel beneath her hands and head. There was a dull ache from her face and her legs, but she could tell – somehow – that nothing was broken, that the skin was healing already over the scratches and tears in her face.

Then Liz Trefoil's freckled face tilted forwards into her view, blotting out the stars. Peri felt herself rising to her feet, taking Liz's hand, walking with her across the road and up the cobbled street towards the quay.

It was like a dream, a sleepwalk. She had no control, her mind already muzzy, vision blurred and gloomy. She was barely aware of what was happening as Liz handed her down into the small boat. It bobbed beneath her, but Peri did not know it. Her mind was cold and numb as Liz took a pair of oars and began to row mechanically, efficiently, across the water.

A minute later, Peri reached down for the second pair of oars. She knew she was doing it, was aware of the effort and the sensation, but she could not stop herself. Slowly, inexorably, helplessly, she was making her way back to Sheldon's Folly in a body that was no longer her own. She screamed, and no sound came. Her mouth was twisted into a smile, but her mind was in tears.

The keypad was dented from where the Doctor had forcibly removed it from the wall earlier. Unable to get it to slot back into its housing, Janet let it dangle from the wires attached to the back of it. She stepped aside and gestured for Sir Anthony to key in the numeric sequence.

'I hope you're right about this,' she told him.

'Don't worry,' he replied. 'Whatever happens, they're not going anywhere. They come out eventually, or they starve. Simple.'

He keyed in the sequence.

Sheldon sat with his head buried in his hands as the Doctor encouraged the centrifuge.

'Come on, come on,' the Doctor hissed as the mechanism continued to spin. His fingers tapped impatiently on the worktop. 'Are you all right over there?' he called across to Sheldon.

'Not really.' Sheldon's voice was strained and muffled by his hands. 'But you carry on.'

'Almost there,' the Doctor said. 'I think.' The centrifuge was slowing as it came to the end of the timed cycle the Doctor had programmed in. 'All we need is just a little –'

The Doctor broke off as the massive door to the laboratory swung slowly open.

'Time,' he finished. 'Pity, that.' He reached out and opened the centrifuge, carefully lifting out the test tubes inside, keeping his eyes fixed on Sir Anthony Kelso and Janet Spillsbury as they walked stiffly into the room. Behind them was a small group of villagers, several carrying spades. Rogers stood beside Bob Trefoil, who was hefting a sledgehammer.

Sheldon slipped from his stool before Sir Anthony reached him. He stumbled across towards the Doctor. Janet stepped briskly towards him, grabbed his shoulder and pulled him back, dragging, pushing. Sheldon slipped to the floor as she shoved him towards the wall, where he remained in a bundle of ragged clothing.

The Doctor pushed one of the test tubes into the wooden rack. He held the other one up, as if in defence, as Janet continued towards him. Behind him, on the workbench, the Doctor fumbled for the syringe. He had cleaned it out thoroughly – all he needed to do now was fill it. If he had time.

Janet ran at him, hands outstretched, fingernails pointing at the Doctor's face as she sprang. He took a step backwards, caught a foot in the legs of a stool, went head over heels, managed – somehow – to right himself and ended up sitting with the test tube still raised, undamaged. The syringe clattered to the floor, its plastic body jumping then rolling away, out of reach even as the Doctor leaned forward and scrabbled for it.

His fingers slipped on the cylindrical surface, grazed it desperately as he tried to reach it. As Janet's foot connected with the side of the Doctor's face, he changed his tactic, sending the syringe spinning away from both of them, towards the far wall. Towards Sheldon.

Sir Anthony was standing, hands on hips, as he watched Janet kick the Doctor again.

'You're an infection,' he said as the shoe connected and the Doctor cried out. 'A blemish on an otherwise perfect world.'

The Doctor was shifting round, spinning on the floor, struggling to crawl away as she kicked him a third time. 'Is that what you think?' he gasped as he rolled clear, gaining impetus from the blow. Still he held the test tube aloft, like a talisman. To no effect.

'A canker that must be cut out,' Sir Anthony went on. 'An open wound that needs to be seared, closed, sutured.'

'We'll see,' the Doctor said indistinctly. He wiped his mouth with the back of his free hand, pulled it away bloodied and damp. 'We'll see,' he said again. Then: 'Here, catch!'

Sheldon seemed to come to life as the test tube arced through the air towards him. Suddenly he was moving, rolling, hand outstretched. He caught the glass phial cleanly in his stumpy new-grown fingers, kept rolling, gathering the syringe as he went.

Sir Anthony was turning towards Sheldon now, as if realising he was there. Bob Trefoil raised the sledgehammer. The Doctor was a blur of motion as he managed to catch hold of Janet's leg as she lashed out at him again. He held on, twisted her foot viciously and sent her skidding across the room to connect with Trefoil. The sledgehammer went flying, bouncing on the workbench and taking equipment and glassware with it as it skewed across the top. It caught the test tube rack, shook it, rolled it to the very edge of the workbench. The wooden rack teetered on the edge. And fell.

The Doctor just made it, his hands underneath the rack as it fell. He caught the rack upside-down. And the test tube fell neatly from it. It bounced on end on the floor, rose, spun, and was gathered by the Doctor's other hand as he dropped the rack.

He looked up in triumph, to see Janet's face close to his, teeth exposed in a grotesque parody of a grin as her long nails reached down towards his eyes.

She blinked, a sudden reaction as she stiffened, froze. Behind her, over her shoulder as she dropped away, the Doctor could see Sheldon. The syringe was still sticking out of Janet's arm as she fell. The Doctor grabbed it as it passed him. Empty.

And Sir Anthony was closing on Sheldon now. The Doctor was pushing himself away across the floor, juggling syringe and test tube. The rubber bung in the top of the test tube was in his teeth as he pulled it out, spat it away, pulled at the plunger of the syringe and felt it pulling oh-so-slowly from the body.

Rogers and Trefoil were helping Sir Anthony as they dragged Sheldon to his feet. Janet was scrunched up in a lifeless ball under the workbench. The other villagers were advancing slowly on the Doctor as he struggled to steady his hand, to pour some of the liquid into the syringe. Not too much, save some for later.

He pushed the plunger back into the body of the syringe, turned it upright and expelled a tiny drop of the viscous liquid. He smiled in satisfaction. But the smile turned into an anguished cry as Janet Spillsbury lifted the syringe from his hands and stepped away from the Doctor.

'It's finished,' she said, and the venom in her voice was unmistakable.

The boat bumped gently against the jetty as Liz threw the painter over a wooden pole. She stepped easily on to the wooden boards, not waiting to see if Peri followed.

The two of them walked, in step, towards the house. The moon was shining bright and clear now through the skeletal limbs of the bare winter trees. Somewhere in the distance an owl hooted, a satisfied, fulfilled cry. Like calling to like across the wooded island.

There was a line of villagers standing across the pathway to the house. As Peri and Liz approached, they stepped aside, made room. Liz Trefoil joined the line, standing beside Jed, from the farm.

Further along the line, Hilly Painswick watched impassively as Peri took her place in the ranks of the Denarian. Then she turned her pale inhuman eyes back towards the jetty.

'Finished!' Janet Spillsbury repeated as she stepped across to Sir Anthony Kelso and stabbed the syringe into the back of his neck.

He shrieked, an inhuman wail of pain, hand clutching, struggling to pluck out the needle. It clattered to the floor, and he sank to his knees after it.

For a moment all movement was frozen. The villagers stood inside the doorway, watching. Trefoil was still holding Sheldon by the shoulders. Janet stood by the prone body of Sir Anthony.

Then the Doctor was moving, on his feet and dashing across the room towards the gun cabinet. 'Keep them back, if you can,' he shouted. 'I need a minute. No more.'

'Right, Doctor.' Sir Anthony's voice was already strong and assured as he pulled himself to his feet. Beneath his left knee was the crushed remains of the syringe, its plastic body splintered and broken. He kicked it away with a sigh, then turned to stand with Janet.

Trefoil pushed Sheldon away with a snarl, and stepped towards them, Rogers at his shoulder.

The line turned, as one, to face the house. The group started to walk slowly back towards the house, all in step, all at a uniform pace. Across the lawn, another group of villagers mirrored their actions.

On the other side of the house too, groups of villagers began to converge once more on Sheldon's Folly. The schoolchildren followed Miss Devlin, formed into a crocodile, marching in step.

There was a look of surprise more than pain on Bob Trefoil's face as Janet slammed the stool into it. She held it by the legs, swinging it in an arc about her head until it connected with Trefoil, sending him spinning away. The red gash on his cheek was already healing over as he staggered back towards her and Sir Anthony. Then Sheldon grabbed his legs from behind and brought him down.

The other villagers stepped forward as Trefoil fell. Sheldon was fighting to disentangle himself from the big man, trying to avoid the fists and feet. Janet and Sir Anthony were now both swinging stools in front of them.

Behind them the Doctor was using a pipette to inject a small quantity of liquid into several of the darts. As he finished with each one he pushed it down into a magazine. And after he had pressed in the last of the darts he snapped the magazine into place beneath the rifle and turned to face the villagers.

Janet was sprawled on the floor, holding the stool above her to try to keep back the two men who were struggling to reach for her neck. Sir Anthony was backing away from Rogers, the splintered stump of a wooden stool leg in his hand. Sheldon was lying on his back on the floor, unconscious, his head bloodied from Trefoil's attentions.

The Doctor raised the dart gun. 'Let's hope its quality that counts, not quantity,' he said to himself, and pulled the trigger.

The first dart found the side of Trefoil's neck. The big man paused, reaching up as if bothered by a fly. He pulled the dark from his neck, stared for a moment at the blood-soaked tip and at the matching crimson of the flights. Then he tossed it away, snarled with anger, and ran straight at the Doctor.

Chapter Sixteen
Solution and Evolution

They paused close to the house, the groups combining now to form a circle. Miss Devlin standing among her schoolchildren, the vicar in the midst of his flock, villagers united in a single purpose. The cordon round the house was complete, each person within an arm's reach of the next.

They stood, silent and still, as the first cracks of dawn splintered the night sky. Waiting.

There was nowhere left to go. The Doctor's back was against the wall of the laboratory, and Trefoil was still lumbering massively towards him. The Doctor closed his eyes, pushing his head against the wall, holding the gun across his chest for what little protection it might offer. And nothing happened.

He opened his left eye a crack, and peered out blearily at the unfocused scene in front of him. When he was sure that there was not a fist or a foot speeding at his face, he opened his eyes fully.

Trefoil was swaying on his feet. As the Doctor watched, the big man stumbled, falling to his knees.

'Ha!' the Doctor gave a shout of triumph and levelled the gun again. Distracted for a moment, Janet and Sir Anthony half turned to see what was happening. And as they did so, one of the village women together with Rogers broke through and came at the Doctor. They obviously knew that he was the main threat, ignoring the others as they ran across the lab.

The Doctor fired from the hip. Once, twice, the gun exploded in the echoing room. Rogers kept coming, passing the Doctor through sheer force of momentum and crashing into the wall behind him, before falling slowly backwards to the floor. The villager, a middle-aged woman with tightly curled brown hair, was knocked sideways as the dart caught her in the arm, spinning her round. She kept spinning, spiralling to the floor in an almost balletic movement. Even when she was on the floor, her arms continued to make circular motions by her sides.

Trefoil was pulling himself upright again now, looking around in surprise and confusion. He was making noises that sounded like they ought to be words, but which were cut off before they had really got started as he tried to make sense of the situation.

Sir Anthony and Janet stepped aside to let the Doctor pass. The final three villagers were backing away now. One turned to run. But the dart caught him in the back of the neck. His hand whipped up clumsily behind him, reaching in vain for the tiny projectile. Then he collapsed forwards on to his face, making no effort to break his fall. The Doctor winced, hoping he had not broken his nose.

The other two barely had time to turn, then they too were falling.

As they surveyed the villagers, watched them clambering groggily to their feet, Janet and Sir Anthony were elated.

'Well done, Doctor!' Sir Anthony exclaimed.

Janet was helping Sheldon to his feet too. He was shaking his head as if to clear it, wiping a hand across his blood-drenched brow.

'I'm sorry,' the Doctor said quietly. And shot him in the arm.

Sheldon cried out in pain. Janet screamed in alarm.

The Doctor shrugged. 'We don't want to miss anyone in the excitement, do we?'

'So what's the plan?' Sir Anthony was rubbing his hands together briskly. 'Shoot the lot of them?'

But the Doctor did not mirror his enthusiasm. 'Hardly, I'm afraid. This is fine for a few people, but there's a limit to the number of darts. And there's the chance of re-infection.'

'But surely if we get all of the villagers?' Janet said.

Sheldon was shaking his head. 'The Doctor's right,' he said. 'Even if we did, it doesn't end there. Does it?'

'Oh, I see,' Janet said quietly. 'The sheep. And cattle.'

'And chickens,' Sir Anthony put in, his voice losing its excited edge.

'And every other animal in the food chain that may have become infected.' The Doctor shook his head. 'This is a stopgap, a respite. No more.'

'I have no idea what you're talking about, Doctor,' Trefoil said wearily. 'But there must be a solution.'

The Doctor turned to him. 'If you have no idea, then kindly don't –' he began angrily, waving the gun by the stock. Then he stopped, frowned, smiled. 'You know,' he said slowly, 'I think you're exactly right.'

'I am?' Trefoil asked warily.

Janet, Sir Anthony and Sheldon were exchanging puzzled looks. Rogers was rising hesitantly to his feet by the far wall. The Doctor threw his arms open and beamed at them. He grinned at the villagers who were watching him with a mixture of fascination and confusion.

'A solution,' he said. 'That's exactly what we need. Something that is absorbed on contact.'

Sheldon was nodding. 'Of course. You mean a solution of the genetic material. That we can disperse somehow and allow the victims, the infected people and animals to absorb through their skin maybe.'

The Doctor laid the gun down on the workbench and looked at the array of shattered and broken equipment. 'Exactly,' he agreed. 'Though that might be more easily said than done.' He set about gathering together various items that were not too badly damaged. 'And we still need a way of dispersing it over this whole island, and the main island too.'

It was a slow process, hampered all the time by the fear that other infected villagers might try to stop them. Sir Anthony, together with Rogers and Bob Trefoil, had organised the cured villagers into a team of lookouts to keep watch up the cellar stairs and along the corridors. The Doctor, Janet and Sheldon were working flat out to distil a straw-coloured liquid the Doctor had synthesised. They had managed to move the huge plastic water container from the corner of the room and position it beside the workbench. Now a length of glass tube worked its crazy way through a collection of flasks and beakers before coming to an end overhanging the container.

'How do we know it will work?' Janet asked as they watched the concentrated liquid dripping into the large plastic container. Each drop became a misty smudge of yellow as it hit the water.

'We don't,' the Doctor told her.

'We should have kept one of the villagers infected to test it on,' Sheldon suggested.

The Doctor paused and looked closely at Sheldon. 'I'd have thought you'd had enough of that sort of thing, treating humans as guinea pigs.' He returned his attention to the dripping liquid. 'Even guinea pigs shouldn't be used as guinea pigs unless it's completely unavoidable,' he huffed.

As the last of the liquid dripped through the tubes and pipes, the Doctor clapped his hands together loudly. 'Right,' he exclaimed, pulling off his coat, 'I want every glass bottle, beaker, flask and container you can find. Even if they're cracked they'll have to do. And things to stopper them with. Bungs, corks, rag, whatever.'

'What are you intending?' Janet asked as they collected together whatever they could find.

'The villagers are the immediate threat and problem,' the Doctor told her as he rolled up his shirt sleeves and started to fill the containers from the liquid. 'We've got a fair few gallons of the solution here. We'll need a lot more. But first we have to make sure it works, and we have to buy ourselves the time to organise it.'

'So we throw these at the villagers?' Sheldon asked. 'One by one?'

'But that's hardly better than using the darts,' Janet pointed out. The Doctor sighed and set down the flask he was holding.

'It's better than the darts because there's more of a spread. You don't have to be so accurate. And we don't have to get all the villagers. Not like that.' He tapped the side of the huge plastic container they had filled with the liquid. 'Now how can we fix handles to this so we can carry it up the stairs, do you think?'

Sir Anthony was at the door, dividing his attention between what the scientists were doing and the villager keeping watch at the door of the anteroom beyond. 'You're not going to throw that over them, are you?' he demanded. 'It would take a dozen of us to swing it. And the stuff would just slosh over the side.'

'Sloshing over the side is fine, thank you very much,' the Doctor said shortly. 'That's all we need.'

'Don't be ridiculous, Doctor.' Sir Anthony was in a huff now. 'No doubt what you've synthesised or whatever here is brilliant, but I refuse to believe that sloshing it over the side of that big bath will do any more than splash a few people's feet. If you're lucky.'

The Doctor raised his finger and waggled it in admonition. 'Not,' he said smugly, 'the way I intend to do the sloshing.'

They managed to find everything they needed in the lab or elsewhere in the cellarage. They took it in turns to carry the enormous container. It barely fitted along the narrow cellar corridor, two of the villagers struggling to lift it by the rope handles that had been threaded through holes in the side of the container. The Doctor led the way, carrying a flask of the solution in each hand. He had others stuffed in every available pocket. Sir Anthony had insisted on bringing the gun. The others all carried as many flasks and bottles as they could manage.

Taking it in turns as they tired, they eventually managed to manhandle the container up the narrow stairway. Trefoil dragged it up, his muscles straining and bulging. The pale liquid lapped over the sides of the plastic and dripped to the floor. The rope handles were damp and slippery with it, which made the task even harder.

But at last they managed to get the heavy load into the hallway of the house. It was getting light outside, the sun filtering through the smoky remnants of the fire in the drawing room. There was no sign of anyone else until they got to the front door.

Then they saw the circle of villagers surrounding the house. Watching, waiting for them.

The Doctor stepped back inside and slammed the door shut. He turned to Rogers. 'I want to get to the outbuildings round the back of the house,' he said. 'With that,' he added, pointing to the container. 'Which is the nearest door?'

'There's a tradesmen's entrance,' he told him. 'Back this way.'

The Doctor nodded. 'That should do. Now,' he turned to the others, 'I need a diversion here at the front. I want as many of the villagers as possible brought round here while we sneak out the back with our little bucket of the Doctor's Patent Remedy. You too, please, Janet.'

'I suppose it's too much to inquire why you want to get out the back, Doctor?' Sir Anthony asked.

'You'll find out soon enough,' the Doctor told him with a wry smile.

'Hmm.' Sir Anthony was not impressed.

As the door of the folly slammed shut, a small group stepped out of the line of villagers. Peri and Liz Trefoil, together with two of the men, turned slowly and began to walk along the path towards the side of the house.

The others closed ranks, filling the spaces left by those who had left.

When the front door opened again, the Doctor, Janet, Rogers and one of the men were missing, so it was Sir Anthony and Bob Trefoil who led out the small group. They stood in a tight group in the doorway for several moments, waiting to see what would happen. The villagers faced them, staring, immobile.

Then, as one, each of the villagers took a step forwards. And then another.

'Now!' shouted Sir Anthony, and the group in the doorway split and scattered. Bob Trefoil ran forwards, almost to the edge of the approaching line of people. But he paused, just out of reach of their outstretched, clutching hands, and hurled a glass beaker towards the nearest person.

It was Old Jim. His pipe still clamped tightly in his mouth as he advanced, his weather-beaten face set. He made no attempt to move aside as the beaker came at him. He raised his hand to smash it away, batting it out of the air.

The beaker was cracked and, as Old Jim's hand connected with it, the thin glass shattered. Viscous liquid spread over Jim's hand, and he waved it, trying to shake the liquid off. But it clung and stained in the pale light.

Old Jim frowned. His forehead became even more creased. His pale eyes blinked rapidly twice. And then his pipe fell from his mouth and he collapsed to his knees, holding his stained hand in front of him as if it burned.

At the sight of Old Jim's collapse, the villagers suddenly broke ranks, driven on by the instinct of the material within them to survive. They were running, screaming, hurtling towards the group in front of the house now. More villagers were coming round from the side of the house, converging on the tiny group that was desperately hurling glassware at them.

Sir Anthony stood in the doorway, taking careful aim with the rifle and picking off villagers one at a time. He was aiming for those in the second wave, letting the leaders run into the rain of glass and liquid. But it was clear that in a few moments the group in the doorway would be overwhelmed.

At the front of the group, Bob Trefoil grabbed Hilly Painswick as she ran at him. He held her hands from his face and hurled her away. He was looking round, thumping, ducking, kicking, hurling his last flask at the head of one of the older school children. All the time, though, he was looking, searching, praying for a sight of his daughter.

Then, as he looked to one side, catching a glimpse of red hair, disappointed to see that it was Mick Robarts after all, he was knocked off his feet by the Reverend Alan Parker. He was on his back, staring up at the dawn sky, arms up, pushing people away. But they kept coming, fingers reaching down, feet kicking. The last thing he saw was the face of Mrs Tattleshall, contorted into a silent scream. For a brief moment the irony of her silence made him want to laugh, despite everything.

Then the noise blotted out his thoughts and the mist came down.

The approach taken by the Doctor's group was more offensive than defensive. As soon as they heard Bob Trefoil's shout from the front of the house that they were about to open the door and go out, the Doctor cracked open the tradesmen's entrance at the back of the house. After just a few moments, the villagers lined up at the back of the house began to move away.

'They're going,' the Doctor said with satisfaction. 'Obviously not tacticians. Now we can't wait long enough for them to be out of sight, I'm afraid, or they'll have finished with our decoy friends and be coming back. And that's not a pleasant thought for them or us.' He turned to Rogers and the other man standing by the plastic container. They had the straps in their hands, ready to heft it up and run with it. 'Ready?' the Doctor asked.

The two men nodded. Both looked grim and afraid. Their hands were grasping and releasing the ropes nervously.

The other person there was Janet Spillsbury. The Doctor looked at her, and she too nodded that she was ready.

The Doctor checked through the crack between door and frame again. 'OK,' he said. 'Time to go.' And he threw open the door.

It was not so much a run as a stagger across the back lawn towards the outbuildings. The Doctor pointed out where they were headed as they set off. As soon as they broke from the house, the villagers who had been heading away, round towards the commotion at the front of the house, turned and began to run towards the Doctor and his group.

The slow, lumbering run of the possessed villagers mirrored the stagger of the men dragging the container between them. Liquid was splashing out of it on to the lawn as they struggled on with it. The Doctor was hurling flasks and beakers into the early morning at what looked like random. But almost all found their mark. Janet waited until she was closer, more certain of her targets.

Behind them they left a trail of groggy, kneeling people rubbing their eyes and looking confused. But still they were coming.

They were pushing their way through a crowd now. The Doctor had a beaker in his hand and was scooping liquid from the container and flinging it in a wide arc to try to clear a path through the sea of people in front of them. Janet joined him and they seemed to be succeeding. Rogers, almost exhausted from carrying the container, slipped on the wet grass, sank to his knees. The container started to tip.

At once the Doctor was there, dragging at the rope handle, pulling the container upright with one hand while pushing away a charging villager with another. Rogers managed to get up, to grab the handle again and resume his progress. They were almost there now.

Janet pulled open the door to the coach house. And as she did so, she caught sight of what was inside. And at last she understood what the Doctor was planning. She smiled thinly, waiting for the Doctor and the other two men to stagger in. Then she slammed the door closed again, hearing a cry as someone was knocked flying.

'Right then.' The Doctor was immediately oblivious to the noise from outside, to the battering at the door and the shouts of the enraged villagers. His attention was completely focused on the next problem. 'Our challenge now,' he said, 'is to sling this bucket underneath. We need to be able to tip it, probably using one of the ropes.'

'We also,' Janet pointed out, 'need to get the helicopter out of this coach house. We can't take off in here. Can we?'

But any further discussion was cut short. The door of the helicopter was opened violently and suddenly, colliding with the side of Rogers's head as he reached under the fuselage. He gave a shout and went reeling, collapsing to the floor, stunned.

The other man backed away, his job only half completed. From inside the helicopter jumped four people. Two were young men, fishermen, from the village. Then came Liz Trefoil. And finally, Peri.

The men were charging at the Doctor, arms out. One had a knife. Liz Trefoil stood beside the helicopter, her face contorted into a grin. Peri closed on Janet Spillsbury, her hands twisted into claws as she reached out.

Somehow the Doctor managed to avoid the knife and send the first of his attackers spinning into the second. They both collapsed in a heap. But after a moment they were rising to their feet again, coming at him again.

'You know you won't succeed,' the first man said. His voice was flat, dead.

'You can't succeed,' the second man added, his voice the same flat monotone as the first.

Behind them, almost casually, Liz Trefoil kicked out at the man backing away from the helicopter. Her foot caught him under the chin and sent him reeling into the shadows at the side of the coach house. 'There is no way you can ever succeed,' she said, as if continuing the same argument.

Peri had Janet by the hair, was dragging her head closer, ever closer to her extended fingers, aligning the eyes with her nails. 'Whatever you do,' Peri hissed, 'we shall still survive. The rule of Mankind is over.'

The Doctor dived forwards, over the arms of the two men approaching him. He had his coat off, was waving it like a desperate bullfighter. As he rolled and flailed, his progress brought him to the helicopter. He turned to see Liz Trefoil's grinning macabre face close to his own. And he smiled back.

'Over for ever,' she said.

As she was speaking, the Doctor ducked away, flinging out his coat. The young woman flinched instinctively. But the coat was not thrown at her. It dipped into the container of liquid. The Doctor kept hold of the sleeve, letting the coat float for a moment on the surface of the viscous brew, then dragging it back. As he pulled it from the liquid, he flicked his wrist, and the coat whirled towards Liz, catching her across the face, spattering her in the liquid it carried in its wake.

She screamed, hands to face, twisting and turning away.

The two possessed men grabbed the Doctor from behind. But he was struggling back into his coat now, and they grabbed him by the sodden sleeves. At once, both let go, staring at the yellowing stains on their palms, collapsing to their knees.

Only Peri was left now. Her eyes were almost completely white as she let go of Janet's hair and pushed the woman roughly away. 'Our survival is all that counts,' she said as she stepped towards the Doctor. 'Everything else, everyone else can be sacrificed for that.' Then she was running at the Doctor, screaming, arms thrashing as she came at him.

He twisted away, the helicopter behind him. And at the last possible moment, dived aside.

Peri's momentum carried her forward, towards the aircraft. She struggled to stop, but collided with the side of the container where it was pushed half under the belly of the helicopter. For several seconds she teetered, trying to retain her balance, arms working, swaying. But then the Doctor grabbed her legs and tipped her headlong into the viscous liquid.

'I don't think you can overdose on this stuff,' he muttered to himself as he pulled off his coat again and rolled up his sleeve. Then carefully, delicately, he reached into the murky depths and pulled Peri's head clear of the water. Her eyes and mouth were tight shut. She coughed once, then spluttered out a stream of the yellow goo before opening her eyes and staring in horror at the liquid. Her eyes were a sudden startling brown.

'Good,' the Doctor proclaimed, and let go of Peri. With a

coughing splutter of surprise and indignation she disappeared beneath the surface of the liquid once more, before emerging again a moment later.

Janet was checking on Rogers. He was slumped against the wall of the coach house. 'I'm afraid he's out cold,' she told the Doctor.

'Ah,' said the Doctor thoughtfully. 'And I suspect you'll be telling me next that you can't actually fly this thing.'

She stared at him, mouth open. 'Is that why you brought me here with you, rather than sending me with the others?' she asked. 'In case something happened to Rogers? Because, no – I have no idea how to fly a helicopter.'

The Doctor nodded, sucking in his cheeks. 'Well,' he said slowly. 'It can't be that difficult. Can it?' He bent down to see how much progress they had made in attempting to sling the container beneath the helicopter's skids. 'I'm sure I've done it before,' he murmured.

The villagers fell back as the doors to the coach house creaked open. They stood, expectant, as the doors reached the limits of the hinges. Then they were crowding round, pushing their way inside.

But not for long. A young woman was striding towards them. She seemed almost to glow in the pale morning light. The sun was rising over the back lawn of the Folly, glinting on her wet clothes and skin. Somehow sensing the danger of touching her, the villagers fell back slowly.

Behind Peri, the Doctor – helped by the recovered fishermen, Liz Trefoil and Janet – pushed the helicopter slowly and ponderously out of its hangar.

The villagers could see what was happening, and they evidently did not like it. Several ran forwards. But Peri was in their way, between them and the others, narrowing the angle. As they touched her, they fell away, stained and coated by the liquid in which she was drenched. She turned for the briefest moment as she heard the door to the helicopter's cockpit click open.

'This stuff had better wash off, Doctor,' she shouted at him as he disappeared inside the cabin.

Moments later the rotor blades swung slowly, noisily, into life, lifting as they rotated ever quicker. The nose of the helicopter dipped slightly, the tail lifting first. Then it was above Peri, the wind from the blades cutting through her, making her shiver. Drying the gelatinous clothes to her body.

Dispersing the liquid was simple in the event. As the helicopter swung back and forth, so the container beneath it swung, sloshing liquid over the side. As the container emptied, so the Doctor was forced to make ever more exaggerated manoeuvres to coax the liquid out.

But spill it did, and in a thick cloud. The liquid fell as droplets, mixing into the air and creating a colloidal yellow mist that sank slowly to the ground engulfing all beneath it.

The helicopter flew low over the line of villagers at the side of the house, banked over the group by the coach house. It swung past the frantic scramble at the front door of Sheldon's Folly. The Doctor caught sight of Christopher Sheldon waving like a tourist to him. He saw Bob Trefoil struggle to stand up again amidst a group of collapsing villagers as the mist around him thinned and dispersed. He saw Peri sitting cross-legged outside the coach house staring down at her sodden clothes. All round the house, villagers were collapsing to their knees, keeling over. Then slowly, as if in a dream, they were pulling themselves up again and staring about in disbelief and confusion as the helicopter whirled and circled above them like an avenging angel.

The Doctor brought the helicopter round for another pass. Not because it was necessary, but because it was fun.

It reminded Peri of their first night in Dorsill. The venue was the same, and the people were largely the same. Only the atmosphere was different. The pub was full, packed with laughing people. There were a few people missing, of course. Most notably Mike Neville, though Peri could not honestly say she was very sorry about that. And Dave Madsen.

No one said anything. It was not the time. But Liz Trefoil struggled to smile, pushing her red hair away from her brave, freckled face. This was a rebirth, a point of evolution not regression. Time for tears and memories later. For the moment, her father enclosed her at regular intervals in a huge bear hug before sending her off on minor errands or to refill glasses.

The Doctor was at the bar, holding forth noisily about the evils of technology and how he envied the islanders their isolation from both people and things. He and Janet had been working with Christopher Sheldon for most of the day, distilling gallons more of the yellowish liquid and then using an improved version of the plastic container to spray it out over the islands from the helicopter. Now the Doctor was noisily confident that every piece of ground had been covered. Certainly everywhere seemed to be stained sickly yellow and was tacky to the touch.

'But it'll soon wash away,' the Doctor promised. 'Rain, mist, fog… You have plenty of all of them. Just a matter of time.' He smiled at Peri. 'Like so many things,' he added softly. And she smiled back.

Sir Anthony, as everyone now knew him, had spent hours on his mobile phone organising all sorts of people and things, explaining away the failure of the experiment, the sad loss of Logan Packwood. Hilly Painswick was chatting noisily to the Reverend Parker while Miss Devlin listened and sniffed nearby. Old Jim sat alone in a corner, puffing on his pipe and watching everything with a creased expression of wry amusement.

Christopher Sheldon had given up trying to convince anyone that he was not responsible really for saving the islands from the developers, and now he accepted the acclaim with patient resignation. As he held up his hand to stem the flow of praise and advice from Mrs Tattleshall, Peri noticed that the middle finger had never grown completely back. It stopped just shy of the nail. As she stared at him across the crowded room, Sheldon caught her eye and smiled at her. She smiled back, and pushed her way to the bar towards the noise of the Doctor.

'Are they really free of it?' Peri asked quietly as they slipped out of the back door just after midnight.

Most of the villagers were tired, their bodies worn out from fighting against the alien material within them, and had drifted off home at around the usual closing time. A strange reversion to normality.

'Oh I think so.' The Doctor took a deep breath of the cold, misty night air. 'There have been no supply boats for a few weeks. Not even the mail boat got through because of the fog between here and the mainland. The islands are pretty much doused now. If we missed anything, it will pick up the cure through the food chain or the water just as it was originally infected.' He paused beneath a gas lamp and turned to look back along the misty village street.

They passed the church and the quay in silence, walking briskly to keep warm. It took them nearly an hour to get back to the TARDIS. It almost glowed through the gathering fog as they approached. In the distance they could hear the sea crashing on the rocky coast of the island. Like when they had arrived. It seemed an age ago.

'Oh no!' the Doctor exclaimed as he inserted the key in the lock.

'What?'

He pulled his hand away from the TARDIS door. It was stained yellow. 'Sticky,' he complained. 'How very tiresome.'

'So we really did get everything,' Peri said. 'You can hardly complain. It's your own fault, after all.'

'It'll wash off in the vortex.' The Doctor made to wipe his fingertip on her nose, and Peri ducked out of reach with a laugh. As she moved, she caught sight of a pair of birds - seagulls - perched on the outstretched limb of a nearby tree, silhouetted black against the grey of the misty night. For a moment, just a moment, she felt a sudden pang of fear.

But the Doctor was already holding the door to the TARDIS open and ushering her inside.

'No,' he said as she passed him and he caught sight of her anxious expression, 'there's no way that any infection could have escaped from the islands. I'm sure of that.'

'Good,' she said. 'That's good.' She nodded as she headed across the console room and towards her bedroom. 'Good night, Doctor. And thanks,' she added.

'Thank you, Peri,' he said softy as the door closed behind her. Then he flung his coat across the console with an exaggerated gesture, clapped his hands together grandly and set to work at the controls. He froze in mid-stretch for a lever as a thought occurred to him. 'Oh no,' he said with annoyance. 'I forgot to ask the date.'

As the yellowish blue shape of the TARDIS became misty and faded into the echoing fog, a pair of seagulls rose from the branches of a nearby tree. They turned their pale eyes towards the sound of the sea, and set off through the thickening night towards the mainland.

About the Author

Justin Richards has written over a dozen novels as well as articles, audio plays and some non-fiction. In the past, he has worked variously as a technical writer, editor and book designer, fiction editor, software architect, business strategist for a multinational corporation, and an odd job man at a hotel for postmen.

In an obvious career progression, he now acts as Range Consultant for the BBC Worldwide *Doctor Who* series. He is registered as an inventor in the European Union and also has patents registered in the USA and Japan.

Justin is married with two children, the older of whom wants to be just like dad when he grows up – playing with computers and watching television.

In his spare time, he… Sorry, in his what?

PRESENTING

DOCTOR WHO

ALL-NEW AUDIO DRAMAS

Big Finish Productions is proud to present all-new *Doctor Who* adventures on audio!

Featuring original music and sound-effects, these full-cast plays are available on double cassette in high street stores, and on limited-edition double CD from all good specialist stores, or via mail order.

Available from April 2000
RED DAWN

A four-part story by Justin Richards.
Starring **Peter Davison** as the Doctor
and **Nicola Bryant** as Peri.

Ares One: NASA's first manned mission to the dead planet Mars. But is Mars as dead as it seems?

While the NASA team investigate an "anomaly" on the planet's surface, the Doctor and Peri find themselves inside a strange alien building. What is its purpose? And what is frozen inside the blocks of ice that guard the doorways? If the Doctor has a sense of deja-vu, it's because he's about to meet some old adversaries, as well as some new ones...

If you wish to order the CD version, please photocopy this form or provide all the details on paper. Delivery within 28 days of release. Send to: PO Box 1127, Maidenhead, Berkshire. SL6 3LN.
Big Finish Hotline 01628 828283.

Still available:
THE SIRENS OF TIME (Doctors 5,6,7)   THE LAND OF THE DEAD (Doctor 5, Nyssa)
PHANTASMAGORIA (Doctor 5, Turlough)   THE FEARMONGER (Doctor 7, Ace)
WHISPERS OF TERROR (Doctor 6, Peri)   THE MARIAN CONSPIRACY (Doctor 6, Evelyn)

Please send me   [ ] copies of *Red Dawn*
                [ ] copies of *The Marian Conspiracy*   [ ] copies of *Whispers of Terror*
                [ ] copies of *The Fearmonger*   [ ] copies of *Phantasmagoria*
                [ ] copies of *The Land of the Dead*   [ ] copies of *The Sirens of Time*

each @ £13.99 (£15.50 non-UK orders) – prices inclusive of postage and packing. Payment can be accepted by credit card or by personal cheques, payable to Big Finish Productions Ltd.

Name...

Address...

Postcode..

VISA/Mastercard number...

Expiry date...Signature..

For more details visit our website at **http://www.doctorwho.co.uk**